GLOBAL WARNING

Ray Blackhall

Copyright © 2020 Ray Blackhall
All rights reserved
First Edition

NEWMAN SPRINGS PUBLISHING
320 Broad Street
Red Bank, NJ 07701

First originally published by Newman Springs Publishing 2020

ISBN 978-1-64801-604-2 (Paperback)
ISBN 978-1-64801-605-9 (Digital)

Printed in the United States of America

To my wonderful wife, Sally

PRELUDE

Anook was born in the dead of winter with the high Arctic winds whipping snow and ice pellets around their igloo, the temperature below zero, with a wind chill beyond any hope of comfort. His father, Manu, was a skilled hunter and provider for his family, also born the son of generations of hunters, who fearlessly ventured into the frozen wastes, bound by honor to not return without sustenance for their families and clan. Armed with nothing more than courage and a hand-fashioned harpoon or knife, they often traversed endless expanses of featureless white ice or paddled far into the syrupy, black, ice-choked sea-seeking seal, walrus, orca, or even polar bear. To return empty-handed did not mean ridicule; it meant hungry children and longing stares. This was justification to take great but calculated risks.

Manu was a well-respected member of the clan and a natural leader on the hunts. He was wise and never pushed the time-honored rules of survival handed down by the wise ones who came before. Tribal leaders looked upon him with favor and recognized the traits they sought for the honor of high council and made him chief. In his youth, Manu had been impetuous and was often too enthusiastic for his own good, but wisdom came to him at an early age, and he always showed an eagerness to learn.

When Anook was born, his mother, Shano, struggled near death to deliver him, he being of much larger size than most Inuit babies. Shano was a proud woman of stout build, with a strong back and gorgeous dark wavy hair. Her warm smile and beautiful skin had captured Manu's favor at first glance. With his grandmother as midwife, the family was otherwise alone to deliver this newborn child of the village chief. Struggling for hours, Shano finally succeeded in bringing him into the world. His loud cries brought a warm smile to the proud grandmother. She held him overhead, announcing that the chief now had a son, an heir, a reason for the clan to celebrate. It was just as the old ones had said. He would be born in this way, on this longest night of winter, in a terrible storm, when the dogs felt the icy chill and howled at the moonless night sky.

Exhausted, Shano lay prone on the sealskin bedding covering the floor. Manu helped clean her and comfort her, knowing full well that if the birth had not come soon, both mother and child would have died. Manu caressed her face and spoke softly to her, but sleep took over, and he let her rest. Grandmother had cleaned up the child, wrapped him in a fresh warm skin, and rocked him until she placed the newborn into Manu's calloused hands. The baby was healthy, large, and already seemed to look him in the face. The bond was instant.

In the years that followed, Manu and Anook were inseparable. The child accompanied him on almost every hunt, unless the often-wiser Shano said that conditions were too dangerous. From his earliest years, Anook was larger framed, taller, and stronger than the other children his age. He could have become a bully, but his father's patience and stern hand helped mold him into the man he became. Kind and gentle to his sister and mother, he joined his father at an early age in pursuit of stores for the long, dark Arctic winter.

Anook learned his father's lessons well, but his spirit of independence led him into serious dangerous situations on more than one occasion. He fell into the freezing sea several times, turned over his kayak, or got far too close to a polar bear den. His daring allowed him to become a good judge of just how far he could push himself, how long he could take exposure to the winter elements, and how much he could get away with before his dad's strong hand would cuff him back to his senses.

His early life was filled with bravery and hardship. As he grew into a man, Anook's exploits became the inspiration of legends. He became a great leader with a pleasant smile, but he possessed an unwavering resilience, and an iron will, no matter what challenge he faced. In person, he was an impressive physical specimen—very tall and broad shouldered for a member of his ethnic group. His prowess and exploits as a hunter and provider for the clan fueled stories that would be embellished by time and became the subject of evening storytelling sessions, a common social interaction on the long winter evenings. Anook often went to hunt alone, convinced that other members of a hunt could compromise the results. He was a hero, a survivor against sometimes incredible odds, and a savior to the clan in times of greatest need.

Before his father, Manu, passed on, he spent his time creating intricate scrimshaw art carved on walrus tusk ivory. His eyes began to fail, but he completed one final piece: an amulet depicting his son's great achievements on one side and their clan's symbol on the reverse. It became Anook's symbol, his prized possession. The elders said that it had magical powers, embellishing the growing legends of his prowess on every possible occasion. When his father died, Anook held the amulet over his heart and swore to never remove it.

Anook married the daughter of a nearby clan's best hunter. He had two children of his own, a boy and a girl. At the age of thirty-two years, Anook hugged them all, left his family for an expected two-day hunt, but never returned. Though his friends and family searched for days, no sign of him was ever seen or found again. On the night of his disappearance, the aurora borealis shimmered across the evening sky, much more vibrant than seen for many years. The stars in the black crisp sky twinkled with an uncommon brightness. The clan took it all as a symbol. They hoped for his return but knew in their hearts that he was gone, taken by the sea or the ice or the bears that had nurtured him. The only certainty was that Anook and the amulet would never be forgotten.

CHAPTER 1

THE ATTACK

Crossing the barren, rocky, windswept no-man's-land was a perilous journey for any living creature, man or beast. Traversing it this night meant certain death if any of the insertion group were detected. In his heart, Pakesh felt that his actions were justified. If he'd known in advance the ramifications of his actions, he would have wished to Allah that he'd never been born.

Pakesh crept forward, knowing that only by the grace of Allah would he see morning. Rivulets of perspiration trickled from his brow and underarms, even in the cool mountain air. He was oblivious to the chill, adrenaline coursing through his body. Feet wrapped in soft velvet cloth to muffle the sounds of boots on loose talus, each man in his column stepped with precision into the footprint left by the man ahead. There were thirty well-trained special force commandos, each a volunteer, all willing to die tonight, and he was their leader. He was not first in line but third, the two ahead wearing full-body armor and Kevlar pads, offering some protection from undetected booby traps or mines. Pakesh was too important to be at point. He was the explosives expert as well as commanding officer, carrying the fuses, detonators, and timers necessary to trigger the pyrotechnic destruction he was charged with delivering to the enemy.

They were crossing the barren no-man's-land between two low opposing ridges, an area festooned with motion detectors, trip wires, and various sensors all set up to expose human trespass. A narrow ravine provided minimal protection from visual observation by an enemy bent on their destruction. Months of reconnaissance and the subsequent deaths of a dozen infiltrators provided some detail of the defenses. During the previous two nights, sophisticated countermeasures were put in place by technicians, who braved the defenses to provide his group with the least perilous approach. The crumpled body of one still lay where he died in a hail of bullets only two meters to the left of their present path.

His men moved with maximum stealth, every rattle silenced, hand signals only, each man trained to move with deliberate precision and absolute care. One mistake, a single squeak, loud crunch, cough, or sneeze would mean discovery and a near-certain quick death. They would not survive one hundred meters in retreat if the searchlights illuminated their position. All knew their jobs, all were specialists, and all knew the result of any mistakes.

Dawn was still four hours away. This determined group of volunteers was now almost three kilometers from the safety of their own positions and closing fast on their intended target: a rocky crag of windswept rock housing the command and communication headquarters for the Indian mountain division guarding this sector. If Pakesh and his men were successful tonight, this blow to the enemy would cause the loss of key personnel and their command and control for this entire sector as well as boost the sagging morale of his own troops in the region.

Creeping forward, Pakesh thought of his beautiful wife and three children back home, and the idea of not seeing them again knotted his stomach. He could not afford any distraction, so he dismissed the thought and instead mimed his favorite prayer. He also prayed that he and his men would be able to cover the final distance and that success would be their reward.

Pakesh joined the mountain frontier defense brigade two years to the day prior to the mission tonight. A bony sprite of a man with a grisly beard and pointed bent nose, he was anything but handsome. Well educated, he was street tough and very physically fit for a man of forty years. The young, normally reckless men in his charge called him the old man or dad, but none would dare challenge his veteran special force's sharpened fighting ability or courage. This night, they all depended on his leadership for their lives.

Pakesh had a difficult childhood and joined the Afghanistan freedom fighters while still a teenager. The freedom fighters were a terrorist cell, a branch of al-Qaeda. He believed in the Muslim insurgent's cause and joined the mujahideen in their jihad or holy war. That was until he saw and was repulsed by their atrocities carried out against innocent targets in the name of religion. He fled from the cell after killing its leader and returned to Pakistan ready to find a way to fight against their terror. What he did now was for his country, to secure the border in an area that their foe claimed.

Carried on the clear mountain air, the sound of voices froze each man in midstep. Crouching and listening, they knew from the sounds that they were close to their target, very close, and that they were within striking distance. Of absolute necessity, all communications were now by sign only. Pakesh gestured, and two men passed his position moving silently forward, their task the elimination of the sentries, who had now given away their position. The rest of his group waited in silence, a last brief respite before the attack, a time to make peace with their maker or to recheck their weapons one final time.

An almost imperceptible sound of a silencer caused the first of two guards sharing a shielded cigarette to slump forward onto his stunned comrade. A moment later, before he could even react, the second sentry's face sprayed red, and the back of his head littered the cold rock behind him. Two shooters slipped silently over the stone bastion into the trench-like fortification. They signaled Pakesh, and the others began their final approach. Moving to their right, the first two killers searched for the next sentry post intelligence had spotted twenty meters to the south. They were crawling forward one behind the other; the first stopped and pointed ahead, holding up two fingers. These two guards were awake, alert, and surveying the area to the west. Good fortune for the assassins, the guards were looking away, and two more silenced shots dispatched another third of the sentries on duty. Such laxity and such poor security were laughed at by the shooters. They retraced their path to the first post, meeting Pakesh there, then crept forward toward the third and final two-man guard post to the north. Seconds later, the last pair were dead, one while urinating and the second one studying the terrain through night-vision glasses but, unfortunately for him, looking the wrong way.

Satisfied that no other guards were on duty or active, the two point men returned to the first post and rejoined the now assembled and waiting commando group. As he approached Pakesh, the first into the trench whispered, "Allah is with us. The sentries are all dead, and clouds continue to block any moonlight. We are ready to complete our mission."

Pakesh signaled his men. They all knew their tasks, having rehearsed the planned attack more than twenty times. During their wait, Pakesh and his assistant finished preparing the charges, brick-sized blocks of high explosives, detonators now attached, timers set. They had ten minutes to distribute and plant the explosives and return to a point approximately one hundred meters back along their original approach path. The rendezvous point was the deepest place in the shallow ravine that would offer at least a minimum of protection when the detonations began. If anyone was discovered and shooting started, each man was prepared to hurl himself and his explosives onto the enemy or deep into any entrances or passages into the tunnel-and-bunker complex.

They fanned out into the complex, searching for the weakest points or places where they would cause the most damage. Aerial drone reconnaissance and photography had provided a basic layout, but so much was unknown to the attackers since much was subterranean. An awakened enemy or alert could still spoil the attack, subsequently minimizing the inflicted damage.

Pakesh led the advance into the tunnels, he knowing the most about the explosives and where best to place them. Without hesitation, they bravely moved ahead, still being vigilant of silence but now determined to penetrate as far as possible without discovery.

Simultaneous with Pakesh's attack, an explosive-laden food supply truck was pulling into the back entrance of a quiet hotel. The sleeping representatives and officers of the provincial government were resting before the parliamentary meeting starting in the morning. Crippling the regional government and a strategic military base in one lightning attack was the overall military objective of the planned attacks. This attack was also planned to push the pacifist government to finally agree to new borders and relinquish their claim to the long-disputed area called Kashmir.

A silenced nine-millimeter Taurus barked twice, ending the board game between two more tunnel entrance guards. The attacking group was now inside, and the carnage would soon begin. Charges were set, bodies were booby-trapped, and the backpacks filled with explosives were quickly placed in the locations deemed best. Looking at his watch, Pakesh signaled for his men to begin their extraction. They now had less than four minutes to clear the area. They were almost back to the main entrance when a surprised young man stepped yawning from a latrine door. Pakesh's first lieutenant killed him with his knife as the young man flailed his arms, useless against the aggressor. Unseen by his assailants, a second soldier behind the first carried a sidearm, and his first shot killed the lieutenant. Surprise was now lost as the sound of the shot resonated down the corridor. Pakesh tossed a grenade into the lavatory. His assistants threw three more behind them as they raced for the entrance.

Emerging to the cacophony of alarms, with automatic spotlights clicking on and with less than two minutes to go before the detonators did their job, they sprinted for the perimeter. Blinking soldiers emerging from another entrance took up positions and began tracing their retreat with machine-gun fire. Two men behind Pakesh were cut down just as they reached the wall. He felt the graze of a bullet tear through his pants below his knee; a searing pain soon followed. Most of his men were already gone, running down the shallow ravine. He glanced back one last time to see two more of his men cut to pieces by the rapid-fire guns. He stopped and stooped once more to look for any more stragglers. Satisfied there were none, he again ran as fast as he could toward the limited cover, blood now flowing down his wounded leg.

He scrambled into the lowest part of the depression where two of his comrades were crouched low, rifles aimed to cover his retreat. As he plunged headlong into the shallow cover, incoming bullets throwing rock chips over him, the first charges exploded, followed by the deafening concussions as the entire top of the mountain fortress seemed to rise up and be engulfed by a brilliant red-black fireball. Rocks and debris showered down around them. The surviving members of his group made a hasty retreat under the cover of dust and destruction. A younger member of the team, flushed with the thrill of their successful attack, was struck in the head by a falling rock and killed.

They gathered at the second planned rendezvous point to look back at the smoldering hilltop behind them. There were no longer any searchlights, sirens, or machine guns firing, only the glow of fires burning and the explosions of ordinance. Satisfied, Pakesh bandaged his bloody leg, counted his survivors, and all disappeared into the night.

Miles away, two food service truck deliverymen walked casually away from the hotel, chatting like two boys enjoying an evening stroll. One produced a black plastic object from his pocket as they rounded a corner. Extending a small antenna, he flipped open a cover, revealing a small red button. He pushed the button while stepping into a recessed doorway, and they covered their ears. A split second later, the hotel was enveloped in a monstrous explosion.

The first irreversible steps were in motion. Tensions between India and Pakistan were at a point they had never reached before. Arguments over land ownership and the border placement were frequent. Cross-border incidents were not uncommon. Mutual distrust and hostilities were the norm. The two countries had been at odds over the mountainous stretch of disputed land known as Kashmir for more than half a century. Mounting tensions reached the boiling point on several occasions, and a mutual distrust only fueled the tension, but cooler minds normally prevailed.

In 1947, the partition of India took place, creating two independent dominions—India and Pakistan. The dominion of India became the Republic of India in 1950. The dominion of Pakistan became the Islamic Republic of Pakistan in 1971. Millions of people were displaced or forced to move.

The princely state of Kashmir and Jammu was ruled by King Hari Singh, who preferred to remain neutral and independent. Following uprisings and attacks by rebel raiders, the maharaja signed an accession instrument whereby he would join the Dominion of India for military aid. Pakistan considered the territory of Kashmir theirs because of its Muslim majority. Pakistan still claims all of the state of Jammu and Kashmir. India's official position maintained that all of the area of Jammu and Kashmir was theirs. The disputed ownership and border between India and Pakistan became a flash point and remained that through the years. Three wars were fought along with many skirmishes. The Indo-Pakistani War of 1947 was the first following the accession. Wars broke out again over the region in 1965 and 1971.

A cease-fire line now known as the Line of Control refers to a military line between the Indian—and Pakistani-controlled parts. Established by the Simla Agreement in 1972, the line does not constitute a legally recognized international boundary but is instead a de facto border. This "border" is considered one of the most dangerous places in the entire world.

Uncontrolled Muslim extremists in Pakistan have always been a potential international danger. According to Amnesty International, Indian forces in Kashmir have been accused of committing many human rights abuses. Each side blames the other for fanning the flames.

To the Indian authorities, the Pakistani government did nothing to restrain or stop the terrorists who planned and carried out the attack on and total destruction of the base and may have been complicit in it. India's patience was gone, and the people demanded retribution when the Pakistani government did nothing, and the Pakistani military was believed to have been involved. Massive air and land attacks were launched by India along the border, overrunning the Pakistani border defenses in only hours. Pakistan's leadership underestimated the resolve of their Indian counterparts after the latest attack. Their border defenses were formidable, but troop morale was poor, and command structure had deteriorated. The degree of response was less than enough to repel a major invasion.

Threatened with a collapse of their border defenses, a devastating loss of face, the loss of any influence in Kashmir, and a crippling defeat, Pakistan declared war and launched a nuclear missile attack upon several Indian cities. Use of nuclear weapons had been banned by earlier treaties, and stockpiles supposedly destroyed or limited, but both sides were nuclear powers. In reprisal, the Indian military unleashed a furious nuclear counterattack. Millions died or were dying within a few days. The actual war lasted only four days. Resultant debris and ash clouds carried by upper-atmospheric winds covered most of the northern hemisphere within a few weeks.

CHAPTER 2

CHANGES

2031, Chicago, Illinois

Wayne Adams studied it, pondered it, measured it, and had spent most of his adult life immersed in its ramifications. His passion for studying weather and the atmosphere was real, a zeal to unravel a very complex science. He knew that the earth's climate was changing, but he also knew that this dynamic macrocosm called the earth had gone through many such cycles and episodes in the past. Wayne heatedly argued his science while listening carefully to his detractors.

The new climate problems started after the Pakistan-India conflict. Wayne found it hard to believe that to this day, the media still did not refer to it as a war. It was referred to as "an escalation of lasting hostilities," "an overreaction to domestic pressure," "an international incident of dreadful consequences," but it was not called a war. Wayne thought it incredible and purely political.

Pakistan and India had been at odds over borders in Kashmir for years, in fact, for over half a century. Many minor skirmishes marred the efforts to bring peace to the region. Both countries developed the nuclear bomb and the means to deliver it, while the rest of the world pushed for disarmament and removal of nuclear threats. The burgeoning populations of both countries were overwhelmed by their government's abilities to plan for or control the growth.

Recent crop failures, potential for famine, unemployment, and social pressures caused by extremist groups escalated the border conflicts. International pressure and the fear of annihilation ended the confrontation quickly. After only four days of nuclear conflict, the damage was done. Cities were destroyed, and areas of both nations were laid to waste.

When both sides agreed to end production of nuclear devices, they began destroying their stockpiles in 2028. International supervision supposedly confirmed the treaty agreements were carried out. The consequences of the hidden weapons and their use now accelerated the changing weather conditions.

The nuclear detonations created vast clouds of dust and debris and contributed to an almost unbroken blanket of low-lying clouds throughout the northern hemisphere. At first, everyone feared the radioactive fallout, but the bombs were fairly clean. Though a serious consequence, the radioactive fallout was a much smaller problem. The dust cloud circled the globe, and much remained as a sun-blocking barrier. This new phenomenon became a particularly interesting study for Wayne and his meteorological comrades and researchers.

They saw many factors contributing to a potential "nuclear winter" scenario. These included the present solar cycle, the nuclear detonations, climate change, and unexpected volcanic activity in the Arctic and Pacific Ocean Ring of Fire. They all knew that the situation was deteriorating, and their climate models simply could not handle all the varying parameters. One thing they did agree on was that weather conditions were going to deteriorate.

From his south-side office in Chicago, Wayne monitored a vast array of climatological information from numerous sources around the globe, graphing data, measuring and comparing variations, no matter how incongruous. This year in Chicago, spring was not happening. Wayne saw that the changes were gradual, subtle, beginning in the late twentieth century. By the millennium, climate change was a hot topic for the world governments, national leaders, and a hungry press and media. Weather and climate became a regular controversial topic of conversation around the globe. At first, scientific debate raged, but gradually, more and more members of the scientific community began to realize that some undeniable changes were taking place all over the world. Whether caused by human's contributions of pollution, known as anthropomorphic, or caused naturally, changes were evident almost everywhere from the high Arctic to the equator. At first, the phenomenon was called global warming, then climate change, then almost anything that would garner grant money or political notoriety.

Wayne also studied changes in the sun and solar radiation, which can also be responsible for significant climate variations over time. Cosmic rays can influence cloud formation. The sun's solar wind or stream of charged subatomic particles helps shield the earth from cosmic rays. Cosmic rays collide with particles in the atmosphere, leaving them electrically charged or ionized. The ionized particles then seed the growth of cloud-forming water droplets. Lower solar activity means higher cosmic ray bombardment, thus more low clouds and a cooler climate.

Clouds that form low in the sky are relatively warm and made up of tiny water droplets. These clouds also tend to cool the planet by reflecting sunlight back into space. High clouds are cooler, consisting mostly of ice particles, and they have the effect of warming the earth by trapping heat. The northern hemisphere was now wrapped with an increasing coat of low moisture-laden clouds.

Wayne also studied the alignment of the gas giant planets, their relative positions with Earth and how that could affect volcanism on Earth, even ocean currents, and thereby climate conditions. He understood that their present positions and combined gravitational effects could cause more volcanism on earth, something that was already happening. This in turn was putting additional gases and ash into the atmosphere, thereby exacerbating an already serious problem.

His latest cause for concern was the recent increase in volcanism. A feature called the Gakkel Ridge runs under the Arctic Ocean and beneath the North Pole. It is a northern branch or continuation of the mid-oceanic ridges, representing another area of upheaval and a place where new crustal material is created. These unobtrusive areas of intense geothermal activity and subsea volcanism only occasionally reach the surface, exposing themselves as newborn islands, Iceland being the most well-known example. The Columbia University Lamont-Doherty Earth Observatory began tracking more activity on the Gakkel Ridge as early as the year 2000. Wayne added their studies to his growing database.

Little was known about the Gakkel Ridge because few direct observations were possible until the advent of subpolar ice voyages of the nuclear submarine fleets from Russia and the US. When data was finally gathered and assimilated into the growing volume of information concerning the hot seafloor spread centers, scientists, including Wayne, discovered that the hydrothermal activity on the Gakkel Ridge was almost twenty times the average along mid-Atlantic and other subsea ridges. More data was needed, and both nations began crisscrossing the polar ridge, making numerous measurements. It was also the perfect opportunity for the implementation and deployment of another top secret defense project by the Navy disguised as a base for studying the weather.

In his studies, Wayne found other historic events of similar consequences and duration on world climate patterns. One was the eruption of Krakatoa near Java in the South Pacific in the 1880s. The year following the eruption was called the year without summer. Volcanic gases and ash effectively reduced solar radiation enough to cause a brownish sun, decreased daylight, and very cool temperatures. The second was the eruption of Mount Pinatubo in 1991 that injected enough aerosols into the stratosphere to cool the earth over one-half degree Celsius for two years. The Little Ice Age from 1450 to 1850 was a classic example of longer-term changes that have now been linked to excess volcanism. Volcanic eruptions cool by injecting particulates and sulfate aerosols into the atmosphere, which reflect sunlight back into space.

The dust from the brief nuclear holocaust and increased volcanic releases further intensified the already occurring weather problems. The world had been making headway before the nukes were unleashed. International agreements and trade pressure had been cutting down on pollution and particulate effluents on every continent, and improvements were noticeable.

GLOBAL WARNING

This year, the winter was long and cool, and the humidity in Chicago was setting even higher records. The average daytime temperature last year had fallen again. The winter this year was long, wet, cold, and not over yet. Wayne knew inevitable unrest, potential for civil problems, and the emotional strife of a short, wet summer would follow. He planned to leave Chicago this time. Last year, unrest in his decaying neighborhood nearly forced him and his girlfriend to leave.

His monitoring stations were all now focusing on and compiling data about the unusual high humidity. For days, the air was thick with fog, an increasing stench of mildew and mold, and laden with the bothersome burden of excess moisture. Chicago had steadily become more air-conditioned in the early part of the century to deal with the increasing summer heat, but that was a thing of the past.

Last year's winter "storm of the century" should have sent the final warning. But that type of storm had already been repeated several times. This year, the Midwest and most of the US were blanketed in record snows. Flooding from the late melt-off would inevitably be horrendous in various northern hemisphere locations.

Wayne could see that something different was happening again this year. Vast blankets of fog formed off the west coast of Canada and Alaska. Similar blankets were present west of the European continent. Instead of the turbulence of the warm unstable air masses clashing with the cooler polar fronts, quiescence had settled. The polar jets moved south, leaving most of the northern hemisphere in a stagnant stalemate of unprecedented character.

The warming period at the end of the last century and early twenty-first did cause more atmospheric instability and a few more storms, floods, tornadoes, hurricanes, and typhoons. The number of weather-related deaths rose. But that period was good to farmers, crop yields were excellent, and there was abundance to feed the world's burgeoning population.

Now crop failures were common and widespread; famine an increasing concern. A shroud of thick sunlight-blocking clouds and excessive moisture was having a devastating effect on agriculture. A shroud of gray—a blanket of fog and smog—now cloaked an enormous area of the northern hemisphere. A vast amount of moisture was present in the northern latitudes with little wind or jet stream to move it away. This meant serious trouble for many millions.

Wayne's various weather data displays began to show the changes some time ago. High humidity and fog reached far north into Canada and the Arctic. The most northern latitudes were still cold. Coupled with the crippling moisture-laden air over the northern expanses of Canadian forest and tundra, snow was still falling at amazing rates. In some areas, nothing was moving, and there was no sign of any letup anytime soon. Spring simply was not happening north of the Thirty-Fifth Parallel.

The changes were no longer subtle. Years of slow warming were over for certain. Wayne could see that things were adjusting again. His computer models and simulations were changing. Wayne reviewed and re-reviewed his data. It was clear that the nuclear exchange and subsequent widespread of dust clouds were causes for concern and sure to have some brief climatic effect. The eruption of several volcanoes on the Arctic ridge, in Iceland, and the Pacific only contributed more particles and gases to the already existing problem. Wayne was not certain of what was taking place at present, but he was alarmed that it was so rapid. All indicators now pointed to serious cooling, more precipitation, and therefore more problems in all the northern latitudes.

Wayne monitored the Canadian Rockies every day. For two winters in a row, the snowpack was incredible. Many peaks and passes remained snowbound for almost the entire year. Ski resorts never opened because they were buried, and access to any remote location was difficult and dangerous and, in some cases, impossible.

This year's snowpack was again unprecedented. Some mountain resorts and towns had tried to prepare and fight for existence, but the mountains reclaimed their turf. One particularly severe storm dropped almost twenty feet of snow in less than ten days. In places, even the trees were buried. Calgary, Alberta, was paralyzed, and supplies were dwindling. The northern stretches of the Arctic, normally dry with limited amounts of snow, were receiving unprecedented measurements. Fed by record snowfalls, glaciers began to grow and advance, some for the first time in many years.

Wayne feared that his associates at the new Arctic research base were now facing serious trouble. Several scientists were stranded at two Inuit settlements. The villagers of Inuit heritage had long since pulled out. The weather scientists chose to stay. He felt responsible for the people under his direction at the base. He enjoyed the cold and isolation that the job required, but he felt that he should be there rather than in Chicago.

He grew up in the Chicago suburbs, the child of poor parents who scraped together all that they could to help him through his undergrad years. But if he had not gotten some scholarship assistance, he never would have been able to afford college. He worked hard as a painter and handyman every summer and worked in food service to afford his board.

He was not tall, standing five foot ten, with straight dark hair and big blue eyes. Wayne was muscular and handsome if you liked beards. His athletic prowess was limited only by his time constraints. He wrestled in high school and did very well, but jobs and hard work limited his athletics in college to intramural baseball, where he excelled. It also limited his social life and dating, but he could party with the best of them. Accepted into a master's degree program, he pursued his weather and climate advanced degree with a passion. The hard work paid off when he received his present position, which led him to a symposium on climate where he met his fiancée, Becky Cottingham. Their wedding was planned for later that year, when Becky returned from her assignment at the base in the Arctic.

CHAPTER 3

KENUIUT SOUND
AWRB 1

Arctic Weather Research Base Number 1 (AWRB 1) was situated on spectacular Kenuiut Sound along the Arctic fringe of Northern Canada. Located a short distance from a long-ago abandoned Inuit fishing village, the base slowly became a mecca for a number of scientists and technicians studying various climatological and ecological fields.

Reaching AWRB 1 in good weather was no easy task. During the prolonged period of malicious Arctic weather, ingress and egress were virtually impossible. Igloolik on the Melville Peninsula was the jumping-off point. Weekly air service connected remote Igloolik with the outside world, but Igloolik was still a long way from nowhere.

From the village of Igloolik, a place made famous by the Inuit Eskimos' ice homes or igloos, the scientists and their vital supply planes had another arduous flight to their base camp. Kenuiut Sound, the home of AWRB 1, occupied a barren, rocky cove on the south side of Baffin Island, a vast expanse of tundra. From the camp inland stretched a spectacular coastal fjord.

AWRB 1 occupied a site that, on several occasions in the past, had been the summer home of the Sin Inuit Native North Americans. These Native peoples had inhabited the coastal fjords, venturing inland to hunt caribou in summer and subsisting on the bounty of the sea the remainder of the year.

Around Igloolik, the Natives were Iglulingmuit. Both were Eskimos or Inuit, which means "the people." Several worked at the base camp in various capacities. All had warned the scientists well in advance of the present problems, and several had wisely departed. The scientists refused to acknowledge the sage advice of their non-professional colleagues. It would prove to be a case of very poor judgment. Most of the degreed team recognized the situation well in advance but were too preoccupied with their work to abandon the assumed safety of the well-provisioned base.

The scientific teams were at the fjord base station to not only gather and interpret real-time weather and climate data but also research ancient climates and changes. There was no better repository of climate data than that preserved in the myriad layers of crystalline ice. They had obtained and preserved numerous ice cores, allowing more detailed analysis of ancient climates.

An especially hardy group of Canadians were studying the Barnes Ice Cap on the eastern central end of Baffin Island. They had already made some startling discoveries, but sadly, now much of their work area was being buried by expanding ice fields and would soon be wiped away by advancing glaciers.

All this area was well north of the Arctic Circle, the parallel at 67° north latitude. The entire region was underlain by rock and permafrost or perennially frozen subsurface soil. At these latitudes, the Arctic precipitation was normally scant, more like a frozen desert. In the long months of winter, temperatures could drop as low as -46° C (-50° F) and seldom rose above 10° C (+50° F) in summer.

Life-giving solar energy was in short supply during winter that consisted of months of long polar nights. Even in April, the midnight sun, its rays prolonged and slanted, brought little heat.

Everything was changing and had been for some time. Now heavy snows were common and often continuous for days. Snow was accumulating at beyond-record rates. A heavy crust of deep snow, uncommon on the near-desert Arctic, could spell disaster for both land-bound wildlife, such as the caribou, and man.

The ice landing field at Kenuiut was impossible to keep clear of snow. Light planes were able to land with their life-supporting supplies up until this spring. Snow removal or packing equipment had managed to keep the aircraft moving, but this effort was abandoned when the equipment became too deeply buried. During the recent past, there were few days clear enough for aircraft to be airborne, and few pilots were willing to risk the unpredictable conditions. Long-range helicopters and hovercraft flights were risky but had become the only tenable means of reaching the base. Overland travel was now out of the question. Deep drifts and thick snowpack, often overlain by a thin unstable crust, made surface travel dangerous and arduous.

Wayne knew that all the scientists and support people should have gone home. The Greenlanders and Danes had recalled their group to Greenland where conditions were just as bad. The Canadians had pulled a fair number out. Wayne was not alone in the decision-making process regarding his team. He knew that several of the group were also government agents planting a vast array of sensors and relay points for satellites. They had multiple assignments and what was called "strategic importance."

Among the latter was the one individual most important to him: Ms. Becky Cottingham, a beautiful and remarkable young lady who wore his engagement ring on her left ring finger. He missed her, even more so than during the riots last year when he asked her to marry him. She laughed at him and said, "Not a chance, buster!" He had been startled and was taken aback. She let him wallow in his bewilderment for a few moments before consenting with a warm and wonderful hug.

Becky was a mid-US, small-town girl of modest background. She was pretty but not beautiful by magazine model standards. She was shy and modest but warm and friendly toward everyone she met.

Wayne loved her smile and calm demeanor but, when it came to her science, knew her personality could change to argumentative in an instant. She could debate with the best of them and knew her facts. Becky also had a penchant for remembering her favorite jokes and telling them with a flair that surprised everyone. That sense of humor he truly loved. It had cheered him out of depression on more than one occasion.

Her hair was silky brown and long, but, much of the time, she wore it in a tight bun clipped to the back of her head. It made her look professorial. She was teaching some classes while earning her advanced degree. With penetrating green eyes and high cheekbones on a smooth blemish-free face, she always looked amazing to Wayne. He was immediately stricken when he first saw her in a climate symposium that they both attended. They exchanged contact information. It took Wayne several attempts at setting up a date after that before she finally relented. She agreed to meet for a quick lunch between classes at the student union. That led to several nice dinners together but no intimacy for several months. She finally kissed him when he dropped her off one evening. It was long and meaningful—a moment he would never forget.

CHAPTER 4

ICE SECRETS

Becky was torn by the omnipresent snowstorms and raging weather outside AWRB 1. She longed to return to the sight of her discovery. It really was hers. She had stumbled upon her incredible find completely by accident. Now she could only long to return to the site in order to search further and retrieve more invaluable material. But the present weather and the impending forecast called for more of the same. There were no breaks in the forecast, no letup in sight long enough for her and her team to search anew.

Bob Meadows, Carl Long, and Eluk, better known as Cool Hand Luke, their Inuit assistant and "guide," had been exploring the base of a very active nearby glacier. Bob was a leading and widely published authority on glacial geology. Fellow scientist and avid explorer Carl coauthored a number of papers on paleoclimates with Bob. Becky was excited when she received word that she was accepted to work with them at the base. Bob and Carl were glad to have her on their team. Becky's credentials and academic achievements were exemplary. Her energy was inspiring, and that sense of dry humor and endless jokes kept morale high even with the terrible conditions present when they worked outside.

Good weather and relatively clear conditions in which to work became a rarity. It was a struggle just to keep the base area free enough of thick snow to use their helicopters. Trips anywhere had to be of short duration and returns to the base immediate if the weather deteriorated or poor conditions for flying or exploring set in. When they did at last get a respite from the raging storms, the machines were readied, and equipment that stood by was loaded as fast as safely possible. The three scientists and their guide climbed aboard, and the machine lifted off swirling clouds of loose snow in all directions. The cloud cover was thin for the first time in two weeks and the wind speeds low enough for the short flight.

They choppered in and landed on a moraine hill, a small drumlin, at the head of a river of blue ice. This particular glacier was spectacular because of the brilliant clarity of the ice and its magnificent light-blue hue. The top of the glacier, normally visible in the past, was now covered with a thick blanket of snow many meters thick. Where deep crevices were once visible along with rock and stone debris trails atop the river of ice, only white drifts now appeared, stretching toward the glacial source.

Their primary assignment that day was to walk to the tongue of ice and set up devices to monitor and measure its movement. The second task was to drill several ice cores and pack them for transport back to the lab. Aerial photographs suggested that this was one of the most rapidly advancing glaciers in this entire region. They were planning to obtain the ice cores using a new piece of apparatus, a laser cutter designed specifically for this purpose by Bob Meadows. If it worked as designed, his new tool had the intended purpose of speeding up ice core collection several times. The new tool worked nearly flawlessly in tests around base camp, but this would be the first true field test. Bob was worried, concerned to see if it would still function as planned after transport, loading and unloading, and then being packed over to the edge of the mass of moving ice.

This glacier had no official name. Becky had named it Long Glacier for Carl. He was flattered and eager to actually explore it. It was Carl who spotted the possible ice caves along the lower left side of the ice flow on a previous reconnoiter. Though potentially very dangerous, these ephemeral caves often allowed penetration deep into the ice in a lateral direction. This could allow much deeper sampling of the internal parts of the glacier itself. The dangerous caves were always a temptation to the scientists.

After landing and unloading their gear, Bob and Carl went to work, assembling their new toy. Becky and Cool Hand Luke decided to make a preliminary reconnoiter of a nearest ice cave. They received their mandatory warnings and cautions from the rest of the group. Several of the caves showed the obvious signs of earlier warmer periods when water flowed more freely from them. Though this was an almost clear day, above freezing, only a trickle of crystal clear water bubbled forth from the opening. Luke was not averse to Becky exploring a short distance in, but he did not like ice caves. He decided that he would wait by the entrance while Becky looked around, cautioning her to not venture too far inside. She slipped her ice cleats over her boots and walked with care into the crystalline blue interior.

Luke received his peculiar moniker because of his extraordinary ability to go gloveless in relatively severe weather while the scientists needed well-insulated gloves. Besides being acclimated better to the conditions because of his background, Luke had amazingly good circulation that allowed his hands to stay comfortable for a considerable time without his thick caribou mittens. Carl Long named him Cool Hand Luke, and the name stuck.

Becky headed into the cave, sure-footed in her heavy boots festooned with the steel ice-climbing cleats. She crunched forward over the glistening path, gazing about with a light in one hand and an ice ax in the other. She hadn't proceeded very far within when they were all startled by her shrill scream. Her comrades all momentarily froze when they heard the scream. The sound had emanated from a total nonscreamer. Becky was not a female who was inclined to get overly excited. Something really frightened her. That was evident from the intensity of the cry. They feared that she had fallen into a hidden crevice or broken through a crust of thin ice.

The thin safety line connecting her to Luke was still limp. Luke was startled and frightened for her. He only took a few steps inside when he spotted her. She was standing frozen, staring up at the ceiling of the cave, and it appeared as though she was ducking. Her gaze from her half-crouched position was fixed on the clear ice directly above her head.

Luke trotted gingerly over the clear blue floor of the cave to join her. As he approached Becky, Bob and Carl reached the cave entrance with complete bewilderment and deep concern etched on their brows. Luke shouted back, "Wait there until I know the reason why she cried out." He had drawn his seal-skinning knife and was brandishing the sharp blade when he reached Becky's side. There in her light was a sight that made his skin crawl. Above them, a face stared directly back at them from a frozen sprawled person in a laid-out position, who appeared to be falling straight down on Becky from above. The personage looked like an Eskimo floating in clear blue water. The face was frightened and confused, the eyes wide open. It was a visage frozen in the ice, frozen in time.

Luke was far from comfortable, and his highly superstitious nature determined that this was a very bad omen. Becky regained her composure and was enamored with the surreal face before her. All she could say was an unladylike "Holy crap!" She quickly followed that with, "Bob, Carl, you've got to see this. Come here! This is beyond belief."

As they assembled below the figure, Becky shone her light on the frozen man. They were all entranced by the apparition encased in the sparkling ice. It appeared that the being above them had somehow become trapped in the ice and was perfectly preserved. The face almost appeared to be alive, like the entrapped person was pleading to be released from the entombing frozen water around him. Carl fumbled through his backpack for his light and switched it on. The sight of the hominid figure in a thick fur parka encapsulated in crystal clear ice shocked him. The gleaming ice distorted the details of the figure, but the face was only a meter or so away.

Bob had his digital camera equipment out and was already dictating into it as he snapped the first pictures. "We have found a person, a body in the glacier. It is not crushed and mangled. It appears to be intact and undamaged." He snapped pictures and took several short videos of the mysterious figure. He added the time, GPS points, and basic location information.

Becky realized that this was something very special and that the day's assigned duties were going to be abandoned. They had just made an interesting and potentially very significant scientific discovery. Carl's immediate reaction was to begin extracting a small sample of the adjoining ice for analysis. His work and apparatus back at the lab would age-date the ice and fix a potential time for the entrapment of this casualty of the Arctic's unpredictability. He guessed from his experience that the surrounding ice here was well over a thousand years old, maybe even much older. The group gathered around to stare at the transfixing face and body before them.

The rumbling and crackling of ice and rock interrupted their examination of the mysterious frozen figure. Emanating from deep within the moving ice, the sounds brought a chilling reminder of the dangers involved in exploring ice caves. None of them believed that the strange corpse floating above them in the azure ice could possibly be very old, much less ancient. The state of preservation was much too good. Anything trapped in moving glacial ice would normally be pulverized beyond recognition.

Carl was quick to point out that this section of the ice flow was cut off from the main part of the glacier and therefore could have been relatively stable. The ice was not cloudy and cracked by immense stresses. It was clean and clear, virtually pure, and permanently frozen.

Luke was not pleased to be viewing a potential ancestor under these conditions. He objected vehemently to Becky's suggestion that they try to remove the body and take it back for research. Since this day was a rare, almost clear day and bad weather was not expected again until later the next day, Becky made the decision to set up the tents and camp by the helicopter. The pilot would make the final decision. He and their second Inuit assistant, John, were busy getting a lunch ready. She expected no objections to the slight change of plans, and the weather forecast did look good. Becky assured Eluk that the corpse could ride back in his seat. Eluk did not appreciate her humor. His eyes told her his genuine feelings about the body with a look of disappointment and displeasure.

They decided to break for lunch and plan a means of extracting the frozen figure with the least potential for disturbing it. Bob wasn't sure that they should even try. He thought it was important to bring in an anthropologist and archeologist before disturbing it. After a short discussion, he agreed there was no way that they were leaving without it.

As a group, they made a plan. They would cut a block of ice out of the cave ceiling big enough to not disturb the discovery, yet of a size that could be airlifted back to the AWRB camp. The helicopter could not possibly lift them and the block of ice, so they would call in a Canadian Air Force heavy-lift chopper while weather allowed. The block of ice would be cut using the ice-coring laser and dropped onto a cushioning pile of snow and inflatable life raft from the helicopter. It sounded like a good plan, but no one was sure that it would succeed.

After lunch, they used a life raft to scoop up loose snow and built a pile beneath the targeted section of the ceiling. Upon completion of this objective, they briefly rested and prepared to begin the extraction. Eluk helped gather and pile the snow but refused to help with the actual removal of the frozen corpse. Instead, he waited near the ice cave entrance and feigned disinterest.

It took Bob and Carl considerable time to decide on the position for the ice incisions. It was necessary to remove sections of the overhead ice to facilitate actual removal of the target block. The danger of falling chunks of ice was very real for the laser operators below. Premature breakage or a large falling chunk would create serious problems for the ice cutters.

John and Carl operated the cutter. Bob and Becky stayed at a safe distance, ready to help if or when it became necessary. The superhot laser cut through the ice like butter.

The initial cuts were smooth and efficient, almost exactly as planned. Surrounding ice was removed in small enough pieces to be of limited danger. When enough ice was removed from the side and ends to expose the target block, John had Carl move away. He alone would make the cuts behind the block to free it. Working alone gave him more room and allowed him more freedom to get away fast if the block broke free prematurely. This was the tricky part. They had planned their cuts like a lumberjack felling a huge tree. If it went as planned, the block would fall away from the cutter. The crude snow hill and life raft cushion was shaped and positioned to dampen the fall and to hold the huge ice chunk.

The eerie sounds of the moving glacier made everyone nervous. Just before the block broke free, the surrounding ice field groaned as if uttering an objection to their endeavor. With a loud snap, the block broke free. None of them expected what happened next.

Eluk had removed his parka to enjoy a brief sunny period and relative warmth of the day. The temperature was hovering near thirty degrees Fahrenheit. He was going through his exercise routine. He heard the loud crack of the block breaking free and the dull chunk as it landed on the target cushion below. His eyes grew wide as he beheld the ensuing surprise.

Much to everyone's chagrin, the block landed intact as planned but did not stay where it should have. The extracted block, measuring over a meter and a half thick and plus two-meter long and almost one and one-half meter deep, slid off the pile and headed down the slight slope toward the cave entrance. It became a very large ice slab projectile heading straight for the startled Eluk.

"Look out!" Bob screamed.

"Luke!" Becky shouted.

In the blink of an eye, Luke was going to either be another victim of the ice slab or find a way to avoid it. He dove to his right as the slab careened toward him. The impact when it stopped was horrendous. The sound was almost sickening. His comrades gasped in horror. Becky's stomach turned when she saw smears of red on the still-moving block. "Luke!" she again shouted.

Carl had covered his mouth in anticipated horror. John saw nothing. He ducked when the block broke loose.

No one wanted to look, but they heard the cursing. It was coming from Eluk. He was alive. His back was very badly scraped, and there were two sizable bleeding abrasions. He jumped to his feet with a look of shock and anger. A string of expletives rang through the cave. They were all elated to see him standing and were oblivious to his ranting. The ice block had torn his heavy shirt and with it a sizable section of skin. He needed immediate medical attention.

The nearly lethal ice block passed over Eluk's parka and shredded the back of his shirt. The parka miraculously changed its direction by a fraction. Without this change, Eluk would have been crushed. The block had slowed just enough that it came to a stop only a few feet outside of the ice cave entrance. If it had not slowed down, the block would have hurtled over the edge of a small drop-off and smashed on the rocks below. It was chipped but intact, its occupant still suspended in the crystalline capsule of ice.

Except for the injury to Eluk and near escape of the giant ice cube, things had gone as planned. The pilot saw the block emerge from the cave and heard the shouts. When he saw the red smears, he feared the worst. He grabbed the first aid kit and ran for the cave. He reached the cave about the same time that the others gathered around Eluk. In his haste, he slipped on the wet ice, landing on his back with a loud "Oof." The first aid kit went flying. It opened on impact, and medical supplies scattered everywhere. Streaks of red appeared beneath his motionless head as his now limp body slid toward them.

"Oh, God, not Mitch too!" Becky was almost in shock from the two injuries in rapid succession. Even Eluk was silent. Concern replaced pain on his face. Carl was packing snow and ice on Eluk's back. The snow quickly became a red mat. Bob raced to Mitch's side. Becky scrambled for the medical supplies, wondering how things could possibly get worse.

John answered her question. They all turned toward the roar. "Oh, shit," he muttered. "My gun is leaning on the helicopter landing strut." They all looked toward the helicopter, questioning why he would be concerned with that at this moment. The problems at hand seemed far more important. Then they saw it standing upright next to their helicopter, sniffing the air. It was a large polar bear. It was swinging its head from side to side, nostrils flared. Seeming oblivious to such close contact with humans and their machinery, the huge animal roared with apparent rage. The figures in the ice cave watched in disbelief, each now aware that they were trapped, unarmed, and had two bleeding injured, one unconscious. The starving bear was hungry and already smelled blood. The bad situation had just taken a turn for much worse. Fear filled Becky's eyes and heart.

CHAPTER 5

RECOVERY

The group at the ice cave had serious injury problems, but none were more threatening than the new one confronting them. The bear circling the helicopter snorted and continued to sniff the air, nostrils flared. To the trapped explorers, it looked like an older animal, gaunt and hungry. Polar bears seldom attacked humans, preferring instead to avoid them. This bear appeared agitated, and the instinctive reaction to extreme hunger was a serious motivator. It could have ripped the helicopter open with its massive forelegs and heavy claws and shredded the interior, but instead, it was homing in on the smell of fresh blood.

Carl had his satellite phone with him and tried every way he could to connect to the web of communication satellites now blanketing the globe. Carl tried to raise AWRB 1, Canadian civil defense authorities, the RCMP, or anyone. He simultaneously sent a distress signal and a plea for assistance to anyone listening. The devices worked well almost anywhere, but they were in a deep rock valley enclosed within an ice cave. He received no response and had no idea if his emergency communications went through.

Eluk and John engaged in a heated but subdued debate, speaking in their native Inuit tongue. The conversation was serious by their grave intonations, concerned faces, and arm gestures. John assisted in temporarily patching up Eluk, while Bob listened with intense interest, understanding nothing. It did not take understanding the words for any of the group to know that they were discussing what to do about the great white bear. Both Inuits had drawn their shining blades and appeared to be discussing how to handle an imminent attack.

All knew that the last two winters had been very hard on the ruminants and carnivores. Heavy snows were horrendous and caused many deaths among the caribou that had remained too far north. The bears were initially able to gorge themselves on the dying animals. This year, the caribou were few, and the seal catch was light due to the difficulty the bears had finding them. Many surviving bears were desperate, and by its appearance, this one fit into that category.

It continued to sniff the air and circle the chopper for ten minutes. The pilot could not believe he had been stupid enough to leave their lunches in a box on the portable table he had set up near his machine. The bear had already made short work of that. They watched their situation get worse when an additional problem appeared. The mother bear had not one but two starving juvenile cubs. If the mother was starving and her cubs were very hungry, she would find them sustenance or die trying.

John explained the problem they all faced while they retreated farther into the ice cave. No one really needed the explanation. The danger was obvious, and, they all recognized their predicament. They had to protect themselves and get word out for assistance.

They also had a new problem. The bear was beginning to mall the helicopter. There was more food inside; her nose told her so. Her cubs continued to squall while sitting on their haunches behind the helicopter.

Mitch was beginning to come around. He had hit the ice so hard that the back of his heads-up flight helmet was cracked. If he had not been wearing it, his head would have broken like an egg. He was groggy and dizzy, but very lucky. Smelling salts from the first aid kit worked to bring him around, though he was still dazed. Mitch was roused to semiconsciousness, but not without a cost. As he regained his senses, he shouted and flailed his arms. The sound aroused the bear, which now stared in their direction. They were downwind, but she picked up the unmistakable scent of blood. It was only a matter of time before she zeroed in on their hiding place.

In spite of Eluk's and Mitch's conditions, they had to take action and move. They had no chance of escaping the cave by leaving from the way they had entered if the bear attacked. Eluk and John hurried them deeper into their glacial chamber. If they left the shelter even as a large noisy group, the bear's reactions were still unpredictable. She might decide to protect her cubs by bolting and running if threatened and intimidated by their sheer numbers. While they had watched and debated, Mama Bear made the decision for them. She lowered her head after gulping several more wafts of the breeze, growled with a guttural menacing tone, the hair on her back bristled, and she began lumbering straight for the cave.

None of the group waited to see. John remained behind to watch the bear's approach to be sure it continued toward them. Bob and Carl whisked Mitch along at a too rapid pace. Becky attempted to assist Eluk, but he pushed her ahead of him. John did not stay behind for long. Eluk looked back to see him running toward them with his knife in his hand, taking an occasional glimpse back over his shoulder. They had only two lights and two small ones from the emergency first aid pack. The batteries in all were new, but those in Bob's satellite phone were not. Carl had his GPS unit on his belt, but it was of little use.

Becky asked if Bob could somehow use his core cutter as a weapon. It produced a laser energy heat that could vaporize the ice it cut, making it suitable for use in the Arctic. The unit produced tremendous concentrated heat, but only in close proximity. It might scare the bear, but she could be on top of the operator before the tool produced any damaging effects.

The hungry bear stopped at the cave entrance. It was close enough for them to still see it while they fled deeper into their frozen trap. It stopped by the entrance to inspect the ice block. Eluk had retrieved his parka after being bandaged but not his bloody shirt. The animal shredded the shirt. It circled the ice block and licked the traces of Eluk's blood. If it could have smelled the iceman, it too might have been a frozen dinner.

Before the bear caught another glimpse of them, the group rounded a corner and were out of its line of sight. The bear's curiosity with the remnants of blood on the block of ice and with Eluk's shirt bought them some time.

Mitch was feeling the strain of moving in his condition but was holding up well. Becky thought that Eluk was amazing in his ability to withstand the pain she knew he was feeling. It was obviously excruciating and, though bandaged, was still losing blood. They all looked down in horror when they discovered the trail of blood droplets leading from the entrance.

"Leave me." Eluk struggled. "Save yourselves."

"No, I'll face the bear," John stated.

"Very noble of you both," Becky shot back, "but we are all in this together."

Bob, Carl, and Mitch moved ahead, the glistening blue palace around them sparkled in the beams of their light. With a blood trail path to follow, a blind bear could find them. Bob switched off his light when they rounded another bend because its reflection in the crystal clear ice was blinding. The passage ahead became narrow, low, and dangerous, sharp ice stalagmites protruding from the floor. Next, what greeted them was their worst fear. The ice tunnel abruptly ended. It continued on as a narrowing crack, but the passageway was too narrow for them to pass through.

Bob turning off his light when he did was a stroke of good luck. They might not have seen it. The narrowing cave came to a near dead end, but from it rose a vertical crevice, a slowly narrowing crack in the ice with a faint glow at the top. The only way to go at this point was up, and that looked like a formidable task for an experienced ice climber.

Becky joined the other three, looking up the near vertical shaft in the ice. They told her to turn off her light. She did so and saw the faint light above. Without hesitation, she scrambled up into the crevice with a boost from Carl and Bob. She still had her ice-climbing cleats on and was an avid ice climber. In a flash, she was well up into the narrow crevice and pushing steadily higher. A fall would mean instant death or, worse, impaled on the icy spires below. Her light backpack always contained a length of strong nylon rope. She dropped one end of the rope to Bob's feet and pounded two ice pitons from her pack into the ice with her ice pick hammer she kept attached to her equipment belt. She tied the other end of the rope to the pitons with a secure knot and used the pick to move even higher.

Bob and Carl tested her first securing point with all their weight. Becky wedged herself at her next stop. They satisfied themselves that the rope would hold a person's weight. The strong anchor and rope gave them a chance to climb high enough to be out of the reach of the bear and perhaps save themselves if they were all fast enough to scale the crevice. Carl suggested that Bob go next. Bob didn't argue. He was very strong, so he would be more capable of pulling the rest of them up. They had gone through a similar routine during a basic survival training course after arriving at the base. They all did some much easier climbing for fun. This was real and very dangerous, but escape was now the goal. They needed all their expertise and a fair amount of luck to get them away from the hungry bear.

Bob scrambled off the floor and reached the first small ledge where Becky had secured her pitons. He was greeted with a face full of ice from the climber above. He did not utter a sound but began hauling the still groggy Mitch up toward him.

Carl uttered a strained "Hurry" when John brought Eluk to his side. John was very nervous. Carl could see that. Eluk leaned against him in obvious pain.

"The monster has found the trail and is following us. I went back to the first corner to check, and it looked straight into my eyes." John did not have to convey the gravity of the situation. His countenance said it all.

Mitch heard the voices below, understood the problem, and strained to force himself upward. With Bob's assistance pulling hard on the rope, Mitch rose to the ledge and forced himself higher. He was the only one without ice cleats and began slipping back. As he clambered past Bob, he felt Bob attach one of his own cleats to his free boot. He thanked him and pushed himself to go higher. The pain in his head raged.

Three were now safe, and Eluk pushed his knife into Carl to make him go next when the free end of the rope hit the floor. Carl struggled to pull himself up, falling back twice. With his dwindling strength, Eluk pushed Carl while Bob grunted and heaved from above. Carl slid up into the crack. He was the most physically unfit one in the group and struggled to pull himself upward.

There were only two left below when the unwelcome bear arrived. It snorted and bellowed ferociously when it found its quarry. It was too late to climb for the stranded Inuits. Their ancestors had faced the largest predator of the north numerous times. To face the beast trapped in a cave with few weapons was a true nightmare.

Both Inuits had learned the behavior of these creatures as a part of their heritage. They both began shouting, creating a great commotion. It was a bluff, but it beat the odds of hand-to-hand combat. John had saved his best surprise for last. As the bear rounded the final corner, confronting them face-to-face, he lighted a signal flare from the emergency kit and threw it straight at the beast. The glare of the intense red flame stopped the charging creature in its tracks.

The bear was startled and blinded. It became momentarily disoriented. The rope dropped to the floor beside Eluk. John wrapped it around his companion and jerked on the line. Bob, nearly exhausted, pulled hard on the rope but could not lift Eluk, who grimaced and winced in pain. A foot came down next to Bob on the ledge, and a third hand began pulling frantically. Carl had returned after securing Mitch above, and together they pulled Luke to safety in the crevice.

John was now alone to face the even angrier beast. He had bought just enough time for the rest of them to climb to safety but was unsure if it would be enough for him. Eluk was now up to the overcrowded ledge. Carl pressed him against the wall with his body and released the rope. It dropped to John's side. The blinking, enraged, desperate bear found him by both scent and movement. He had stood motionless after Luke disappeared into the crevice. Now he flung himself into the crack with a furious burst of energy as a last-ditch effort to save himself. He threw his parka over the charging bear's head and hurled himself to the side, clambering and scratching for handholds to climb upward. The wild animal smashed through ice pinnacles, scattering shards in every direction.

The still somewhat disoriented bear crashed headlong into the ice wall, just missing the dodging guide. John was climbing farther up the crevice, forcing those above him to keep climbing. Carl was straining upward, helping Mitch, whose slumping body now blocked their escape route. They were all temporarily out of reach but far from out of danger.

Becky was well overhead, perhaps fifty or sixty feet above the others. The bear bellowed angrily, standing on its hind feet and scratching at the ice. They were all dead if it could reach them. If one of them slipped or fell backward, the bear and its cubs would have a large meal.

A second ledge protruded from the crevice about forty feet above the floor. It was wide enough to sit on and rest. As the crack finally widened above, the climb became progressively more treacherous. Carl and Mitch were exhausted by stress and strain and out of energy by the time they reached the second ledge. Breathing heavily, they all huddled together, sharing the limited space on the ledge. Steam rose from their perspiring bodies and mouths.

Bob had unstrapped the heavy battery pack he wore on his waist. In his haste, he had neglected to drop it earlier. He gathered it in both hands and threw it hard down the shaft at the snarling bear now struggling to climb after them. It struck the bear's snout with a dull thud. The beast roared in anger and pain. Blood burst from one of its nostrils, mixing with the blood from Luke's trail.

They were temporarily safe. Luke sat up as straight as he could and positioned his bleeding back against the slippery cold. He was shaking from weakness and cold. His situation would soon be desperate unless they got him more medical attention.

Becky had run out of pitons before reaching the top. Her final climb showered those below with icy shards. They did not dare look up. She strained to gain a secure final foothold. With one last exhausting push, she reached the top of the crevice where a thin layer of translucent hard snow covered a narrow opening at the surface. Someone crossing this hidden crevice without probing for weakness would have plummeted to an icy grave. A cold chill ran up her spine. She envisioned the poor iceman possibly meeting with this very demise. She poked with her ice ax, and snow and ice fell away, cascading onto her fellow climbers huddled below. A cloudy sky with a few blue patches greeted her. It was a welcome sight.

Becky had shoved Carl's satellite phone into her pocket. It was packed with snow and ice when she extracted it. Cleaning it off, she turned it on and tested for a signal. She heard a static crackle and a voice speaking on the other end. "Who is this?" she screeched.

"This is the Canadian Air Force Search and Rescue Unit Four Zero" came the static reply.

"This is Becky Cottingham, director AWRB Base One," Becky countered. "We are in immediate need of assistance."

"We received your distress call and have been closing in on your triangulated position. We are twenty-eight minutes out and closing. What is your situation?"

"Thank God," she responded. "We have two injured and a serious bear problem.

"Roger that. We have a medic on board. Hang tight."

CHAPTER 6

THE ESCAPE

When Rescue Unit Zero Four arrived at the glacier, they had no problem finding Becky. She continued to give them a status report until just before she heard the sound of the rotor blades. The satellite phone lasted long enough, but the battery was weak by the time the chopper arrived. Although they could have located them without the constant communication, Becky and the group felt more assured with continuous conversation.

The angry bear finally gave up trying to climb up the crevice after them. Becky had cautioned the others to remain on the ledge and keep Luke and John warm. She did not want anyone else attempting the final climb. She too was very fatigued. There was still the possibility that the bear would come to her new hiding place if it spotted her and force her back into the ice. Becky knew that she could descend again if she had to but wondered about the injured. Staying quiet and concealed was safer while they waited.

The Mounties arrived before the bear even looked for her. Becky was more than impressed by the massive animal's persistence at finding sustenance. It had returned to the helicopter while cuffing and scolding the young bears. They had followed her initially but then returned to play around the curious-looking human contraption. When Mother Bear rejoined the cubs, they licked at her face and received a stern reply, demonstrating her disapproval. She knocked one over backward and tackled the other nipping it until

GLOBAL WARNING

it yelped. She then turned her full fury on the unsecured helicopter. Angry, venting her frustration or just driven by instincts and desperate for food, the mother bear ferociously tore at the machine. Her powerful forepaw pried open the rear-side larger door and tore it from its hinges.

In a few minutes, she scattered equipment, a notebook computer, and several boxes of food and emergency supplies onto the snow. Her nose found the food, and this distracted the white creature from further mutilation of the aircraft. Mother Bear shredded food containers. Her cubs feasted on the contents. Becky thought about their close escape, watching the hungry animals shred what could have been one or more of them.

The CAF rescue chopper came in low and swept over their position to survey the situation. Becky had described the nearby landmarks and her relative location with respect to the helicopter and bears. The second helicopter and its noisy threat were too much for the three bears.

Mama Bear rose once and waved menacingly at the airborne threat. Then she and her youngsters beat a hasty retreat down the snow-covered rocky incline and straight across the base of the ice mass. After chasing her with a third close dive, the rescue helicopter turned back, and the side door slid open. A Canadian Air Force rescue specialist stepped out the door, balanced on the landing bars, and swung free on the winch, descending as they approached Becky's location. She waved her arms and shielded her face as the helicopter hovered above her and set the rescue specialist down beside her.

They used the helicopter winch line to lift the others from the crevice one by one. The pilot had to hover with care and be patient in order to extract them from their precarious location. Time after time, the winch line was lowered, and a shivering body appeared at the surface. A second rescue specialist was set down to go and assess the damage to the wounded helicopter. He was left there alone with a high-powered rifle and instructions to use it if any of the bears returned. The three bears were satisfied with their thievery and now had some food in their bellies and were very far away. The specialist reported that except for the damaged door, the chopper was still airworthy.

Four from the exploration party were set down next to the wounded helicopter. Mitch and Eluk were hoisted aboard the Air Force chopper for more medical attention. Eluk was okay but had lost a fair amount of blood from the scratches and two deeper gashes. Mitch's head cut needed a few stitches, and he was feeling the effects of a concussion.

After hoisting everyone from the crevice, the larger Air Force helicopter landed as close as it safely could to the damaged machine. The copilot insisted that he would fly their helicopter back even though both Becky and Bob were qualified to operate it. After their ordeal, he would allow either of them to fly it.

The Air Force team took a few minutes to go and to inspect their discovery. Enthralled, they realized the importance of the discovery and checked for the availability of a heavy lift unit. They scheduled a pickup for tomorrow, weather permitting, but the weather was starting to look stormy again.

Rescue Unit Four Zero was ready to leave within less than a half hour. Eluk received enough first aid to stabilize him just short of slipping into shock. He was a tough character, young and very strong. In spite of this, everyone could see that exposure, loss of blood, and pain were starting to take their toll.

Mitch was doing better but was unable to focus clearly and was quite unsteady on his feet. The onboard medic bandaged his head and had him lie down and strap in while the rest of the crew tended to Eluk. Carl needed to get out of there too. His stress level was very high. He argued, but none of the group would listen to him. Bob would have stayed, but they mutually made the decision that he would also ride in the rescue unit back to base. The rescue unit needed to refuel there before its long trip back to its base.

The speedy heavier rescue chopper lifted away, leaving Becky, John, the Canadian Air Force pilot, and the armed guard behind. Becky and John gathered up what they could salvage from the scattered debris. They piled it in the back and policed as much of the remaining trash, adding it to the pile. The main cargo door was bent and damaged. John found a large intact roll of duct tape and, with Becky and the new pilot holding it in place, began taping it back to the craft. It would have to suffice to hold the door in place for their return flight. For the ride back to base, they would all have to enter the front side door and crawl over the instrument console to the rear of the craft. Satisfied that the temporary repair would suffice, the pilot tested the engine. It sputtered to life in an instant. They were ready to leave.

None of the four remaining at the site wanted to stay longer than was absolutely necessary. Where there was one bear, they all understood that there could be more, and the smell of food and blood was a powerful attractant. Becky wanted to return to her discovery now laying exposed at the ice cave entrance. She had already kept her promise to Mitch to recover as much of his precious equipment as possible. The Canadian rescue specialists simply said, "No way." They were sticking together, staying close to the helicopter until it lifted off.

After the cleanup and repairs, they all climbed inside. Becky watched the rifle-bearing Special Forces rescue specialist seated in the front seat. He was focused on the semisteamed window before him. Becky tensed with the thought that the bear had returned. She glanced at his hand on the weapon across his lap. His hands looked warm and relaxed. He was not tense or primed for action. Becky followed his gaze out the window and smiled, beholding the beauty outside. The days were short, but the spectacle of an Arctic spring evening was descending upon them. Floating in the air outside were innumerable tiny glistening ice crystals. Beyond the crystals shimmered an astounding display. The still visible aurora borealis was dancing across the evening sky. Sinuous curtains of glorious hue waved tantalizingly from the heavens. It was an unusual occurrence. A splendid beauty played out its magnetic choreography before them. Becky had witnessed nature's Arctic wonder many times, but none seemed more beautiful than this occurrence.

They watched transfixed for a few minutes. John's stomach growled loudly. They were hungry but not eager to release more food aromas in the almost absent breeze. Most of the food stores had been ravaged by the bears, with remnants still scattered about. There would be no food until they returned to base.

John's demeanor became spiritual. He was highly superstitious and was always respectful of the teachings of his forefathers. To him, as to his ancestors, everything was a sign, a portent of something. He did not like disturbing the iceman. The suddenly brighter than normal pastel shimmer of the skies was another sign. How he would interpret this one was of curiosity to Becky. She needed a good omen. They had had enough bad things for one day.

The deep rumble and crackle of the moving ice mass nearby added an eerie feeling to the scene before them. The ice field was never quiet. This particular glacier had grown and advanced in the last two seasons. It was advancing at an ever-increasing rate as it was fed from the compacting snowfields at its head. Though not perceptible to the human eye, the cumulative movement was obvious to their instruments. The rate of movement was the astounding factor. Glaciers simply were not supposed to move at rates anywhere close to what they were recording.

More deep groans of grinding rock and ice filled the air, omnipresent evidence of continued activity. The glacier seemed to be speaking to them. Five minutes later, they were ascending to follow the other helicopter back to AWRB 1.

CHAPTER 7

CHICAGO

From his office in Chicago, Wayne was in contact with his folks at the glacier through the Canadian rescue team. Before they completed their return to their base, he completed a short evaluation of the situation and rendered his opinion to the team who were at the glacier as well as to his superiors. Everyone had agreed with his recommendation that they all needed to get out of there before anything else went wrong or the weather turned bad. Wayne was in no way angry at the situation that had developed and the departures from normal procedure. His team had virtually unlimited freedom to operate on their own, within established safety limits. Small departures were normal. Breaches of safety were not tolerated.

Wayne talked to Becky and Carl for several minutes while the rescue helicopter prepared to leave. The present milder weather allowed for good communications. He wanted both Becky and John on that rescue chopper, but Becky finally talked him out of it. At least that was what she thought. John's comments and those of the Canadian pilot made him relent to their request. They were allowed to remain behind and salvage what they could but ordered to stay as a close group with further directions to leave as soon as they completed the immediate task. If there were any problems with their transportation, there was no other unit to dispatch to get them out of there.

The CAF told John that they had a heavy-lift jet-propelled vertical takeoff and landing craft available to bring their prize back to the base after he told them about what his team had found at the glacier. Becky was beaming with excitement, stressing the importance of their discovery. With the unit available, depending again on weather factors, the recovery of the iceman within days was possible.

The importance of Becky's find could not be diminished. Ever since the discovery of a perfect mammoth specimen at the turn of the century, numerous scientific teams had been searching for and recovering other specimens. From the description of their find, it appeared quite old and perfectly preserved. If they could recover it, the credibility of their research would be greatly embellished. They had already cleverly extracted it, but with near-tragic consequences. The price was already high. Wayne hoped that the importance of this find would mitigate the potential negative publicity of the injuries and following expensive rescue operation. The Canadian rescue teams were already overworked and stretched far too thin.

This iceman was an unexpected bonus to their otherwise rather droll research. Measuring the relative motion of the rivers of ice was important again. The recent return of growing glaciers was replacing the many years of receding ice. Their work now received new interest and importance in the last two years. The corpse discovery was an added big bonus.

Wayne was anxious to see the pictures the team captured at the site. He made Becky promise to get some rest upon arrival back at the base and then send him pictures of the frozen hominid. He knew her personality and figured that she would send him the pictures first. He also knew that she would not handle the problems that developed and injuries well at all. He wished he could be there to help her cope and hoped that the excitement of the find would keep her from getting too anxious and upset.

Becky could be overzealous, but to Wayne, that was a fine virtue. He had fallen for her only a short time after they had first met in that research symposium at Loyola. She could carry on a conversation with anyone and was never shy about telling anyone exactly how she felt. He liked that a lot about her, but more than once, that had gotten her in social trouble. Her green eyes were piecing, her nose a bit too long. She carried herself with an air of confidence that he just adored. Her intelligence matched his any day, and her stamina often amazed him. She was perfect for tough Arctic duty. She was a perfectionist too, something that often caused her problems and consternation. Her temper fuse was not short, and she handled disappointments rather well, but patience was a virtue of which she came up a little short. He knew that if she was allowed to dwell on the problems at the glacier, she would get more and more upset about it and blame herself for everything negative. He loved her and missed her terribly, especially the physical contact.

Wayne fell asleep dreaming about Becky and their last night together before she left for the base. He was asleep before the pictures came in on his computer. He was correct that she had sent them to him first before resting, and the tone of her attached note sounded like he expected.

The next morning, the weather was not as bad as the predicted storm and good enough for the heavy-lift unit to depart by early that afternoon for the base. Becky slept restlessly and was basically despondent over the injuries and damages suffered the previous day at the glacier.

She waited, nerves fraying, alone, outside in the cold for the incoming HLV (heavy-lift vehicle) to arrive at AWRB 1 for the return to recover her precious ice block. She longed to begin the recovery effort or at least do anything to help prepare the iceman for transport. She talked to Wayne several times. The day dragged on. His calls calmed her demeanor. She longed to return before adverse weather started again. A few ice crystals settled from the air, and the chill of being outside began to lessen her comfort. Though fairer weather was again forecast, a fierce storm was expected that night or early the following day. After being at the base for weeks, she knew how fast conditions could change. She shivered in her parka and drew the hood closer to her face. The bear had wreaked havoc on what had seemed like a wonderful day. It would be a short, very cold flight back to recover the block, but there was nothing that could keep her from returning.

Becky could feel the drowsiness of fatigue and the aching in her legs and shoulders from the strenuous climb up the crevice. It was a constant reminder of the frightening escape. She shuddered. John had joined her and noticed. He gently patted her shoulder.

"Go back and rest awhile," he said. "You look like you could use it."

She smiled and said, "I'm okay, just bummed out by what happened to Mitch and Luke."

"Hey, we all are, and it's not your fault." John gave her a hug. "The person that is most bummed out right now is Luke because Doc said that there is no way he is going back today. They almost had to restrain him." Frosty breath was trailing from his lips with each word.

Becky left John and went back to warm up inside while he waited for the arriving HLV. She sat down on a bench beside the double doors, put her head back against the wall, and was asleep in seconds.

Becky's phone rang. It was Wayne. She did not hear it ring at first, but Wayne let it ring for a long time. John joined her and answered it for her. John handed her the phone with a quaint "It's your boyfriend, boss." She groaned, yawned, and said hello, fighting back another yawn.

She noticed that the accent was on the word *boyfriend*. She stored that in her brain for later consideration, *fiancé* would have been more fitting. She took the phone from his grasp and began to listen intently to the excited voice on the other end.

Before she said anything else, she asked him to start over. He was talking about the pictures; that much was obvious. Wayne began again. "Carl forwarded his images, and I got your pics from before the extraction. He also forwarded his ice-dating data and everything else he measured. It really looks remarkable. The face, the eye you can see, the body almost looks alive."

Becky could not get a word in edgewise, so she listened, yawned, and smiled. John copied her smile in mockery and then crossed his eyes and stuck out his tongue. His face and Wayne's staccato chatter through the phone simply broke her up. She laughed and laughed, nearly dropping the phone when John repeated his face.

"What? What? What is so funny?" Wayne was confused and curious.

"Sorry, hon," Becky retorted. "Are the pictures that good?"

"I still want to know what was so darn funny? Yes, the pictures are that good, in fact, sensational!"

"John was making me laugh, and I'm glad he did. I needed it."

"It is so good to hear you laugh after the travails of yesterday," Wayne said softly. "You sounded pretty ragged earlier."

Becky felt better. Even the cold was tolerable that day, and the weather was holding.

"We will have a few logistics problems with the recovery, but we should be ready for it at the base. The Canadian authorities, the Nunavut representative, and the Inuit elders committee all have to be properly informed. It should not slow the retrieval of your find, but it may complicate further study and, more particularly, by whom."

"I know. That kind of stuff is to be expected." Becky was saddened by the bureaucratic paperwork that was sure to follow. The brief summer would not allow a great deal of time for decisions. If this year was like the last, they would have to be out of the base in less than three months or face the potential for more freak storms like last year.

Wayne interrupted this last bit of reverie with his final comments on the photos. He wished her good and safe travel and closed with an "I love you" before signing off. She blew a loud kiss into the mouthpiece, eliciting a whistle from John.

CHAPTER 8

FINAL EXTRACTION

The HLV arrived, landed on the cleared landing pad close to the tiny village, picked up Becky and John, and took off for the glacier in less than ten minutes. Heavy clouds were moving in. They did not want to wait a minute longer than needed. John recounted the tale of their near escape with great precision, raising the eyebrows of the Canadian pilot and recovery team with his own particular embellishments. Becky shivered perceptibly each time he mentioned the polar bear. To him, the near escape rivaled stories retold by the elders. To her, the stories reinforced her genuine fear and adrenaline-peaked exertion of the previous day. John would have a fine tale to relate to his peers, but he also expressed his genuine concern for his wounded compatriots back at the base. Becky anguished about Luke and Mitch. She was jointly responsible for the health, safety, and welfare of every member of her group. She was not looking forward to the grilling and endless paperwork, only to return to the remote, frigid, desolate location of the ice mummy.

The steady drone of the HLV and John's constant chatter softened her somewhat depressed state. The Canadian pilot switched on his searchlight and watched his GPS closing on the coordinates he had entered. Becky helped him pinpoint their target by directing the search beam, and they started into a descent circle to survey the landing area. Little conservation took place between the two except a few exchanged pleasantries and the description of the suggested approach and point for touchdown. The HLV was much larger and heavier than the rescue craft and their own helicopter. They flew over and checked the entire area around where the other craft had landed, surveying by eye for the most advantageous point to set the larger vehicle down. In a giant swirl of snow and ice, the HLV tilted backward on its axis and landed with a gentle bounce. The twin turbine engines changed to a low idle, and the two great rotors slowed and sagged to a stop. Once on the ground, the entire group unloaded the lift harness and the hookup equipment and prepared for the extraction of Becky's prize. They planned every precaution to prevent damage to the ice-encapsulated Eskimo body and the block holding it captive.

When the HLV was first summoned, the pilot was requested to bring heavy-cargo lifting nets. He assumed that his mission would be to lift and retrieve the smaller, damaged helicopter. Upon finding out that his efforts would be rewarded by carrying back a large ice cube, in a land of endless ice and snow, he was not amused. His attitude changed upon learning that the block contained a body. He was not looking forward to being laughed at by his macho mates later for rescuing an ice cube. He was from Australia and took a normal ration of good-natured ridicule on a regular basis from his Canadian compatriots.

It seemed like forever to Becky, but after only a few minutes, the HLV team were ready to drag the nets and lifting cable to the cave entrance and attach the netting. They surveyed the scene, the remaining scattered debris from the bear rampage, and the glistening block that Becky prized. Her total fascination was beyond the imagination of the Aussie, although he too was transfixed by the apparition encapsulated in frozen water. He soon became fascinated by John's newest recounting of their tale when they noticed the few remaining blood smears. He finally beamed a wide smile while remarking, "Bonger, mate." Becky was patient while waiting. John finished the last tidbits of his story. She was cold again, depressed, still exhausted, and just a little frustrated by the entire situation, but one look at the frozen surface of the large block, now highlighted by John's flashlight, reversed her state of mind.

Her elbow was nudged gently, and the face of one of the crew appeared over her right shoulder. The smiling young airman handed her a steaming cup of hot coffee. Once safely on the ground, he had started the brewer. The wonderful aroma drifted to her senses when he extended the cup to her. She wrapped her chilled fingers around the spill-proof mug.

"Thanks," she said.

"There will be warm stew in the heavy when we're done, ma'am."

The new serviceman missed the conclusion of John's story, but at this moment, he just wanted to make Becky more comfortable. The stress was obvious on her continence, and the crewman was genuinely concerned. "Let the gents hook it up." Becky followed him to the HLV and, once close enough, picked up the aroma of warming stew. Her stomach gurgled in anticipation. She had been unable to eat before they left the base. A pang of concern made her wince, thinking of the starved bears sensing the aroma, but she realized that not even a desperate bear would dare to approach the present scene.

Becky and the young serviceman waited by the HLV, the young man not moving far from the large bore antibear rifle he leaned by the door. They both consumed the welcome treat of hot food, watching the pilot and support personnel begin their extraction plan in earnest. The ice block rested in a location where removing it would be difficult. Moving it wrong by shifting it prematurely or by letting it slip would send it crashing down the rock talus sloping away from the ice cave entrance. The fact that it had not already gone over the edge was a small miracle.

The block was in a slight depression below and over forty meters from the HLV. They had to raise the block in order to spread the heavy thick cargo net under it, thereby securing it for final drag uphill and subsequent removal. The fact that the ice block was sitting in a slight depression allowed them to slip two strong straps under the block. Stability was poor, but at least they had it relatively well secured from sliding away down the rock and ice slope. To Becky, the potential for recovering it intact looked good. The laser cutters had done an amazing job to remove the giant ice chunk. Though irregular on the edges, the ice block was roughly trapezoidal. The fall had broken off a few pieces, and small cracks were apparent, but even after the slide out of the cave, the chunk was still intact.

Clay Morris, the Aussie pilot, took over command of the recovery effort. Born in Brisbane, he had joined the Canadian rescue team after acquiring a similar specialty, working for the Australian armed forces. An argument with a superior following a flubbed rescue effort at sea had made him a scapegoat. A wicked left hook settled the argument but landed him in the brig and cost him his career in Australia. He missed his native land, but he came to love Canada, and his job here brought him more respect as well as the constant adventure he sought.

Clay's initial hesitancy was replaced with a genuine enthusiasm. He welcomed any challenge, and this was one he liked. He calculated the approximate weight of the entire lift assembly, including the ice. Clay returned to the HLV, powered up, lifted off, and hovered over the block. The winch operator took up slack in the lines to the straps. Clay lifted the block using the hovering vehicle, just enough to allow the positioning of the two strong lift nets. This saved having to dig under the ice block and taking any more chances of breaking it.

Once in position, the HLV lifted the block just enough, and the heavy-cargo netting was secured under the block for the final lift and transport. His crewman let out slack in the cable again, and he set the large craft back down. After a final inspection of all connections and a check that the cable was clear of obstruction, they were prepared to leave. They all enjoyed the warming stew and coffee. John circled the block several times, leaning to look at the frozen figure inside, and said nothing.

Becky wanted to help but was forced to watch. The others took over the care of her precious specimen. The recovery operation went without a hitch even though hers had been a near disaster. Becky knew that if she at least returned with this prize, the results might mitigate the feelings of disappointment she felt due to still blaming herself entirely for the injuries and near disaster. *What a mess*, she thought. *I hope that this is the last time I'm involved in something like this.*

Clay gave one of his crewmen his permission to go inside the cave just long enough to find and retrieve Bob's precious laser cutter apparatus. Shining his light off the glistening ice, he passed the place where the ice block had been cut from the glacier ceiling. He was gone for less than five minutes when he exited the cave with it. The bear had spared it, and damage looked minimal to Becky upon inspection, just a few scratches.

Closing her eyes and thinking again about the terror she had felt, she was startled out of her brief reverie by Clay's accented voice relaying the message to his base and to Igloolik that they were ready to lift off. After a final policing of the area to clean up remaining scraps and debris, everyone climbed aboard and fastened their seat belts. Becky watched Clay apply full power to his engines and felt the vibrations of the huge craft as the motors came up to speed. The friendly airman, who had handed her the wonderful cup of coffee, took his seat beside her and smiled warmly. The HLV slowly rose into the air in a swirling cloud of ice crystals and debris. It had more than adequate lifting capacity. Becky watched out her small window. The vehicle rose, and she heard the cables stretch and groan as their cargo swung briefly but then stayed centered and suspended beneath the giant craft. They were on their way back to base after relayed affirmatives from the pilot. She closed her eyes and tried to relax to the monotone repetition of the turbine engines and great whirling blades.

"We've got it, Becky. It should be a piece of cake from here. Estimated time back with the load is thirty-five minutes. We will be going against the wind and have to keep the load centered. We won't be moving as fast as we were on the way here. Weather is good all the way. We should get back and be able to unload before that next system moves in." Clay's voice gave her confidence that the nightmare was almost over.

The trip back to Igloolik was uneventful. Becky was more than just thankful for that, though she was not looking forward to the questions she knew would lie ahead. There was no reason to return to AWRB 1 yet since transport of the body or storage and study of their find would not be practical there. Igloolik had numerous unused small buildings from the ruined fishing industry, any of which would suffice for their intended thorough examination.

At present, the weather situation in the tiny northern town was bad, but nothing like it would be if the coming winter were anything like the misery of the year before. Much of the village was abandoned to the elements, and all would be if the weather deteriorated again. Igloolik would be a brief stopover for their find if there were no problems with the elders or council, a few members of which still remained as residents in order to supervise the final evacuation of their lifelong home.

Arriving in Igloolik, Becky and the others were surprised by the turnout. Word of the discovery had spread, coupled with the tale of the close encounter with the hungry polar bear family. A frozen body was nothing to cause excitement among the locals. They were used to this occurrence as a normal result of carelessness in their daily lives. Close encounters with the king of the north were also very common. The combination coupled with the HLV and rescue was just too much for the curious few remaining in the village to ignore. Add to that the official position of the council having to put its stamp of approval on the disposition of the iceman, and everyone wanted to see what would transpire.

The HLV maneuvered to the designated landing area near where the smaller damaged helicopter was parked. What would have normally been a muddy or cleared asphalt landing zone this time of year was still blanketed in ice and snow, even heading into the end of a mid-Arctic spring. Hovering with the block, the reception crew guided a large dolly under it. Once on the carrier, Clay's winch operator lowered the block onto the trailer and released the netting and cables. The HLV rose and banked landing a short distance away. Because of the deteriorating surface conditions, they had to leave within minutes in order to return to their base.

As soon as the nets were removed from around the block, the small group of onlookers moved in to get a closer and better view. Exiting the HLV, Becky hurried to inspect the condition of their cargo with John at her side. Word had just come in over the radio that Luke had been treated at the hospital and was already aggravating the nurses. Carl and Mitch were also fine, though Mitch's concussion had temporarily left him only a vague recollection of the entire incident.

Carl could not wait to get an update as to the status of the iceman. He was part of the reception group. He also was already making plans for the next part of their study and extraction of the corpse for further evaluation. Once extracted, the closest coroner would have to examine the body and decide if an autopsy was warranted. A mountain of paperwork would be next, and Becky knew that she had to complete a lot of it. Becky was reluctant to discuss this very much with anyone at this point, but she thought of nothing else during the return flight from the glacier.

CHAPTER 9

RECOGNITION

After the commotion of their arrival was over, the curious locals dispersed. The weather again turned inclement. Large insulating tarps were wrapped around the ice block and corpse on the oversized dolly, and it was moved to a new temporary home inside a nearby storage unit. The ambient temperature in the building with the heater off was low enough that with the extra insulation, there was almost no chance of any melting by the next morning when the Canadian coroner was scheduled to arrive. He was expected to make a cursory inspection and sign off on removal of the body to allow transport to a medical facility for more detailed scrutiny. The coroner also had the official duty of dealing with the local Inuits, complying with their wishes and assuring them that complete care would be taken to handle the body with dignity and to preserve any artifacts obtained.

Luke was the most curious about the frozen victim since he was there at the initial discovery. He wanted to see the face again that he saw in the ice and the clothing of the victim. Since he was hurt during the process to extract the block, he was still upset that he had been unable to return for the recovery at the glacier. Neither he nor the initial onlookers could have seen very much detail through the frosted and chipped exterior surface of the now translucent block. The interior ice was still crystal clear, but the external surface was rough and abraded enough to make a more detailed analysis or to identify any distinct features. The iceman as he was now called continued to be a mystery.

His mind raced, and his side hurt. Luke wanted to see and know more. He followed the four-wheeler, the block, and dolly through the double front doors of the old drab wooden storage shed. The wrapped frozen ice block and body were unceremoniously unhitched from the towing vehicle and positioned in the middle of the shed. One helper guided the four-wheeler back outside and drove away on it back up the main and only street. Luke and the other two men who accompanied the iceman turned off the lantern illuminating the shed, closed and padlocked the doors, and turned to leave. One man handed Luke the keys to the lock, lit a cigarette, and said goodbye. With a nod from the other, the two workers plodded off to the one small pub and eatery in the tiny village, leaving Luke standing alone outside the shed. He looked down, turning the shiny key over and over in his gloved hand. To Luke, their disinterest was palpable.

The visage of the iceman would not leave his head. He held out his hand and stared at the key. A few glistening snowflakes drifted down and settled softly around it. Evening was falling. He thought about Becky's scream when she first saw it, what looked like a body falling straight down toward her, and then the recovery of the ice block from its glacial tomb. He had the key, and he would be the first there tomorrow morning when the wraps were removed.

Luke spent a restless night. The searing pain in his side and shoulder was incessant, but he handled it without painkillers. Continuous thoughts about the icemen also contributed to his lack of sleep and kept him awake for several hours. He was not sure what it was, but something about the frozen man and his garments bothered him.

Morning came too early for Luke. When Becky roused him from a dream of his youth, he was glad his agitated night was over. She brought a message that the arrival of the Canadian coroner would be delayed due to more weather problems en route. He arose, splashed as much cold water on his face as he could stand, and dressed in his traditional Inuit garb for the day. When Becky saw him later, she was puzzled at his particular choice of clothing. Luke had no appetite. He should have been very hungry. Instead, he grabbed one cup of tepid black coffee and headed straight for the shed. He even chose to forego the pain medicine he had been given to lessen the throbbing ache in his bruised shoulder. Becky decided to make a fresh pot of coffee and get something to curb her hunger. She would join him later.

The morning sun broke over the horizon with hues of red and orange behind wispy clouds in the eastern sky. A partly clear sky that morning was unusual. To Luke, it was a good omen. Luke crossed the quiet street between the sleeping quarters and dark storage shed, shuffling through freshly fallen overnight snow. He loved this time of day. The only sounds were sled dogs barking for their morning feeding. No one else had ventured outside. He was alone with his thoughts while the rest of the settlement awoke to another chilled morning.

Luke removed one glove and searched in his pocket for the key to open the rusted old lock sealing the storage shed. He opened the hasp and swung open one of the two double doors. The overnight temperature left no chance of any melting. He wanted to have warm water to pour over the ice to clear up the outside when the elders arrived for their inspection.

With no one else around, Luke began the process of removing the layers of wrap. He unfolded the first layer of heavy canvas tarp and let it fall to the floor. Next, he unwrapped the plastic inner layer, exposing the block. He walked back to the inn and brought back a five-gallon bucket of water to pour over the ice. The slight amount of surface thawing it induced left the block with a watery sheen and again a crystal clear surface perfect for observing detail that was hidden before. Luke picked up a lantern from a nearby workbench, turned it on, and hung it from a rusty nail in a roof support above the block. The shed also had one bare light bulb near the door that he had turned on when he entered the first time.

Luke took his trusted flashlight from his deep pocket, and using it, he shined it on the parka, noting the excellent hand-sewn stitching with sinew and boots handmade in the same manner. Moving around the body, he noticed details that were invisible before. The body was still facedown suspended, just as it had been in its permanent position in the ceiling of the ice cave. Becky and Carl were the only ones who had gotten a good look at the face prior to the extraction. The bottom of the ice block was now scraped and gouged from the fall and slide out of the cave. Luke could still see a few traces of crimson left behind by his own blood. They were subtle reminders of how close he had come to being crushed.

Luke shined his flashlight from several angles but was still unable to see much detail of the face. For that, he had to cut away the tarp and plastic from beneath the block using his trusted and always sharpened knife. The tarp and plastic were no match for his blade, and he was able to pull most of it from under the block. He rotated the block just enough to expose the end where the face was located. He lay down prone on his back on the damp dirt floor using the shredded tarp for insulation. He inched himself under the protruding end, working to where he could at last look into the face of the entombed occupant.

Only a foot and one-half from the frozen face, Luke saw how the iceman had met his demise. Several large rips and gashes were apparent on the left side of the head, which showed blood and parallel tears in the parka hood. The claw marks were unmistakable, and by the spacing and severity, Luke could tell that a very large and powerful polar bear had caught the iceman with a deadly swing of one enormous forepaw. The hunter had likely become the hunted. Nature's top Arctic land predator had won the battle.

Perhaps knocked into a crevice by the blow or making one last futile effort to avoid death, the Eskimo had escaped being eaten but had died and become entombed in the ice. Luke understood from the clothing that this was not a recent incident but instead a very old body and that except for the damage to the head, it was in a near-perfect state of preservation.

Light glinted off something beneath the iceman's face. Luke stared and strained to see the object suspended beneath the Eskimo's chin. It was an amulet connected around the neck by a sinew cord. Luke focused on the object. The circular amulet was ornately carved from walrus ivory. He recognized something familiar about it. He remembered a likeness drawn by the elders, preserved in their records, its appearance unmistakable. Luke gasped and shuddered at the thought. There before him was a thing he could scarcely believe—an Inuit treasured memory, something of extreme reverence. He was shaken and awed. It was the amulet of the legendary Anook, "the great one."

In near shock, Luke slid out from under the ice block, banging his head on the edge. A small drop of blood trickled down his face, the second time that this iceman had drawn his blood. He was speechless, his mind racing about the discovery he had just made. At that moment, the two workers who had assisted him in bringing and storing the block overnight appeared in the doorway of the shed, puzzled looks on their faces. One carried a gas heater and the other a butane torch, armed and ready to begin thawing and melting the large block.

Even if they had permission, Luke had to delay them, so he asked them if they had stopped for breakfast and told them that he was buying. He also informed them that the coroner was going to be late. They happily trotted off toward the little diner, leaving their tools behind on a workbench in the shed. When they were clear of his line of sight, Luke checked that they were not looking back, relocked the doors, and sprinted toward the house where two of his Inuit friends were staying.

Reaching their residence, Luke pounded on the door and burst through in one continuous motion. His startled friends leaped from their chairs, spilling coffee and plates of food across the table. Luke shouted, "GRAB YOUR ICE AXES. JOHN, BRING YOUR RIFLE. COME WITH ME!" Luke's staccato shouted words were almost unintelligible, the sounds running together in one excited jumble. Neither man said a word. Ice axes and a gun they understood. That meant trouble, and John's agitated state backed that up. The blood dripping down Luke's forehead and cheek further enhanced their concern; adrenaline was now coursing through their veins. Luke disappeared back out the door as quickly as he had burst in on their peaceful breakfast. Without a word, they grabbed their parkas and the requested gear and matched his pace into the morning air.

At the shed doorway, Luke began to explain the situation in their native Inuit language. The change from English heightened their sense of curiosity. Luke stated, "Lying within entombed in the ice is the one who is most revered by our elders, the subject of our songs and folklore, whose legend is loved by every child ever raised in our clan. I say our clan because the amulet around his neck matches our totem. The amulet is that of the chief of all chiefs, the spiritual leader of our people, the greatest of all hunters, revered among all of the clans, a sacred symbol of all Inuit people. It is that of Anook. We are bound by the honor of our clan to guard him." The look of disbelief was evident on the faces of both of his close friends. "I know that this is hard to believe! But I have seen the amulet around the iceman's neck. It is the sacred mark of Anook, and his clothes are very old, the style of the ancestors."

Both men facing him had a look of utter shock. Anook was lost so many years ago, the subject of handed-down songs and legends. If he was really here, if it was really him, the three Inuit men were about to make sure that no one was getting a chance to touch him.

Luke described the detail of the clan totem and the amulet. John crawled beneath the block and checked Luke's description for himself. When he looked back up at Luke, he just shook his head in the affirmative. His close examination of the facts left little doubt.

"I believe we have discovered Anook." Luke was proud and jubilant. "I will inform the council and summon all of the elders," Luke continued. "John, you must guard this place and stop anyone from disturbing his body. This will be a great day of both celebration and sorrow for our people. A mystery of many generations may at last be solved."

"It will be done as you wish, Luke." John's voice was stern in his commitment. "No one will touch this place."

Luke removed the lock and opened the shed doors. The three men approached the block and placed their hands on it. With their heads bowed, Luke said a few words in their native dialect, reverence and sorrow evident in his voice. When finished, Luke relocked the shed, gave the key to John, and left to report his find to Becky and the clan elders. Modern communication would accomplish in minutes what a dogsled-delivered message took days to deliver not many years before. Luke knew that the clan chiefs had already given their permission for the body to be removed for further study. His preliminary identification of the body would change that and move the council to immediate action. All he could think of was protecting Anook, keeping him from the hands of the authorities at this point. He anticipated the potential for a confrontation.

Becky was checking the records of the list of any hunters lost at sea or in the ice fields, any disappearances of any kind in that area. Two were reported, but none matched the clothing worn by her discovery. His clothes and boots were all of the very old handmade style.

Satellite phones had replaced shortwave radios as the most trusted form of intervillage communication. Luke did not care much for them but kept one of the devices at his temporary residence in the nearby small village inn. He returned to his room and made the call. He thought carefully how he would word his report. His first call was to his brother, a more traditional Inuit who took great pride in passing down the traditional customs to his five children. A sleepy voice answered, "Oh, hi, brother, what's up?" Luke relayed his message. His brother was incredulous, but he knew that Luke never spoke anything but complete truth. Sitting bolt upright on the edge of the bed, he realized at once the importance of what Luke relayed and how this might be the most significant event for his people in many years. "I'm on it, brother. Thanks for the call." With that, Luke's brother grabbed his clothes and left his wife rubbing her eyes and wondering what was happening when he dashed from the room.

Luke's brother called his most trusted friend on the council, who in turn relayed it to their chief, who then called for an immediate meeting of all the remaining elders. Last he called Luke back to tell him that he had delivered the message.

Putting his satellite phone back in his pocket, Luke closed his room door behind him, stopping only long enough to grab a fresh muffin on his way out of the inn. Returning to the shed, he arrived to find a confrontation taking place between the Inuit guards and the two local workers eager to start their assignment of melting the block, thus freeing the corpse. Luke walked up to the scene of the foursome in time to hear a string of expletives from one of the workers and a promise to return with red jackets, members of the Royal

Canadian Mounted Police. The Inuits said nothing. They just stood their ground like stone pillars in front of the shed door, one with arms crossed, John standing menacingly pointing his rifle at the closest and loudest arguer.

Roger Coleman, chief coroner for this entire territory, was a thin, frail, bespectacled man over sixty years of age. He despised flying, in particular to remote places in small airplanes. Already sick to his stomach from the rough flight and always looking pallid, he preferred to have corpses brought to him at his uncomfortable cold laboratory. His bush pilot assigned to deliver him to Igloolik could hardly concentrate on flying with all the coughing he heard. Bundled against the cold, Coleman coughed into his soaked handkerchief, looking irritated at having to be there. Many years of smoking had taken their toll, and Roger never stopped fidgeting unless he had a lighted cigarette hanging from the corner of his mouth.

Coleman had been completing an autopsy when the report of the recovered ice-encased body came in. Coughing up sputum, Roger took the brief report in stride but was very perturbed by the order to respect the wishes of the Inuits and fly in person to their remote settlement to complete the formalities of his job. He was never comfortable leaving the confines of his medical facility, especially having to fly any distance in a small aircraft. If his assistant had not been out on another assignment, he never would have made this trip. Now he was sitting in a small plane, cold and uncomfortable, flying over a barren wasteland and suffering from nicotine withdrawal since the pilot would not let him smoke. He promised himself that someone was going to receive a major butt chewing when this foray was over.

The weather was deteriorating when the pilot started his steady decent toward the short runway at Igloolik. Permafrost heaving and ice and snow mixed with gravel and dirt made the landing strip rough and uneven. Roger's pilot had listened to a near-constant litany of complaints for the last forty-five minutes of their flight. He wanted nothing more than to get his craft on the ground and make it a rough landing for his one cantankerous passenger. He brought the airplane in at a low angle and then let it drop fast, bouncing hard in order to make the unfriendly coroner as miserable as possible. His plan succeeded. It caused the coroner to fill his mouth with vomit and then swallow it again. Satisfied with his idea and glad the older man did not spit up in his craft, he taxied up to the windswept one-room terminal and stopped with an extra jolt.

When the pilot switched off his engine, Roger swung the side door open and cursed the pilot for what he called a terrible flight and even worse landing. The pilot grabbed him by the shoulder and jerked him back in to prevent him from getting out before the prop stopped turning. Roger's breath filled the small airplane cabin with nauseating odor. The pilot mumbled something unintelligible and wished the coroner a nice day.

Moving away from the aircraft and pilot, Roger responded with a terse "Go to hell, but I guess that you've already brought me there. Just be ready to get out of here as soon as possible, and I hope that your takeoff beats the heck out of your landing."

The "Mountie" on call was one John Cochran Morris the Third. He was a fourth-generation RCMP or Royal Canadian Mounted Policeman in the Morris family. A recent graduate of the academy, he received his first stripe in spite of breaking too many rules and a drinking problem that nearly cost him his commission and first assignment. Both his grandfather and father finished illustrious careers and retired with many honors and accolades. By tradition, he was expected to follow in their footsteps and maintain the family tradition. Where they had graduated at the top of their respective classes, Jamo, as he was nicknamed, graduated near the bottom, barely making the final cut by a narrow margin.

Jamo was born and grew up with very fair skin, red hair, and a very slight build. He often had to defend his masculinity against bullying foes half again his size. Two broken noses, numerous scrapes and black eyes, and a broken tooth or two were ample evidence of his fiery personality and short temper. These same traits contributed to an early demotion and his near discharge from the Mounties and also caused him to drink too much. If not for calls to the top brass from his father and grandad, he would have been dismissed from the service.

He arrived on a separate flight two hours before the coroner. Finding the inn first to warm up, he ordered two hot chocolates with double shots of schnapps. He was not officially on duty yet, but either way, he did not care. He felt self-pity for his plight, assigned the lowly duty of meeting the coroner sent to examine some fool who had gotten himself frozen in a block of ice. He dreaded his next assignment: to inspect and provide security to a damned weather base in the middle of nowhere. Jamo knew that he had no one to blame for such lackluster duty but himself, but at least he was still wearing the uniform, and that gave him the right to bust some heads if circumstances warranted it.

Jamo heard the low drone of an airplane engine passing over and gliding on low throttle onto the nearby runway. Straightening and smoothing his crimson uniform, he plunked down enough money to cover his drinks and added a modest tip. Alone in the small bar and dining area, only the proprietor had noticed his presence in the village. He slipped out the front door with a mock salute. "Duty calls, Max. Remember I only had a hot chocolate, right?"

"Sure, Jamo," he responded, wiping the short bar and picking up his empty cup.

In case the coroner was a stickler for protocol, Jamo entered the one-room terminal, used the unisex single bathroom, combed his hair in the cracked faded mirror, and freshened his breath. When the foul-smelling, fast-talking, disheveled little man burst through the door looking like he had slept in his clothes for a week and cursing like a drunken sailor, Jamo realized that this was not what he expected. He was not prepared to deal with foul language and bad manners.

Roger disappeared into the bathroom. The pilot came in to wait his turn. Jamo looked at him and asked, "What the hell was that?"

The pilot smiled and said, "That's a real case there, that one is. He's mad about everything and nasty as heck. If I had my way, I'd have chucked the creep out of my plane and said he never showed up." Just then, Rogers came out of the restroom smelling and looking better. The pilot ducked in and wished Jamo good luck adding, "You'll need it."

"Let's go, Mountie," Roger demanded, putting his heavy coat back on and slipping thin black leather gloves onto his chilled hands. "What's your name?" he asked. Jamo was certain that he knew his name because it was on the paperwork that he and the coroner both had. He said nothing and, with the small man in tow, started up the street for where he had seen the guarded storage shed. Before they got very far, they were met by the two disgruntled workers wanting to talk to Jamo. The coroner believed that they were there to talk to him, but they just ignored him, instead blocking Jamo's path until he would listen to what they were complaining about.

The taller one exclaimed, "Jamo, we need you at the shed right now. There are two friggin' Eskimos stopping us from doing our job. One's got a rifle, and one's got an ice ax." Jamo explained that they were heading there now and that he would take care of their problem. After having nothing to do for two days, he looked forward to a little excitement and was more than ready to use his authority. He realized that the coroner was going to get even madder if the body he was supposed to examine was not even thawed yet.

Jamo had no idea what the Inuits were up to. He hoped that he would get a chance to impress the coroner and get a good report, maybe even bust some heads. Roger Coleman in his official capacity seized the moment to take control of the entire situation. Without confronting the Native men, he ordered Jamo, "Officer, take me to the inn where I can freshen up from that awful flight here, and I am hungry. I also need to inspect the medical facility where I shall conduct my examination."

Jamo just laughed. "That small shed on the right with the two cigar store Indians is your facility, and that ramshackle dump ahead of you is the inn, restaurant, bar, and store. I hope they will do."

The elder man snapped back, "We'll see about that." Angered even more, the flustered little man pulled out his cigarettes and shuffled toward the weathered inn door, expecting the worst. He glanced at the faded sign above the door that read End of the World Inn.

Jamo shouted, "I'll go see what kind of problem we have with the locals."

The pilot brought Roger's bag and medical kit to the door in time to listen to the last part of their conversation. He placed the coroner's medical kit on the one chair in the cramped room that served as check-in and dropped his overnight bag from high enough that it made a loud bang when it hit the floor. Turning, he exited the building to another chorus of low-toned cursing, trying not to laugh on his way to check over his aircraft.

Jamo and the two workers crossed the rutted road in order to confront the two Inuit guards. He wondered why they were so intent on guarding a dead man. Jamo thought about going back to his bag and retrieving his sidearm since the workers told him that the guards were armed, but he could not believe that he needed anything more than a bit of diplomacy to straighten things out. Approaching the Inuits, Jamo smiled, extended his hand, and wished the two men a good day, the two workers flanking him to each side.

John, holding his rifle in a relaxed position across his body, spoke first. "Good day to you too, Jamo. It's been a while. Haven't seen you since you arrested my uncle for getting drunk. We don't want any trouble, but those two are not going inside."

"Well, then just give me the key, and I'll open up, aye?" Jamo's voice became much sterner. "What's the deal? Why are you two acting like you're on guard duty? Don't you two have something better to do? These guys are supposed to melt the ice and thaw the body enough for the coroner to do his job. And I don't want to have to deal with that creep any more than I have to."

"Sorry, Jamo, can't do that." This time, the second Inuit spoke. "In fact, nobody goes in there before Eluk returns with the elders.

"I have my orders and an executed release from a member of your council, and the chief coroner from this province office is here to do his job." Jamo was irritated and getting more agitated, and his diplomacy had failed. "Step aside and put down your weapons, or I will be forced to arrest you both on charges of obstruction. If you refuse to obey my orders, I will increase the charges, and that will earn you more time in the slammer."

The shorter Inuit took John's rifle, raised the weapon, and pointed it straight at the Mountie's gut. His smile was gone, replaced by a stern jawline, and Jamo saw a resolve in his demeanor that frightened him. The look was deadly.

Jamo stepped back in disbelief. His two accomplices backed away. He shouted, "THE CHARGES JUST BECAME ASSAULTING A FED-

ERAL OFFICER WITH A DEADLY WEAPON. PUT DOWN THE WEAPON! THAT IS AN ORDER! YOU BOTH ARE UNDER ARREST."

The satellite phone in John's pocket rang. He answered it, never taking his eyes off Jamo. Before he could say anything, a shot rang out. The shorter Eskimo fired a shot into the air. No one was hit or injured except Jamo's pride. Whether just frustrated or fortified by the four shots of alcohol, he rushed the Inuit holding the rifle. Met by a downward sweep of the rifle butt, Jamo was knocked unconscious and was now sprawled facedown in his sparkling red uniform in the dirt-and-snow-mixed mess. The white-faced, shocked workers turned and ran away.

Luke heard the loud report of the rifle through the satellite phone, followed by, "Shit, you just killed a Mountie!" His stomach knotted, and his throat went dry.

CHAPTER 10

JAMO

Three tribal elders, two being council members, arrived from the remaining small settlements in the area. Luke sent them a message while they were on their way about the confrontation between the guards he posted and the young Mountie. If necessary, John and his friend were to be sent to another village, a place more remote, where they would remain until they found out if the "red coats" would pursue the issue and bring charges against the men. The chiefs decided to treat the officer like a hero, play to his oversized ego, and make him feel like the savior of the ancestral treasure.

Becky stayed out of all the commotion. When the dazed officer was brought into the inn, she had him placed in her room and bed and took care of him like a well-trained nurse, tending to his bruised chin and bruised ego. He basked in the attention, enjoying the pretty face fussing over him. The innkeeper found his bottle of dry-cleaning fluid and removed the soiled spots from the uniform, rendering it spotless again in minutes. Jamo's anger and resentment subsided. When Becky explained the importance of her find to him, he even stated that he had been foolish and probably owed the Inuits an apology. Becky assured him that an apology was not necessary and hoped his attitude would not change later. The innkeeper brought Jamo his clean uniform and a sumptuous breakfast of hotcakes and bacon with a large mug of schnapps-spiked hot chocolate. Jamo was happy. He smiled.

The elders visited Jamo, first wanting to know how he felt about the altercation. Assured that there would be no further ramifications, they waited for him to don his uniform, and acting like an escort for him, they all returned to the open shed. One elder patted his shoulder and called him a hero, adding that he was going to be famous when the news of this discovery got out. It worked. Jamo was beaming with pride. The workers had returned and were allowed to melt most of the ice block under close supervision. John and his compatriot apologized several times for the blow inflicted. Luke appeared at the door and joined the others surrounding the body still preserved in a thin veneer of clear ice and much easier to scrutinize. Becky held Luke's and John's hands. They all formed a circle around the corpse, and the elders chanted a prayer, tears forming in the aged eyes of the eldest.

Jamo was carried to the inn on the shoulders of the two shed helpers. It was time for a celebration, and to Jamo, that meant it was time for another drink.

Upon completion of the brief informal ceremony, Becky and Luke returned to the inn. Roger Coleman passed them, going in the opposite direction without saying a word. He was busy coughing into his moist handkerchief. Luke and Becky stopped him and took him aside, explaining as quickly as they could about what was happening in the shed and the importance of this historic find. Roger's countenance took on a whole new look. He now understood the serious nature of what lay before him.

Becky went to her room and packed her bags and equipment for her scheduled trip to AWRB 1 the next day. Luke needed to prepare, but she did not think that he should leave with her and John. Becky believed that he should heal and come at a later date. Luke's assignment was base adviser. His new job entailed teaching Arctic survival at the new weather station 150 miles closer to the North Pole. John had been to the base twice before and was returning with him and Becky.

Luke decided to show Becky the bandage under his shirt. Becky had noticed that Luke's side wound was seeping a little blood from the old bandages and rebandaged it for him. They hated to leave the body behind, but their new assignment at the base began tomorrow.

That is if the weather held, and they could get there. Luke knew that the pay would be good but wondered about the wisdom of accepting the new assignment. He had been present to check over the specialized technical equipment that was delivered to this tiny village and then on to the base. Some crates were obviously military, and that bothered him. He preferred his less cluttered lifestyle still practiced by an ever-shrinking number of his people, and except for Becky, he distrusted the so-called scientists from the land of lights and smog.

Roger entered the shed, a lighted cigarette dangling from his lips. Coleman was taken aback by the scene before him. He was surprised by the Inuit countenances and stern but friendly expressions. The three elders were gathered around the body. He bowed to the elders and asked politely if he could begin his examination. They nodded assent, but none were leaving.

Roger Coleman became somewhat irritated by the group of locals and Inuits looking over his shoulder when he began his examination. The most senior member of the Inuit group approached the coroner to speak, but with a perfunctory wave, Coleman ignored him, procuring a scalpel from his medical bag. As soon as he began scraping at an exposed part of a hand, the stoutest Native of the group picked him up, slung him over his shoulder, and plunked him down on his behind outside the shed in the same muddy spot previously occupied by the Mountie. The now infuriated little man shouted, "HOW DARE YOU! DO YOU KNOW WHO I AM?"

The Inuit elder answered, "Yes, we know who you are. You are the little doctor who smokes too much, complains too much, and you have come here to take Anook away from us. This will not happen. You will not cut him up. You will not take his things."

Though angry and puzzled, Roger heard him say the name Anook. Becky and Luke had not used a name earlier. "I know that he is important to you all. Becky told me that. How do you know his name. Was he a friend of yours?"

The most senior elder stepped in front of Roger and stared into his eyes. "All Inuits know Anook or about him." His English was perfect, and he sounded more like a student of English literature than a full-blooded member of North America's most northern Native people. He continued, "Anook is our most revered ancestor, the greatest hunter ever and folklore hero. His stories have been handed down for many generations. His symbol you can now see on his amulet is found on many of our totems. Now he is back among us. His body is sacred to us beyond what you can comprehend. He belongs only to us. Do you understand?"

Coleman said only, "Yes, I do. My job is done here." With that, he turned and walked away. Jamo appeared at the door, a steaming mug of something in his hand, at the same moment that Roger said his perfunctory goodbye. He watched the coroner leave and said nothing, following him out the door and back to the inn.

Jamo's jaw ached now. He eased into one of the barstools at the serving bar and ordered a double shot, this time straight Canadian whiskey. The innkeeper's wife, Edna, was the closest thing the village had to anyone with medical education. She bad basic training in first aid and had worked as a physician's assistant in Edmonton a few years before she and Max bought the old inn and moved to remote Igloolik. Edna also assisted the traveling doctor who visited the settlement on occasion to treat the inhabitants. She was concerned for Jamo, but except for the bruise on his face, he looked fine to her. For his pain and ache, Edna gave him several pain pills. Becky continued to try to soothe him, with a stern warning about drinking alcohol and mixing the potent drug with it. He felt a little dizzy and stepped outside for a few deep breaths of fresh air.

Roger Coleman was entering the inn front door when Jamo swung it open to step outside. The door slipped from his hand, swung back to close, and hit Roger hard. There was an audible *oof* sound followed by a puff of white smoke and the clack of eyeglasses hitting the floor. The old man collapsed in a disheveled heap outside the door. "Oh crap" was the only thing that the Mountie said.

"Wow, another patient." Edna sounded pleased. "Counting you, Jamo, Luke looking for sympathy, and that crab, I feel overwhelmed. We haven't had this many hurt people around here in a while. Our place is looking like a real hospital." Edna looked down at Roger and smiled at Jamo. "Looks like you just about KO'd him." Jamo was not amused. He bent down and helped the stunned man to his wobbly feet and guided him to a chair inside. Edna added, "When he gets his senses back, he's gonna be mad again. You'd better disappear for a while." She put her arm around the frail coroner's shoulder, picked him up, and carried him to his room.

Jamo returned to the bar and ordered another double. Two other patrons sitting in the corner snickered at him when he reordered. He looked at them with obvious anger and disdain, his face sullen. Max pointed out that it was his third double and suggested that he slow down. His answer was "I'm not on duty. I feel like crap and hurt, and who cares?" He downed the third double in one gulp. "Never thought I'd be glad to see tomorrow and be out of this godforsaken hole for some damned weather station." He no sooner uttered those words when the room began to spin. He slammed his shot glass down on the bar, sending shards of glass in all directions. The spinning in his head increased, and the lights went out. He collapsed to the floor with a loud thud, hitting the back of his head on the bar on the way down.

Max peered over the bar at him and said, "Oh, that is going to hurt in the morning." He came around and leaned over Jamo, shaking Jamo's head gingerly. "Three cheers for Jamo, our illustrious officer." The two locals from the corner picked up his limp body and started to carry Edna's next patient to his room. Brandishing his peacekeeping baseball bat from behind the bar, Max looked at the exiting patrons and stated, "You didn't see any of that, right?"

Jamo awoke the next morning with a pounding in his head unlike anything he had ever felt before. When he looked at the old clock ticking next to his bed, the sound made his head hurt worse. He discovered that he only had two hours to bathe, sober up, find something to eat, and pack for the flight to the weather base. Becky knocked on his door to remind him two minutes later to make sure he was up and see if he was all right. He felt the raised knot on the back of his head and assured her that he would be ready. Jamo had many headaches before from hangovers and thought nothing more about it. The internal cranial bleeding at the base of his brain stem went undetected.

CHAPTER 11

FORTY DAYS AND FORTY NIGHTS

The uneventful flight to AWRB 1 for Luke, Becky, John, and Jamo went as planned, though it was bumpy and most of it above and through swirling falling snow. Their pilot circled the base, breaking through the low clouds, trying to provide himself with an overview of the surrounding landscape. John noticed a few changes, new antennas, and a larger improved landing area where they set down. The base below the landing area was marked by a series of low Quonset hut-type buildings connected by translucent heated tubes. It was possible to reach any part of the small jumble of buildings and labs without ever venturing outside. A few utility buildings, storage sheds, and a snowmobile garage completed the main section.

Behind and landward from the base rose a rocky promontory with a steep front side and a flat windblown top. Constant breezes kept the top relatively snow-free between storms. This fact was part of the reason for the selection of this particular location for the base. Being windswept and relatively snow-clear provided a good, solid landing area for helicopters and vertical takeoff aircraft. The rock cliff protected the base below it to some degree, though large drifts were a potential problem when storms dropped prodigious amounts of white.

Engineers constructed a tube tunnel with a long stairway through the rock from the topside landing area to the base of the cliff, connecting the two. They also fashioned a shaft for an equipment elevator through the rock to the topside landing zone. Safe sheltered passage was possible in all conditions. A rudimentary hangar was constructed at one end of the rocky landing area. The base was in a good location, a safe choice, and its function well worth the cost.

The new and returning group unloaded their gear and descended the stairs to the base where they settled into their dorm-style rooms and prepared to go to work while the good weather lasted.

Eluk insisted on accompanying the others to the base even though he was not healed. His sense of loyalty to his friends and especially to Becky gave Wayne comfort back in Chicago but also a twinge of jealousy. Wayne knew that she was very loyal to him, but he missed her more with each passing day. As a final surprise, with a made-up excuse to his boss and as a gesture of his affection, Wayne decided to fly north and catch the last ferry helicopter run to the base.

Wayne visited the weather research base during its construction. He met Eluk for the first time on his initial trip there. Thinking about Becky's story about Luke's injuries, Wayne was amazed at his resiliency and his quick recovery. Wayne originally objected to Eluk coming to the base so soon after his injury.

During the final leg of the trip back to AWRB 1, Wayne reread the latest reports. He suspected that there were gaps in them or that someone had removed information about certain activities.

Upon his arrival at the base, Wayne noticed some changes. He saw new construction close to the landing area that he knew nothing about. Located on a rocky projection of land at the end of a glacial fjord, Wayne noted that this part of the fjord was normally at least partially open water in the summer, thick pack ice in the winter. This year, he could see that the pack ice never broke up. Pressure ridges of jumbled ice marked the seaward side of the base. Beneath the ice and a short distance from shore, the seawater was dark, deep, and dense.

Wayne was concerned but not alarmed by the much deeper than expected snow around the base. He had seen videos and reports, but the camera angles did not show the amazing buildup of snow. A thick satin shroud covered everything. He wondered if the cameraperson was instructed to de-emphasize the snow depth. The base looked nothing like it did two years ago when he supervised the layout and first phase of construction.

When the copter door opened, Wayne was greeted by a blustery wind that blew ice crystals and snow into his face. He left behind subtropical conditions at home. He had prepared himself for it, but he never was comfortable in extreme cold. Eluk was there to greet him, helping him out of the door. The Inuit smiled, breathed in the cold air, and seemed to bask in it. Wayne knew that it was for his thin-blooded benefit. Eluk was on his turf. He was not. After greeting him and feeling that strong handshake, Wayne was glad that Luke was there.

Gathering his gear on the way to the door and the stairway, Luke described his ordeal and progress. Luke's version of the incident at the glacier was far more entertaining than the official report. He was especially descriptive when he compared his near escape from the sliding block to a hunted seal being skinned. Wayne knew that his version of Anook would be long and wonderful to hear, but at this point, he was thinking of Becky and the unexpected surprise of his arrival.

It had snowed at least some every day for over two weeks before their arrival. The new total accumulation was growing fast. Snow was removed from around the base and pushed into immense piles nearby. These were strategically left out of the last photos sent to Wayne. Since his arrival, snow was starting to fall quite hard again. They hurried to the entrance to the lift and stairway down to the main part of the base. Wayne, their pilot, and copilot entered the small elevator. Luke took the nearby stairs. Luke disliked elevators, but he never explained why.

Once in the base, Wayne greeted the remaining crew and one not-so-surprised fiancée. The secret of his visit had slipped out, but Becky met him with a very big hug and long kiss and a look of complete delight. That caused a few groans, moans, and whispered comments. Wayne could feel her pent-up warmth, and she sensed his.

By mid-August, the brief Arctic summer was waning. AWRB 1 was a bustle of activity as all nonessential personnel packed for departure. Wayne, Becky, Luke, and John were slated to be the last to leave along with two government personnel, listed as scientists. Wayne was not happy about this arrangement, but his superiors had insisted on it. An ulterior motive was evident to him. When everyone else was gone, the government would be free to further experiment and evaluate their second purpose for the base without too many sets of eyes watching. Wayne was not too concerned about himself and the Inuits. He was worried about Becky remaining too long, but he knew that she enjoyed the sense of adventure and loved her job. The last thing Wayne wanted was to be trapped there by incessant storms.

At the end of August, the Arctic weather began to deteriorate even more. Last year, the base had been fortuitously abandoned prior to being inundated and then buried by incredible snowfalls. The blanket of glistening white did not melt off at all this summer. Arctic wildlife in the area of the base was decimated. Migrating waterfowl had found no normal, open tundra nesting grounds. Scientists feared that some species had been irreparably damaged; others wiped out. Arctic biologists were overwhelmed by the new problems. Drastic changes were taking place, changes without precedent.

The snowstorms were earlier, more frequent, and far too heavy for their location. Luke and Wayne both understood that major changes were taking place and that it was not another freak summer or early winter. Wayne began rethinking the wisdom of still occupying AWRB 1 at all. The future weather forecast was not good. The people still occupying the base remained his responsibility. He had returned to personally assess the situation and make the decision as to when to evacuate for the season.

The base was designed to operate year-round, but last year had shown the foolishness of considering it. Parts of the base had been buried so deep that several structures had collapsed under the weight. An avalanche from far up the fjord valley had come within a quarter mile of reaching the base. The advancing nearby glacier at the head of the fjord could bring such an occurrence even closer this year. Wayne decided that they would take no more serious risks. He informed the remaining personnel that they would all leave very soon, well in advance of more problems.

Two days later, the weather worsened. As good as the aircraft performed in bad conditions and as skilled as the pilots were trained, there was no chance to leave. Another prolonged Arctic storm overwhelmed the base, settling in with a steady fury. The AWRB crew consisted of Wayne and Becky; Luke and John; Carl and Bob; Canadian scientists Richard Hall, Blake Edwards, and Charise Lacoure; pilot Mitch; and his new Canadian pilot cohort Francois and officer Jamo, who wanted nothing more than to be anywhere but there. There were twelve in all, and if the weather did not improve, they were stuck there for a long and isolated time together.

For the first forty-eight hours of the newest storm, work went on. In the evening, they all shared stories of the trip back to Long Glacier and "Discovery Valley." They discussed their climate data and glacial monitoring. Wayne and Becky also reviewed notes they found on the purpose and function of the more clandestine operation of placing an advanced sensor array for the US and Canadian governments.

After seventy-two hours of unabated high winds and fierce stormy conditions, the pilots were nervous and impatient to leave. Francois and Mitch had been planning to depart two days ago to fly out Blake, Charise, and Carl. They were tiring of playing cards and taking turns attempting to keep their craft clear of snow and ice and flight-worthy. As the storm intensified, their job became more difficult. Nervousness and claustrophobia began to set in. It had now been snowing with severity for five days with no forecast break in the foreseeable future. What they did not know was that this storm would not let up for an almost biblical forty days and forty nights with no breaks long enough to safely depart.

The Canadian pilots insisted on being ready to go at a moment's notice. They were ready to leave twice by the end of two weeks of containment but were ordered to sit tight. Even if they could lift off, the atmospheric problem was widespread and pervasive. When it was better and possible to take off from the base, there was no place within range to safely land. This storm had the entire region in an icy grip. It was better to sit tight and continue to ride it out. The stranded group had adequate supplies for a stay of long duration.

Communications were still good, and taking unnecessary risks was deemed foolhardy. They had to wait, but no one knew for sure for how long.

Two weeks passed, and the snow began to reach alarming depths. The snow removal equipment was now buried, and several of the huts started to groan under the ever-increasing weight of accumulating snow. Keeping equipment and the landing area cleared became impossible.

The team at the base and the persons waiting at their final destinations began to worry about how long the continuous bad weather would continue. They also all wondered when they would be able to or be allowed to flee their remote corner of the world. The patience of the stranded occupants of the base began to wear thin. Everyone shared in the various duties, including snow removal, which at this point was almost futile.

They passed the time reading books from the small library collection and watching old movies. The recreation hall had a table tennis table, and there was a nice card table with comfortable chairs. Games varied from poker to solitaire, depending on the time of day and interest level. Blake was winning at poker until Charise pulled four kings and crushed his full house. Doubles ping-pong was the favorite daytime sport. Morale remained high even though everyone showed signs of anxiety at times, and Jamo looked very bored and depressed. Carl helped that situation when he discovered that Jamo really enjoyed cribbage. They played every day, sometimes for hours into the night.

Meals were taken together unless duty called or someone was outside. Cooking chores were shared among the group, though Eluk and Becky enjoyed it the most. Wayne deferred that talent to Becky, who was a gifted cook and enjoyed experimenting with their supplies to make meals more interesting. Since resupply was not in store for the group, they had to make the best out of what they had on hand.

Becky and Wayne found more time to spend together as the dreary days went on. Their bond grew with each passing day. They became a formidable table tennis team. Becky's jokes had long since run out, but her warm sense of humor continued to keep everyone in good spirits. She was writing a daily log of their time at the base, wanting to someday turn it into a novel. She added short comments from each occupant, keeping everyone focused and engaged.

CHAPTER 12

WITHOUT WARNING

Eluk and John made daily brief sorties into the surrounding area to check for and assess avalanche danger. Though both were experienced outdoorsmen, on one occasion, John became disoriented in the blizzard conditions, was separated from Eluk, and struggled to return. The snowmobiles were almost useless because of the snow depth. They had no sled dog teams at the base. Snowshoes made it possible to go short distances without great fatigue, but a long-distance walk was ill-advised. The drifts and piles of snow were terrible and still growing with each passing day.

Carl and Bob took their turn one evening to check on the helicopter and make sure the hangar was still holding up. They had to clear snow from the roof to keep it from collapsing. The drifted snow against the leeward side now reached a height even with the roofline. Everything was done by teams. No one ventured anywhere outside alone. Eluk and John returned from a brief sortie, tired from shoveling and clearing the entrance to the hangar. Becky and Wayne decided to greet them all at the top of the stairs in the cliff with a surprise mug of hot coffee. That fateful decision saved their lives.

It struck without warning. The only real precursor was a distant rumble and shutter in the huts. It sounded like thunder from a brewing storm. Becky and Wayne did not feel it while ascending the rock stairs within the cliffside. Carl and Bob were chatting with Eluk and John at the top of the stairs. The aroma of fresh hazelnut-flavored coffee wafted to their noses. They heard the sound of Wayne's and Becky's footfalls on the stairs and their voices below. Eluk stiffened and sensed the impending danger. They all stopped when the rumble became discernible and audible. Wayne looked down and noticed circular ripples in his cups of coffee. He and Becky froze in their tracks.

The six still within the base were split into two groups. The pilots were in the recreation room playing ping-pong. Charise was flirting with Mitch, much to the delight of the other Canadian pilot. The other scientist Richard Hall and Jamo were relaxing in front of a blaring television, watching a recorded movie in the adjoining TV room and library. They never even heard the icy onslaught until it was too late to react.

The white wave of terror moved down the valley at high speed. It was an avalanche, a huge avalanche, sweeping toward their location with deadly purpose. In the blink of an eye, AWRB 1 was inundated, shredded, and swept away by the roiling wave of snow and ice. The destruction was complete and horrific. No trace was ever found of Richard Hall or Blake Edwards. The recreation hall took the full brunt of the wave of debris. It shattered and was torn to pieces, as was most of the rest of the base.

Part of the flow of snow was partially diverted, redirected before it struck the recreation hall. The Quonset hut was ripped from its base and pushed ahead of the deflected mass. It was crushed like an empty beer can and crumpled against the rock wall behind the base, but it was not buried entirely.

Pilot Francois was killed instantly, crushed between the collapsing structure and heavy contents. Unfortunately, Mitch met with the same fate. They probably never knew what hit them. Charise was literally launched over Mitch by the explosive force of the avalanche as it breached their shelter. She flew over the ping-pong table as it buckled, landing on Jamo. It happened so quickly that she and Jamo had no idea what happened and ended up pinned there together under heavy furniture, remnants of the ping-pong table, and the crushed outer shell of what used to be the recreation hall. They were trapped but alive, in shock, but still breathing.

The entire disaster happened in less than five minutes, during which their haven became a nightmare of death and destruction. To the lucky ones who happened to be in the rocky stairwell, the rumble of the avalanche was over. The ground had shaken like an earthquake. Luke and John knew what had happened. They scrambled down the stairs to check on the base. Hot coffee lay spilled on the cold rock steps. The lights in the stairway remained on. The generator was protected within their rocky lair and still functioning.

At the base of the steep stairway, the horror of what just happened began to sink in. The double glass doorway between the small area at the base of the stairway, the elevator door, mechanical room carved out of the rock cliff, and the first tube leading to the main base module was pushed in but remained intact. On the other side of the damaged doors, there was nothing but white. All six survivors looked at one another with disbelief and dismay. Tortured realization of their situation began to sink in.

Wayne hugged Becky, seeing the shocked look on his love's face. Becky was stunned, realizing their predicament and terrified about the rest of the residents. John bounded up the stairs to assess the situation from above. Carl volunteered to stay with Becky to check the precious generator. Bob and Eluk followed John toward the upper door. Wayne stopped a little over midway up the stairs to cross to a small catwalk along the inside of the rock wall. The builders had put a small insulated metal door with a window across the catwalk. They had used this second entrance during excavation. Though seldom used since, this door provided a vantage point for observing the base.

John reached the top of the stairway and peered outside into the increasing darkness. Several bright lights illuminated the immediate area around the door. The lights illuminating the nearby hangar were not on. He opened the upper entrance door to peer outside and saw why. The hangar was flattened by a large accumulation of chunks of ice and snow. John's heart sank even more. He had to investigate but realized that the helicopter inside could not have survived the destruction.

They were all lucky to have their parkas on, a basic rule when entering the stairwell or elevator area. They could have been lounging without them like their comrades. John volunteered to venture outside to look around. He warned the others to remain inside. He grabbed a pair of snowshoes from beside the upper door, picked up one of the flashlights always on chargers there, and took a walkie-talkie from its charging base. He slipped the earpiece into his ear and clipped the miniature microphone to the fur beside his mouth and stepped into the growing darkness. His beam was almost useless in the blowing snow. He moved with care to assess the damage and reconnoiter the immediate cliff top landing area.

The strain in John's voice on the communicator startled Bob. John was panting and breathing hard from the effort of trudging through the deep snow. When John reached what was left of the hangar, he shook his head and turned away. Listening to John mumble, Bob and Becky looked up. They heard Wayne's words from the side door above. "Oh my god, it's gone!" His voice broke with emotion. He repeated, "The base…it's gone!"

Full realization of his words hit Bob hard. A rivulet of sweat ran down his back, soaking his T-shirt beneath his flannel shirt and parka. "What happened out there? What can you see, Wayne?"

"Nothing, no lights, no base, no nothing." Wayne's voice became somber and weak. "All that I can see is snow and more snow. It's piled up almost to this door. I can't see anything else." His words carried downward to Becky. He heard her sobs. He could also hear Carl praying. Carl recited the Lord's Prayer. They all joined him. It seemed to give them a bit of inner strength.

Wayne snapped out of his depression. They had to take action. Adrenaline perked up his senses. He knew that destruction of the base meant destruction of their precious supplies. It also meant that communications were cut off, unless someone had their satellite phone. He had already heard John's comments about the destruction of the hangar and their only means of escape.

Luke and Wayne met at the base of the stairs with the others. Everyone looked at Wayne as their leader, expecting some encouragement. He had none. He began the process of fully assessing their personal situation, their resources at hand, and formulating an immediate plan for survival. In addition, he, Luke, and John had to at least attempt to search for survivors. It was the beginning of an

Arctic autumn night and darkness, though not complete, allowing inadequate ambient illumination for searching. They would have to wait for daylight. From his cursory evaluation of the scene outside, the rest of his crew were either buried or swept away. Once John completed a preliminary evaluation of their former base from atop the cliff, Wayne knew that he would need a solid plan. Their future survival might be dependent on it.

John proceeded as far as he could in the direction of the hangar and then circled back along the top of the sloping cliff. Semidarkness and swirling snow limited his vision. Poor visibility limited his ability to understand the full impact of the avalanche until he reached the edge of the cliff behind the upper entrance. There was a large spotlight still anchored there. He switched it on and rotated the beacon beam down toward the base. What he saw made his skin crawl and put a genuine lump in his throat. Through the falling snowflakes, he saw only white. An erratic chaos of ice and snow lay where a beautiful, fully functional, Arctic research station had been. There was no sign of life.

"Wayne, this is John. I'm at the overlook. The news is bad, very bad. I don't see any sign of the base. The avalanche debris must be at least ten meters or more in thickness. I'm afraid there's nothing left." The emotion in his voice relayed the message with dagger sharpness.

"Wait! I see something! It looks like one of the huts smashed up against the side of the cliff about one hundred meters to the west of my position. Yes, it's definitely one of the huts, but its half-buried and pretty mangled. I am going to try to climb down and check it out."

"Negative that." Wayne shouted as he raced up the stairs. At the top, he took the walkie-talkie from Bob, who had climbed back up and repeated his message. "Do not attempt to climb down or check it out alone. Leave the light pointed at it and rejoin us here. We can organize a search, but we need to do it right, do it together."

"Okay, Wayne. I'm coming in. It's mighty cold and nasty out here, so we better not waste any time. We have to search for survivors and food now. We can't wait."

In a few minutes, John stepped back inside, shaking a dusting of snow from his parka as he entered. Grim faces greeted him. "If anyone is alive out there, they won't last long."

Wayne and John returned to the catwalk with Eluk. They carried a rope from the storage locker at the top of the stairs, two powerful lights, a first aid kit, and the two extra parkas from the locker. Wayne bundled the extra gear and tied it to a rope secured to Luke. They opened the small door, and Wayne moved to the ledge outside. Luke followed him. John closed the door behind them, remaining ready inside.

There was barely enough room for the two of them on the narrow ledge. The crushed hut was discernible in the spotlight beam. Snow was piled almost up to their ledge, even above it in one or two places along the cliffside. The density of the snow avalanche debris was the unknown, but it looked solid enough. Luke knew how hard it could settle and pack, trapping anything caught in it with a very tight grip. Luke took it upon himself to find out.

With his snowshoes tucked beneath his arm, Luke stepped off the ledge and dropped the four or five feet to the densely packed snow. He flopped back and began securing the snowshoes. Wayne was about to join him when Luke waved and said, "No! Not there, over here. Jump into my tracks." He leaned back to where Wayne was going to jump and uncovered a large block of jagged ice. Wayne was thankful for the wise advice and dropped into Luke's tracks.

In a few minutes, they were probing with the ski poles they brought along for that purpose and working their way toward the remains of the crumpled hut. Approaching it, they trained their lights on the more dimly illuminated recesses. Wayne moved toward the twisted remnant of a window frame and attempted to look inside. He heard a moan. Luke did not hear it because he was facing away. "Listen." Wayne repeated, "Listen. I heard something."

Luke pulled off his parka hood, exposing his ears and capped head. He heard the muffled sound too and moved toward the source. Wayne followed behind him. They shined their lights inside the smashed window. The frame was severely warped with layered panes of jagged shards. Wayne leaned close to Luke and told him, "I can't see anything, but I heard what sounded like a low moan."

Charise lay pinned in the wreckage. She could barely move. She had lost the feeling in her legs. She was in shock and could not tell why she could not feel her legs. She feared they were gone or frozen or paralyzed. None of the possibilities seemed real. She fought to stay awake and alive. Her hands were cold, but she could feel them. Her head felt wet, her hair matted. She recognized the smell of blood. Cognizant of one other thing, she felt the warmth of another human under her and had noticed struggled breathing several times. Charise, though barely conscious, lay there, wondering what happened. Questions bounced around inside her head, swirling aimlessly in her semiconscious state. Charise's senses were completely overwhelmed. Nothing made sense. There was pain, awful pain, and cold. Things were beginning to fade. She realized that death was near. Then she heard it.

"Is anyone in there? Can you hear me?" It was Wayne's voice. "Make a noise, any noise."

She vaguely recognized the sound. Then she saw lights moving on the edge of the object pinning her head. Her left hand was holding something warm. It felt like a human hand. Her right hand had room to move. It was cold and stiff and barely responded, but she raised her hand and let her fingernails scrape down the piece of ping-pong table next to it. She tried to scream, to utter a sound, but was not sure if anything came out.

They both heard it. The sound of the scrape was audible. The faint voice sound with it was barely discernible, but they heard it. "Luke, there's someone alive in there. I'm going in. You've led so far, but this time, it's my turn."

Luke checked around the inside of the broken window and began breaking the remnants of thick double-pane glass with his light. He enlarged the opening and assisted Wayne through. The thick parkas, boots, and gloves would afford protection from cuts. Wayne picked his way carefully as he squeezed between broken furniture and broken supports. He was barely inside when his light spotted a hand and then a face matted with blood. The contorted countenance was not pleasant to look upon, but it was Charise, and she was alive.

"It's Charise. She's alive. I'm going to try to get to her."

"Be careful, Wayne. Things could shift." Luke made the comment and activated his walkie-talkie. "Wayne found Charise. She's alive." He relayed the message to the others inside. "I'll let you know if we need more help."

John countered back, "I'm ready if you need me."

"I'll let you know," Luke responded. "Save your battery and your energy. It was tough to get here through the debris."

With great care not to dislodge anything, Wayne moved over to Charise. He was as cautious as possible to check his foot—and handholds. She was obviously hurt and was shivering uncontrollably. He broke open two chemical heat packs and pushed one down to Charise. She was able to grasp the heat pack with her free hand and draw it to her face and neck. It felt wonderful. Wayne assessed the situation around her. The side and roof of the structure had come down around her. She was pinned by part of the game table, a chair or what was left of one, carpet from the buckled floor, and the recreation hall refrigerator. He found it ironic that apparently, a refrigerator had saved her life in the deep Arctic. The building had been crushed and imploded, but the stout refrigerator had propped up the large debris around Charise. Her lower half appeared to be wrapped like a blanket by padding and carpet.

Wayne was elated to find a survivor and optimistic that they could get her out. Nothing pinning her looked immovable. He relayed his thoughts to Luke that they might be able to free her. Luke relayed the same message to John. He also added instructions for John to join them and to bring cutters that will go through carpet, a saw if he could find one, and two ice-chopping bars from by the door.

John rushed up the stairs to the tool locker at the top. Carl, who was with him, opened the upper door and returned with a steel ice-chopping bar. There was a battery-operated cutting saw in the locker but no shears or heavy scissors in the storage unit. Carl looked perplexed, but John patted his side, reminding Carl that he, like Luke, always carried his trusted skinning knife. It would cut almost anything.

Out of the upper hatch and off the ledge, John worked his way to the others in only minutes. Light snow was falling, but through the clouds, he could see a few twinkling stars overhead. The ravages of the avalanche were everywhere, but all had settled.

John handed the saw and bar to his fellow Inuit and climbed into the smashed building. He and Wayne discussed a possible rescue plan with Luke. They all prayed that the hut would not shift. Wayne cut away some weak wood debris with the saw. Luke broke several pieces with the heavy bar. Then he and Luke positioned themselves to use the ice-chopper bar like a pry bar or lever to separate the debris. John joined them to add his strength in order to open a wider gap. Wayne prepared to cut away the carpet from Charise's lower body.

Luke spotted a second person. "Charise, is there someone else there? I see another arm." She did not respond. He reached down and grasped the arm from behind her. Luke drew the arm toward him. It came up easily, too easily. John and Wayne saw it before Luke realized that he was holding a severed arm. His eyes grew wide when he saw the familiar chronograph-GPS unit on the wrist. It was Mitch's. Eyes glistening, Luke placed the arm behind him out of Charise's sight. His stomach turned, and his senses numbed, revolted at the sight of the bloody mangled arm of his friend.

They returned their focus to Charise. She mumbled a few unintelligible words. "There is someone under me, and he's still breathing." Wayne hoped that it wasn't Mitch. John and Wayne strained at the bar to raise the largest debris enough for Luke to attempt to free Charise. He tore at the carpet and padding with his knife, slicing through it with a fury. John warned him to slow down. One mistake could severely slice Charise.

Luke was able to cut away the carpet enough to free her. He felt her legs for obvious breaks. He did not have much time. Wayne uttered a strained "Hurry." She felt limp and cold but somehow managed a brief smile. Luke used all his strength to pull her up and out. He could not believe that Charise was holding onto another hand. He had to ask her to let go of the new hand when he brought her the rest of the way out of the pile of twisted debris. Once he had her free and was able to lay her down away from immediate danger, Luke placed a bent piece of metal wreckage in the pile as a wedge. It worked. John and Wayne slowly let off tension on the lever, and nothing shifted. "Get her inside Luke," Wayne insisted.

"Jamo is down there too," Luke said. Wayne and John peered into the wreckage to see the bloodied face of Jamo. They were elated to find another survivor at his point, but he did not look good. Wayne told John and Luke to take Charise to shelter. He volunteered to stay with Jamo. "I'll put some heat packs on Jamo and stay with him."

Wayne felt the great loss of his friend Mitch. The entire situation was shocking. Luke and John struggled to remove Charise from the mangled hut. She was wrapped in carpet and one parka, and they prepared to drag her to the door on a piece of shredded sheet metal. There was no way to assess the full extent of her injuries. Wayne was sure one leg was broken because of her cries when they moved it. All they could do was move her inside as quickly as possible and then check her further there. At this juncture, cold was her worst enemy, though the numbness it induced helped mitigate the pain.

It took twenty minutes to drag her back, hoist her up to the ledge, and gingerly move her through the small doorway with Carl's and Bob's help. Bob handed them another first aid kit waving and closing the door. Every time they opened the side portal, more heat escaped. The small electric heater in the stairwell worked hard to keep up with what heat was lost. Charise was now in their charge. John and Luke, warmed by the exertion of transporting Charise, returned to the remnants of the recreation hall.

Wayne greeted them with a smile upon their return. His look was unimaginable under the circumstances to both Inuits, but they soon understood why. The Mountie had revived and was sitting up in the space formerly occupied by Charise. He was covered with blood, but it turned out that it was hers rather than his own. Wayne already had a makeshift sling on his arm, and he was holding his head with the other. Jamo was battered, but considering the circumstances and what he had survived, his condition was remarkably good. The group still had no idea about the seriousness of his previous head injury. Now he had another second hard blow to his cranium. The bleeding on the outside, though serious, was bandaged. Bleeding on the inside of his skull was undetectable and exacerbated.

Wayne wrapped his own thick parka around him and worked his gloves onto Jamo's hands. With hot packs on his feet and in his coat, he was doing well. Jamo was marginally aware of what was going on around him. His back ached, and he felt sore all over. It took all three men, but they were able to lift Jamo out of his entrapment. Luke found the back and seat of a chair with no legs. Once seated on it, they tied him to it for transport.

With extreme exertion, the three rescuers slowly lifted their Mountie friend up and out of the crushed hut. They carried him to the entrance where Carl and Bob were waiting. Wayne was exhausted from stress and physical exertion. He struggled to climb back inside. Luke and John decided to return to the hut to salvage what they could. The Inuit's strength and endurance amazed Wayne.

John had spotted several intact couch cushions. He retrieved these as well as shredded draperies, as much carpet as possible, and anything else usable. Luke gathered up several small boxes of snack food, power bars, and chips scattered about the exposed remnants of the rec hall. He then began chopping the jammed refrigerator door open. Beyond tired, John made several trips to the ledge and stacked his materials there for Carl to retrieve. The refrigerator was stuffed with food, mostly perishables, but there were several unbroken containers of juice, sandwiches, yogurts, a number of packages of cheese, and a few other lifesaving food items. Cleaning out the last scraps, they noticed the refrigerator began to creak under the crushing weight of the collapsed roof. John was pulling wiring loose when Luke emerged with a sackful of edibles. His final pull on the wiring brought the remainder of the structure crashing down. The two Inuits exchanged shrugs and a few expletives in their native tongue and dragged the last of their booty to the ledge. Carl could see their fatigue. Luke held his hands like they were frozen. Carl begged them to come back inside where they could inventory their salvaged items.

Becky fashioned a makeshift bed for Charise from the seat cushions. She was thankful to be able to get her off the cold floor. They rigged the elevator as a small hospital room. Locked at the base of the elevator shaft, the room was relatively comfortable with the door closed and one of their two precious space heaters from the storage room turned on. The carpet remnants gave everyone else at least a modicum of insulation from the bone-chilling cold of their enclosure. The rock stairway and foyers at each end also had built-in heaters beside the upper and lower doorways. They cleared the snow and broken glass by the lower doorway and patched up the breaks with duct tape and cardboard box pieces.

John had pulled a damaged hot plate from the wreckage. One burner still worked. Becky melted some snow and warmed water to clean the matted blood from Charise. Bob stitched up her head wound with a suture kit. They were able to stanch the blood flow and control the bleeding. They set her leg as well as possible after removing her clothing. She had bruises everywhere. There was no way to know the extent of any internal injuries. But Charise was hanging in there.

Jamo was a mess too but had apparently been spared serious injury. His shoulder was dislocated, and his wrist or forearm was broken. The swelling was bad. Other than this and potential mild frostbite, he was doing well, actually conversing with Carl. He was lying on another makeshift bed beside the lower-level heater. Jamo was suffering from mild shock and fell asleep after Carl gave him pain pills from the first aid kit.

Wayne was pensive and thankful that two of his comrades had somehow been spared. He passed out from exhaustion while sitting on the bottom stair. Bob insisted that Luke and John eat a sandwich. Both had expended a huge amount of energy and needed the calories. They let Wayne rest and sorted and studied their small inventory of foodstuffs. They melted snow for drinking water and made sure that the Inuits, who had worked so hard, remained hydrated. Everyone was mentally and physically fatigued and very hungry. With rudimentary first aid completed, Carl and Bob began formulating a plan for survival and figuring out a way to get their predicament known to their support folks. Their situation before this disaster was not good but livable. The present circumstances were worse than they could have envisioned. They were cut off and had injured and presumed dead, limited supplies, and at this point, no way to get out. Bob shook his head while Carl sobbed and prayed.

CHAPTER 13

CLIFFSIDE

Night 1 spent in the cliffside was cold and uncomfortable. Wayne could not remember feeling worse mentally or physically when he awoke. The previous day seemed like a bad dream. He awakened several times during his fitful attempt to rest, each time attempting to shift to a more comfortable position. He became fully alert when he heard Charise let out an agonized wail. Becky had gotten her to swallow several pain pills, but the effects were wearing off. The pills worked well for several hours, and thankfully, they had a good supply, but she needed to continue large doses. Jamo was also given some to help him rest. He was now feeling slightly better, though his back appeared to be sprained or at least badly strained.

The ambient light of the Arctic morning brought them another chance to assess their surroundings. Luke remembered to switch off the searchlight before retiring beside the upper heater. The others had huddled together by the lower heater and extra space heater in the elevator. The smell of coffee from the hot plate roused everyone. John had found a box of drip coffee bags during salvage. Becky decided that they all needed it and brewed some in a metal pot.

No one wanted to hear more bad news, but Carl brought it up. None of the six had a phone or communicator with them at the time of the avalanche. A check of Charise's clothing had turned up nothing. They also checked Jamo's pockets and belt pack to no avail. The eight survivors trapped in a cliff stairwell were incommunicado.

Wayne knew that if their home office or relatives heard nothing, it was sure to sound an alarm. When no one could get in touch with them, it was almost certain that there would be an alert and an investigation. But no one was sure how long it would be until a search could be launched. The weather had now been terrible for weeks with one brief interlude. As the winter deepened, it would only get worse.

They all knew that the present food supply and medical situation were their worst problem unless the generator went out. Their fuel supply for it was adequate for a long period. Since they had a backup generator and very little demand at present, they had adequate heat and light. Sanitation was a problem, but they made a plan to cope with it. They simply all had to learn to live with discomfort. Medical supplies would run out in a few days. Charise would have to cope. There was little else they could do for her other than treat the obvious major issues, keep her quiet, and make her as comfortable as possible.

Food, precious food, was in short supply, especially for eight cold people. They had to search the wreckage of the collapsed hut again and then the entire former base area. Bob and Becky were put in charge of the food supply, which they planned to divide equally and ration with care.

When Luke descended the stairs for a cup of weak warm coffee, Becky took Wayne by the hand and led him up the stairs. She had to use the rudimentary bathroom Luke had fashioned beside the upper door. It was two planks and an empty plastic bucket. What she really wanted was to discuss their predicament privately with Wayne. She knew and he knew that there was a way to communicate. It was over the north side of the rock hill a quarter mile past the landing area. To reach it they had to cross a small valley and climb over another rocky rise through towering snow drifts. The subject was the satellite transmitter transponder for the secret clandestine spy sensor network set up with and operated from their weather base.

"Wayne, we must get word out for help. Charise may die if we don't, and we all are going to get really hungry in a couple of days."

"I know, hon. We don't have a lot of choice. Should we try to do it ourselves and preserve the secrecy or just tell them all?"

"Okay, the situation is bad, and we already have four probable dead." Wayne didn't need any more reminders of the potential bleakness of their situation. "I vote for telling everyone now and then setting out for the transponder at best light."

They descended the stairs and called everyone together. All were in good spirits and just glad that they were alive. Becky told them about the secret second purpose for the base, about the array of antennae, and the buried instrumentation. It turned out that it was not much of a secret. Once Jamo found out about it from Blake Edwards after an evening of heavy drinking, everyone knew. Blake was a spook from a government agency whose real purpose at the base was to make sure everything was running properly at all times. He made many trips into the field by himself or with John, who watched what he did from a distance.

If they could communicate using some part of the array, they were all for it. John knew the most about it and where things were on and in the ground. Becky knew the most about how it worked and what they could use to try to reestablish contact with the outside world. With that knowledge, everyone was more comfortable with their situation, and spirits were lifted for rescue and hope for Charise.

Wayne was chilled and hungry. He had purposely reduced his own ration but was now regretting it. They all normally ate hearty meals at the base. Something about the cold, dry, fresh, clean air gave them a voracious appetite. Unfortunately, Wayne had eaten very little the day before the disaster, Becky too. Sitting next to her, he could hear her stomach growling. She was taking her turn sitting in front of the meager heaters. He caught himself admiring the firm shape of her bottom in her tight-fitting jeans. At least she had her warm silks on under them.

Another hunger gurgle emanating from his intestinal area interrupted his stare. It was past noon on the second day. Wayne, Luke, and John formulated a plan to locate the transmitter-receiver brain of the previously considered nonexistent GASS array. It had been easier to explain the clandestine project when he added the point that it might help them communicate with the outside. *Ludicrous, totally ludicrous*, Wayne thought. *How can we be incommunicado in this day and age?* The walkie-talkies had good range, but not enough. They did not have any satellite phones or anything else that would work.

Charise's condition was not improving. It became obvious that she was suffering from internal injuries. She lapsed in and out of consciousness, which was probably a blessing, considering her state. When she was awake, the pain was very serious. Wayne knew they needed to get her some help or get her to a medical facility. Jamo was still miserable and complained about everything but was coping well with his more minor injuries.

In the afternoon, when the howling winds subsided by half, Becky made the decision that they would attempt to locate the transmitter at the heart of the array. The group devised a dual plan for the first sortie into the pervasive near-blizzard conditions. Wayne and Luke would head for the transmitter and attempt to send a distress message. Becky and Luke would return to the hut vicinity to scavenge for food or other useful items. They all hoped that they could be lucky enough to find a satellite phone. Carl's assignment was to stand by at the middle exit, maintaining visual contact with them. Bob's job was to keep continuous voice contact with Wayne. Jamo, being incapacitated, just had to keep an eye on Charise. All had an assignment.

Each pair had two hours to complete their task and then return. Orders were to return immediately if the weather conditions and visibility deteriorated again.

Wayne was unsure that he could locate the transmitter, make his plan to communicate work or send a distress message, and then return in two hours. He had not checked on the details of the physical layout in a while, and the graphics and plans he needed were buried within the destroyed base. In addition, now a thick and deep blanket of snow covered the terrain and equipment. Wayne realized that he faced an arduous trip, but they were desperate, and he had to try. Wayne was confident an alarm had already been raised, but he had to make sure that someone knew that they were in peril and in need of immediate assistance.

Extra rations were proportioned out for those going outside. They would need the food for energy and to maintain their body temperature in the extreme cold and wind. The extra food was mandatory, though John protested vehemently. He relented at Becky's insistence. Before exiting, they shared warming cups of coffee. Then it was time to go. The doors were opened sequentially in order to prevent drafts, thereby losing the minimum of heat. The warmth inside was minimal, but relative to the outside, it was pleasant. Their forays began.

Becky and Luke eased out the middle hatchway first. Carl snapped the small door shut behind them. Wayne and John departed from the upper double-door, closing it as fast as possible.

John had a rough idea of the location of the transmitter from Wayne's description. He had thoroughly explored the area around the base on earlier visits. Luke had stumbled upon several of the array sensors while exploring on his own around the base but had ignored them. They moved steadily ahead, plodding strenuously in their snowshoes. Without them, they would have sunk waist-deep or, in places, out of sight.

After a half hour or so, Wayne could make out a few landmarks. They had crossed the first small ravine with little difficulty. It was nearly filled in with packed snow. They prodded occasionally for unstable places. Although they were moving slowly, they made steady progress. It was an hour before they reached the objective area. Bob reminded them that their allotted time was half up.

Becky and Luke found very little else of any use. Their efforts proved almost fruitless. The remnants of the hut were too dangerous to enter. Deep fresh snow now covered everything. They finally gave up after an hour and one-half passed and returned to the cliffside with nothing more than cold to show for their effort. They were very disappointed.

After an hour and a half, Wayne and John located the transmitter cover with their poles. It was a disguised to look like a large rock but was artificial and hollow. Because of its location on the crest of the ridge, they were able to find it and uncover it just as the weather began to change again. Becky and the rest of the group were anxious about their expected protracted stay outside in the worsening elements. They all hoped that John and Wayne would succeed in sending some kind of distress signal.

It took all their effort to turn the hollow boulder on its side to reveal the interior. Wayne had to remove his gloves to work on the contents of the fake rock. His glove liners alone provided a modicum of protection. The ingenious power supply for the system was dangerous, but he worked around it with care. The system had its own power supply but also received power from the base. He had no way to establish direct communications with the outside world using the array. He did, however, have a rather simple plan.

While John turned his back to produce a yellow icicle on the snowbank, Wayne initiated his plan. He switched the system off manually three brief times. He repeated it three more lengthy times and finally three brief times. John watched him, not understanding Wayne's simple process. Wayne waited a few moments and repeated the same sequences.

A gust of wind whipped snow in his face, nearly blinding Wayne. John had to brace himself when it buffeted him. John gestured that it was time to go. Whether Wayne liked it or not, they had to return to shelter. John was pleased and surprised when Wayne indicated he was ready to go. After putting the cover back in place, they beat a hasty retreat toward the cliffside shelter. The increasing steady wind was a chilling reminder of this inhospitable environment. John led the way, and Wayne did not even look up. It was difficult going. The harsh wind pelted their faces with hard ice crystals and snow. John had goggles he always kept in his parka pocket, but Wayne had none. He followed the Inuit with his head down. Their return was arduous and exhausting. With his eyes almost closed and his parka fur drawn tight around his face, Wayne was relieved when he heard the door open and then slam behind them. He was glad to be back inside. He had not realized how cold he was until Bob began shaking him. He was out on his feet and half-frozen.

All that they could do in the cliffside was hope that someone heard their rudimentary distress call, a basic Morse code SOS. The weather turned bad again. Becky told Wayne and John that she and Luke had no luck finding much of anything of use and no food. He did not show his distress, only nodded. He understood that their meager supplies were not going to last very long.

CHAPTER 14

US PENTAGON– WASHINGTON, DC

Paul Mason saw Colonel Jenkins out of the corner of his eye as the colonel passed his open office door. "Colonel Jenkins, sir, can I see you a moment?" Jenkins turned on a dime and appeared in Paul's doorway.

"You want to see me, Paul?"

"Yes, sir, my system has picked up a glitch in the GASS northern array." The GASS stood for the semisecret Global Array Surveillance System here at the Pentagon. To the US and Canadian public, it stood for Gas Survey System, a supposed remote-sensing system for locating gaseous hydrocarbon deposits and monitoring hydrocarbon pollution in the Arctic. Even though fuel cells now powered many things, natural gas was still the cheapest and cleanest method for heating. It was a simple cover for another "Big Brother" monitoring system. It could detect, distill, and locate virtually any electronic communication, energy source, or transmission anywhere in the northern hemisphere.

"What kind of glitch have you got?" Jenkins inquired.

"Well, sir, part of the grid went down. A small group of sensors went off all at once. That's highly unusual since they are all stand-alone units."

"Yes, that's right." Jenkins also knew that one sensor might go off, but not a group. "How many went off and where? Computer, let me see the grid x34, y35, and y36 in close-up."

"Voice recognition confirmed, Colonel Jenkins. Grid displayed as requested." The machine obeyed with lightning speed.

Mason and Jenkins approached the screen wall and examined the grid superimposed on a topographical map. "Give me a 3D image from the southwest," Jenkins ordered.

The machine again responded in an instant. They noted that the array of sensors that were out were all along the western edge, along the side toward the glacial valley. The location of AWRB 1 was also noted by a series of shapes representing the layout of the base.

"Sir, the array picked up vibrations and sound when the sensors went out," Mason added. "Computer, analyze sound and play it back for us."

"Yes, Mr. Mason," the machine responded. They listened to the dull rumble. When the sound ended, the computer began, "Analysis shows ground vibrations, low frequency." It then did a detailed analysis of the frequencies, wavelengths, and other technical details.

"Yes, computer, but what exactly was the sound?" Mason asked. Jenkins already knew, but he waited for the answer.

"Avalanche" was the one-word answer from the machine.

"Mason, contact the base. See what happened. Find out if they felt it or know about it. At least it was way up the valley."

"I tried, sir. That's the other thing I wanted to tell you. I had the computer contact the base, but all it said was the base receiver did not exist. Then I tried their satellite phone numbers, and only one responded, but there was no answer."

"When did you try, Mason? How long ago?" Jenkins was now becoming concerned.

"Right before you came in, sir. I tried several times but got the same results."

"What was the time of the glitch event?" Jenkins's stance had stiffened.

"Yesterday about 7:00 p.m. Eastern time, sir."

"Nineteen hundred hours and it is now more than twenty-four hours later, and no one else has noticed or informed me? Can we get a satellite look?"

"Negative, sir, it is still socked in up there. We wouldn't see much with anything but radar. Maybe we can get infrared images of the base to make sure it looks okay."

"Mason, send out a precautionary alert and get a long-range, high-altitude side-scan bird up there. Our people could be in bad trouble, and there are a lot of folks who are going to want to know."

"Yes, sir, consider it done."

Mason was on the phone before Jenkins exited, adding, "I'll be on the horn. Keep me informed of progress or contact."

Jenkins could not believe that with high-tech gadgetry of every imaginable type available, they had lost contact with the Arctic station and had no way to know what had happened or what was going on. He decided to waste no time to call his civilian counterparts and see what they knew about AWRB 1 that he did not know. What he did find out after several calls was that no one had a clue. All communications had ceased. The computer stated the base communications center did not exist, not that it was temporarily down for some reason. It did not look good.

The Air Force high-altitude reconnaissance jet streaked over the Arctic, crossing and recrossing the AWRB 1 area several times. Thick storm clouds covered the region, as they had for some time now. It gathered the data, oblivious to the tumult below. Soaring high above the leaden clouds, gliding in the crisp thin air, the pilot enjoyed the glistening stars overhead. It flew over the survivors, who had no idea of its presence. Like any other transpolar air crossing, the jet completed its flight plan, banked south and east, and began the return leg to safe haven.

Colonel Jenkins wanted answers, and thus far, he had none. The side-scan radar images were in processing. He demanded real-time data, but a minor malfunction prevented it. He was angry. His people were not coming through for him. Things were lax; he planned to change that.

GLOBAL WARNING

Paul Mason was pressing the rest of the department for results. He was looking at the infrared thermal imagery and did not like what he saw. A normal picture of the base area would have shown the outlines of the warm structures of the base even through any cloud or snow cover. Instead, he saw nothing warm except possibly the speck from what he guessed was a single light at the highest resolution.

Within minutes, the radar date was loaded and ready for display in the colonel's office. A small group assembled to examine the images. Side-scan radar created excellent terrain images with surprising details. Colonel Jenkins created a split-screen display. On the left, he brought up normal aerial photo data of the base area. On the right, he readied the radar data with an inset of the thermal picture.

"Computer, scale the images identically." The machine obeyed the command and rendered them all to the specified scale. Left-side photos showed the base, the fjord, and the vicinity for several square miles. Beside it appeared the equally scaled side-scan images. He moved his cursor to align the images at the same point. They did not look anywhere close to the same. Much of the lower fjord had changed, and so had the base.

"Overlay the images on the right screen." The computer obeyed.

"My god, the base is gone or covered! Nothing could live through that! Even the hangar is just a mound." They looked at the images from various angles. The computer did several simulations of what might have taken place. There was no model for this particular situation.

The computer in Mason's office beeped three times. The screens blinked and returned to normal. Mason and Jenkins crossed the hallway to his office and changed the display to mimic Jenkins's. Mason heard the beeps before they walked in. "I wonder what made it beep."

"I'm not sure, sir. Let me check." Paul pulled up a database and quizzed the computer. The screen blinked: INCOMING DATA AWRB 1.

They looked at the data on the new screen. Tone on duration two seconds, off two seconds, repeated three times. Tone on duration Five seconds, off five seconds, again repeated three times. Tone on duration two seconds, off two seconds, repeated three times. The machine went on to describe a second sequence repeated exactly as the first.

"Computer, play data as audio signal." They heard the three short tones, followed by three long ones, followed by three short tones. Jenkins knew the significance of the data. "That's an old-fashioned distress call! There are people alive, survivors of that horrendous mess. Get the Canadian Air Rescue people for me. Let's get moving."

Colonel Jenkins was on point. He was back in body armor carrying his M-21. People under his responsibility were in danger; they needed his help. He was much more efficient in this scenario than he was pushing a desk.

"Mason, I want a complete list of all our assets in the area of AWRB 1. I want all of our resources on alert and the Canadians too. I want a list of all of our options. We need a tactical plan, and we need it now. I also want a minute-by-minute update on the weather."

"Yes, sir," Mason responded respectfully. "I can do the asset list now. The weather part is easy, sir. It's bad up there and getting worse every day. The options and resources list will be short and limited.

"The Canadians have a few air bases within range and all-weather vertical takeoff and landing aircraft. They also have at least two icebreakers, but they are a long way off. Ground approach will be really tough, if not impossible. Sir, the sea ice is really thick in that fjord too. It never completely melted last year, and the pressure ridges built by the intense storm winds are enormous. I don't think that the strongest icebreaker could even try to get through."

"Tell me something that I don't already know, Mason. We can't reach them quickly by ground. We can't get a ship there. Flying will be pure hell, but it's all we have."

A young officer stuck his head in Mason's office and reported, "The Canadians have been informed and are attempting a rescue effort as soon as possible."

"Good. Wait a minute. Let's see what the Navy has in the area. They usually have a sub under the ice, a nuke that can stay down forever. It's supposedly just conducting research, but we don't care why it's there, we just need to know if it's close enough to help them. I'll check with our Navy buddies and clear it with the Joint Chiefs. We don't have to go public with this. Just use the asset if we can."

"That sounds like a great idea, sir. Let's hope that they have something close, and it can maneuver those waters near the fjord."

"Those waters are plenty deep enough, but they shallow fast seaward from the base, Mason. Computer, show us a bathymetric chart of the waters around AWRB 1." Jenkins had looked at them when the base was built, but that was a while ago. If his memory served him right, a sub could get in there safely or at least close enough to maybe send a rescue team. There were ridges and obstacles, but they were well charted.

In less than thirty minutes, Jenkins had his answer. It had taken a few calls to breach the classified barrier to the closest sub's location. It was the USS *Longley*, a stealth behemoth, one of the Navy's sleekest, fastest, and most secretive vessels. Since its quiet commission, it had roamed the seven seas with complete secrecy and without detection. It represented a whole step forward in submarine design. It carried top secret weaponry and its own minisubs for even more clandestine operations.

Jenkins had stroke. It was a small miracle to get the Navy brass to even admit that it existed. To give its general location and course was a big step from normal. Jenkins felt that his Navy friends genuinely cared about possible survivors at a destroyed Arctic base, and he knew that they could always use a little good PR. A rescue effort by their Seals would make them look good.

The colonel did not care. He was given the chance to communicate with the sub's captain and explain the situation. The captain of the *Longley* agreed to proceed to the fjord area and, if possible, check out the base. He could not say exactly where they were at present but that the *Longley* was not too far away and could reach the fjord in a day or two. The captain signed off and ordered his helmsman to set a new course.

CHAPTER 15

WHITEOUT

Colonel Jenkins maintained an open connection to the Canadian Air Force. His counterpart with that service was a former wing commander now coordinating the overtaxed air rescue units. Canadian air traffic was chaotic and sporadic due to the often blizzard-like conditions sweeping most of the nation. The commander had his hands full with numerous stranded people far to the south of the Arctic weather base and no unit to spare to go north.

What the Canadian did have available was an American air rescue crew on loan. It was one of many sent to assist their northern neighbors during the prolonged winter misery.

Captain Wales flew one of the vertical takeoff and landing craft or VTL all-weather support craft now doubling as an evacuation transport. He was glad to accept the assignment to make contact with AWRB 1. Colonel Jenkins briefed him on the former base layout and present situation. He uploaded pertinent data to Captain Wales's data center. After they discussed the mission in detail, the final message to Wales was, "Good luck and good hunting." The colonel knew that the VTL would get them there with no trouble. What no one could predict was if the weather conditions would permit Wales's craft to land safely, pick up survivors, and then, though heavier, take off again. The reason they were going at all was the SOS and the fact that it was now a true emergency rescue mission. Any other type of trip to the base or landing was forbidden.

The planned rescue attempt brought together several individuals whose paths had crossed before. Wales had flown attack helicopters in the south Caribbean intercepting drug traffickers. He received his interdiction instructions from the USS *Longley* and its present commander, Captain Brevard. Once again, they were drawn to the same target.

During the drug war, the *Longley* was used to observe and track air and sea vessels suspected of being potential drug transports. The Colombian drug war turned ugly when the drug cartels decided to take out several particularly bothersome US congressmen. They succeeded in killing one US senator and his entire family. In addition, they targeted two other representatives and several more high-level bureaucrats. The senator, his family, and two others were killed by drug-funded hit men. Four others were injured by contract attackers, including one who lost an arm and one who was paralyzed.

As long as the status quo existed in the drug war and it was maintained at current levels, the war was quiet. US authorities intercepted 10 to 15 percent of the shipments, an acceptable loss for the drug lords and a respectable take for the authorities. Pesky senators' demands upped the ante to 25 percent with the use of greater high-tech efficiency. The cartels decided to get even. It was their mistake of misjudgment.

The conflict of interests became a hot war. After the cartel hits, the US authorities struck back with swiftness and a true determination. The policy of never firing on a vessel unless fired upon was replaced with a nothing-gets-through attitude. The smugglers became cleverer, but so did the pursuers.

Small high-speed boats carrying drugs or suspected of carrying contraband that would not stop and be boarded were warned and then stopped by any means possible. Several were destroyed and cut to shreds by machine-gun fire until surrender. Wales flew more than seventy missions and sank a number of fools who were crazy enough to run.

Surface traffic decreased by a large percent. Small subsurface boats, self-propelled or towed behind other vessels, were used more often as a result. Better detection methods and more scrutiny resulted in many of these being discovered and confiscated or destroyed. The end result was that 60 to 70 percent of the illicit drug product shipments were getting captured and eliminated. The smugglers became more desperate and shrewder. They obtained more potent weaponry and decided to ship two huge orders in submersible minisubs manufactured for that purpose. They were towed by cables attached to the keel, pulled beneath, or well behind much larger freighters. The freighters could be boarded and searched without any sign of towing lines or submersibles.

Wales conducted the interception of one of the freighters. His helicopter was shot out of the air by the freighter crew, and the nearby coast guard vessel was badly damaged. The members of the coast guard boarding party were gunned down before they could leave. Wales was able to relay a message before his chopper went down in the sea, killing his copilot friend.

Captain Brevard of the *Longley* was in the general area monitoring the incident. After receiving the report from Wales, he dispatched a high-speed minisub to pick him up. The freighter turned and made a run for a Mexican port. It took the *Longley* three hours to close the distance and intercept the freighter. Captain Brevard put a torpedo into her belly, sinking it and its towed cargo. The mysterious sinking was witnessed by a Mexican fishing vessel whose crew reported the explosion and sinking. They even picked up a number of survivors. The ship sank in international waters with little information about the incident making the news. No official cause was given other than a probable explosion of contraband cargo.

Captain Wales met Captain Brevard after he was picked up and brought aboard the *Longley*. Brevard's parting words to Wales were to remember that he was never there and that perhaps someday they would meet again. The situation at the cliffside set them on a course for that future meeting.

Wales's Douglas TL Six was the finest machine that he had ever piloted. He loved its design, utility, and ease of handling. It would fly itself and go anywhere in almost any conditions. It was ideal for the rescue he was charged with leading.

With him were his copilot, a medic, and an assistant. There were only four of them to leave the maximum room for injured or evacuees. They would fly above the soup for most of the way, but sooner or later, they would have to descend through it. That meant a probable instrument landing, but Wales did not trust instruments alone. He preferred to be flying the craft himself, letting the computer controls assist him.

They took off in blustery but manageable conditions, but the closer to the base they ventured, the worse the weather situation deteriorated. When they departed, the storm briefly abated. Halfway through their journey, it was packing its full fury. The winds were mild aloft but near the surface were strong, nearly gale force. Wales was confident he could handle it.

The radar on the VTL painted a nasty picture: low thick clouds, swirling wind gusts, and very cold air. This was a complete opposite of what Wales normally flew in while working in the Caribbean. What his instruments could not show him was the actual surface conditions. He was flying directly into a complete whiteout, his craft steadily descending through the tumultuous clouds. He also had no way to judge the snow depth and no one with whom he could communicate on the ground. He was flying blind into a bad situation.

On final approach to the base, he made several low passes to get a 3D terrain image and match it to his preset landing coordinates and terrain map. Though he saw little actual detail, he could obtain a near-perfect landing fix. What he did not know was that the avalanche had changed the terrain both in the fjord valley and on the cliff top landing area. He assumed that once the images coincided, all that he had to do was trust his instruments and set the VTL down.

In the cliffside retreat, Luke's sharp ears heard the second pass over the sound of the whipping wind. He and Wayne raced up the stairs and reached the top where they heard the aircraft engine sounds change to landing mode. They were ecstatic, hearing the welcome familiar noise. Luke flashed the exterior light switch on and off. Wayne switched on a walkie-talkie and attempted to make contact.

Back at headquarters, Jenkins and Mason began to make use of the array. They had been giving the supercomputer key words and communicator information to isolate old pre—and post-avalanche communications of any sort emanating from the base. That was what the array was for: intercepting and pinpointing any signals of any type.

They had the data sifted and answers within minutes. A transcript was created of cellular calls and all information before the base went quiet. It was obvious that the base had no warning of what happened. The array's close proximity to the base allowed it to detect and record the walkie-talkie exchanges. Mason included those wavelengths in the search.

By the time the VTL reached the base, they knew who was alive and who was injured from the reconstruction of their communication. Wayne had been smart enough to leave a detailed message just in case the array had picked up his short-range message and someone was clever enough to decipher it.

The Douglas VTL Six came in slow, and Pilot Wales switched to landing mode for its final hovering descent. The merciless wind pounded the craft and created serious instability. Visibility was so poor that he had his crew open the main door to use their visual assistance. Snow flew wildly around and into the vehicle. The wind screamed at the door. He began to abort the attempted landing, fearing for their safety.

There was nothing Wales did wrong, and he could not have prevented what happened next. The raging wind tore at the craft just as they neared their touchdown. A gust raised one wing and its embedded rotating engine. The craft turned to nearly horizontal instead of vertical when the wind tipped the wing. Wales, his crew, and their rescue craft swerved sideways and toward the cliff in an instant. Before they could react, they were over the edge and moving sideways with the ground. Wales struggled to regain control, but it was too late. They crashed into the jumbled avalanche debris.

The wing tip hit first, and the craft cartwheeled, landing upside down in the snow and ice. The doctor and his assistant unclasped their safety belts and wiggled free and out the door. Wales unclasped himself and dragged his injured and unconscious copilot to the door. The four abandoned their craft just in time. In only seconds, it burst into flames behind them.

Those in the cliffside heard the explosion. They had briefly glimpsed landing lights through the whiteout blizzard, which was further exacerbated by the engine wash. The disappearance of the lights, subsequent loud explosion, and flash made them shudder.

Luke was already out of the upper door with Wayne close behind. John, Becky, and Carl were headed for the middle door, looking out toward the direction of the sound and bright flash. What they saw was nearly as revolting as the original avalanche scene. The swirling snow made it difficult to see much at first, but the reddish glow of fire and the smell of burning fuel were obvious when they opened the hatchway.

The would-be rescuers had become victims. The survivors huddled together in complete shock in the blinding snow, watching the glow of their burning craft. John made his way to the burning wreckage first. Looking around, he spotted the stunned rescuers, noting the bloody face of one and the complete dismay on the face of the man holding him.

Back at headquarters, Mason ran into Jenkins's office. The colonel was still there.

"Grey Lady Rescue Six is down, sir. Communications ceased, and I think we have a probable crash!"

CHAPTER 16

UNDER THE ICE

Colonel Jenkins was visibly upset—not rattled but perplexed. Mason's news was disconcerting. It appeared that the Grey Lady Rescue Unit was down, but not as prescribed. They had monitored the radio transmissions from the VTL almost the entire distance to the base. Their secret interpreter array worked to perfection. It monitored the Grey Lady black box until all transmissions abruptly ceased.

They began backtracking to find out what happened. Radio contact ended without warning. There was no sign, no hint of trouble from the crew, only silence.

Direct real-time monitoring of in-flight black boxes was possible using their secret system. It prevented the potential loss or destruction of the data recorders in the event of a catastrophic crash. Colonel Jenkins's staff and the Air Traffic Safety Board began checking for a potential problem when the transmissions ended. Jenkins and Mason feared the worst. All evidence suggested that the rescue effort failed, and their problems were now multiplied.

While the computer ferreted out and compiled the essential data, Jenkins decided to contact the *Longley* to see if the Navy followed the rescue. Contacting the sub through normal channels would have been fruitless. Strict naval procedures, thick layers of ice, and thermoclines blocked normal signals. Jenkins again had to go through proper channels and wait for the request and the answers to be relayed. The means of contact with the *Longley* was also a closely guarded secret and strictly classified.

It took over an hour, but the colonel received his answer. The *Longley* was unable to monitor the rescue. They had no means to penetrate the ice in order to raise the antenna. In the meantime, Mason reconstructed the final moments before the crash. It was certain that the craft had lost proper landing altitude and attitude, tilted too far, and the pilot lost control. Subsequent signs of impact and destruction were pervasive. Grey Lady definitely went down, a probable crash. Another air rescue would not be allowed and was now out of the question. The rescue mission failed. Jenkins could only hope that the crew was all right. He had no way to find out.

At the remnants of AWRB 1, John concentrated on forcing the stunned would-be rescuers to move and began hustling them toward the cliffside shelter. It was tough going in the deep snow with the avalanche debris beneath, and still dangerous.

John jumped from the small doorway with his snowshoes and scuffed along as fast as he could to the four arrivals. Luke shined the searchlight beam from above. Getting them to shelter would not be easy. They were disoriented, confused, and dazed. One was obviously hurt.

Luke returned from the top of the cliff by the inside stairway where Wayne joined him at the midway hatch. They rushed to help John. Pilot Wales identified himself; his slumped copilot, Brad, badly shaken; Dr. Hoffman; and wild-eyed crewman, Joe Stewart. They all looked at the wreckage, realizing that the four arrivals had narrowly escaped death. Shaking his head, Wales forlornly surveyed the burning wreckage behind them.

Wales donned a pair of snowshoes with John's assistance, and he and John began dragging Stewart toward the lighted doorway. All that Wales could make out in the swirling snow was the brighter area in the dark rock wall. Wayne helped hoist the copilot onto Luke's back. The Inuit struggled back to the cliffside with his burden. Wayne waited with the shivering doctor, who clutched his precious bag to his chest. The doctor had stuck his arm through the backpack strap of his supply bag before rolling from the craft. Besides the passengers, it was the only article to survive the crash. Everything else was being consumed by dying flames. When the wind shifted, the fires of the destroyed VTL warmed them. In a few minutes, John returned with the extra snowshoes, and the three retired to their retreat. Before leaving, Wayne took a closer look at the burning wreckage to check for anything useful, but the fire consumed everything.

Once inside, the residents did everything they could to assist the new arrivals. It was supposed to be the other way around. The shock of the crash was profound. Brad was injured but apparently not too badly. Stewart was banged up but was back under control. The doctor's sense of duty was amazing. Within twenty minutes of being inside, he treated Joe and Brad, set a broken finger on Wales's right hand, and bandaged his own bleeding ankle. It was miraculous that none were more seriously injured. Fortunately, they were all wearing their thick Arctic insulated gear and woolen hats when the craft went into its final approach.

Becky could wait no longer. She described what little she had done for Charise to the doctor, who then checked her vital signs and began a more thorough examination. His forethought to grab his medical bag at the last moment proved to be the second smaller miracle for the now expanded survivor group. At least he had the means to help Charise to some degree. When he first saw her, he was amazed that she was alive, and he commended Becky for her astute actions.

The doctor emptied his stuffed pack. The last thing that he put into it before departing was cushioning, a plastic bag filled with high-energy nutrition bars and candy bars. To those who had not eaten today, the sight of them was a true delight. He passed them out to the eager base residents. They each had their own choice. Each in turn selected one and savored it with a relish. Dr. Hoffman could only wish that someone had grabbed the food supply bag from the VTL. His own stomach grumbled.

The next morning, everyone was acclimated to the cramped surroundings. They were all cold, hungry, and dismayed. The doctor completed emergency surgery on Charise in her makeshift elevator hospital room. She survived it but did not regain consciousness. For now, it was all that he could do. He had collapsed in a state of fatigue and exhaustion afterward. Becky remained awake to watch Charise.

By the end of the fourth day, the one comatose and eleven conscious individuals in the cliffside had no coffee, seven candy bars, a few bags of chips, and some packets of instant oat meal left upon which to survive. To this point, they had been uncomfortable, and their bellies sated, but from this point on, it started to look more desperate.

Luke and John were hesitant to leave the others, but now, the situation demanded it. They could find food with a little luck and their inherited skills. While they ventured to hunt, those who remained and were fit enough were tasked with digging around the rubble of the former base to scavenge any food they could find. Using the methods taught by their ancestors, the Inuits had a chance of finding sustenance for the entire group.

At maximum light, the two Inuits departed. They had a basic plan. After exiting from the middle door, they lost no time heading south and west down the fjord. They planned to make their way over the debris and work their way down the valley, seeking thin ice near shore. Both knew that their path would be arduous and blocked by numerous obstacles. Ridges and treacherous irregularities now covered the normally gentle valley and relatively flat ice. No one knew how far down the narrow fjord the avalanche had traveled. Not far beyond the base, the valley widened. The avalanche debris should have spread out and thinned.

John and Luke knew they had at least four to five hours of useful ambient light. The sun was now rising at a much lower angle above the horizon. It remained low, moving parallel to the horizon, before its elongated golden rays disappeared. Their planned trek would have been a reasonable and easy hike before the avalanche, but now every step was hard work.

In two minutes, Luke and John disappeared into the white, while the others settled in to wait and chose teams for their initial search. Wayne reminded everyone that the walkie-talkies were to be used very sparingly. John and Luke planned to be extra careful with theirs. A dead battery meant the cessation of communications, their last and only link with the base. Check-ins were planned every hour on the hour.

Joe Stewart volunteered to begin the vigil beside the middle door. He was ailing and miserable and, at present, of very bad temperament. Things were bad enough, but he chose to be a true malcontent. It did not take very long for the rest of the trapped survivors to begin ignoring him.

Stewart was a lanky mean kid with an attitude. He had originally joined the service to escape an unhappy, abusive home. His ulterior motive was a true desire to cause havoc and kill something if it got in his way. His attitude almost cost him his military career at least twice. Six months in the brig had softened the attitude. He found out that he was not nearly as tough as he thought. He turned it around, convinced an officer of his need for a second chance, and received it. Since then, his record had been exemplary, but now, and his attitude often reverted.

How in the hell did I get stuck in this godforsaken rock? Joe did not want this rescue run since he was long overdue for some time off. His nerves were already frayed. *And now this*, he thought. Joe often felt pity for those he rescued, although he felt little compassion for the bodies. Now he wondered how he would end up.

While languishing in his self-pity, he contemplated starving or freezing to death in this frigid hell. Both would be slow and agonizing. His depression grew. He huddled and shivered by the door. He decided that freezing would be quicker and less painful. He pictured himself stripping and flinging himself from the door directly into the icy teeth of the blizzard. He had almost decided to do it when he was startled by the loud bang on the door.

It was Luke banging on the heavily frosted thick glass portal in the door. Joe had not even been watching. No one expected a quick return by the Inuits. His watch said they had only been gone an hour.

Becky was just starting to ascend the stairs with Carl close behind. She intended to bring Joe a cup of steaming water, flavored with a bit of candy bar. They both noticed Joe was sitting with his back to the door and his face on his knees. His near fetal position and his agonized face were very disturbing to Becky.

Joe swung around to open the door, but the Inuits had beaten him to it. Luke and John made nothing of his irritated continence. Becky handed the cup of steaming quasi-cocoa to Luke, glancing sternly at Joe. He averted her look, eyes askance.

Before anything was said, John spoke up. "That way is no good. It's too rough, too loose and deep, and too slow. We can't go along the base of the cliff, so we are going along the top. It was easier to come back through here than to try to climb it somewhere else. Excuse us. We are just passing through. Haven't we been here before?"

Becky could not help it. She laughed and moved aside. The Inuits took their snowshoes off, tucked them under their arms, trudged past, and began climbing the rest of the stairs toward the upper door. Carl stood, mouth agape, with a shocked look on his face. Joe Stewart was only a bit less menacing, grumbling an excuse for not watching for them. Carl volunteered to take a turn by the upper door.

Luke and John disappeared as quickly as they had reappeared. The empty water cup was the only testament to their rapid transit through the chilly shelter. Becky and a few other voices again wished them a safe journey. Everyone heard the reason for their quick return. Now they had to hope that the Natives would fare better on a trip along an upper route.

John led the way as they moved forward through the backside of the drifts at the top of the cliff. Their new chosen path was much better. Luke knew the lower coastal route from various hikes and walks he had taken to fish in good weather. John used the upper route to the water's edge on several previous trips. He enjoyed the view from the top, and he knew of the existence of several small rocky ravines leading down to small caves and the wide tidal flats at the end of the fjord. The tidal flats remained covered with ice for over two years, and this year, the ice was thick, jumbled up, and piled high by the storms from the south.

After more than two hours of working their way with a steady and deliberate pace down the fjord, the height of the cliffs began to diminish.

"Eluk, look here!" John stopped in his tracks. He then stooped, pointing at depressions in the snow. The tracks were already filling up with fresh flakes but were still unmistakable. "Bear," he uttered in his native tongue. Luke already knew; he also recognized the familiar markings.

They had their knives, and John carried a light hunting harpoon, which also doubled for a probe for measuring snow depth. Instead of avoiding the tracks down the ravine taken by the bear, they turned and followed the tracks. John knew that the bear used an easy way down to the frozen shoreline. They both knew that bears meant food.

A bear would know of a seal breathing hole and wait by it patiently for the seal to return to breathe. If lucky, the bear would catch a meal. If lucky, the Inuits could steal the seal or kill the bear. If unlucky, one or both of them would mean winter survival for the bear. Desperation breeds desperate plans, and at this point or very soon, without rescue, food was their most serious concern.

With caution and stealth, the Inuits followed the tracks down to and then parallel to the irregular shoreline. The break from land to sea was indiscernible. Ice piled upon more ice gave little hint to the exact location.

Crouching and moving slowly, Luke and John crept forward. Rocks and snow rose at a steep angle to their right. Jagged shards of shattered sea ice jutted skyward to their left. The immediate area was a tortured landscape. Between two angled sheets of ice, the trail turned seaward and abruptly ended.

Luke pushed forward, creeping low on hands and knees to the point where the tracks stopped. A one-meter rise blocked the view beyond their surroundings, and the bear's trail went over it and through a narrow notch. Luke reached the blind spot in the path with John watching, his harpoon raised, ready for release. Peering cautiously over, Luke waved John to his side. Together they surveyed the opening in the contorted ice ridges ahead. It was almost invisible, but to their trained eyes, the small darker opening was evident. They recognized that the small opening must be the entrance to the bear's den.

Even with the light beginning to fade, they could see the traces of red in the thickening snow. The bear had made a kill. Perhaps they were in luck. The bear had an ice, A-frame winter den within range of seal breathing holes. Long shadows meant that darkness was coming. They made the decision to backtrack along the shore and attempt to locate a similar suitable natural shelter. They could hack out blocks of packed snow to build a small igloo but decided that perhaps nature had already provided a shelter for them.

For most of their strenuous trip from cliffside, Luke and John had the good fortune of light winds and snow flurries. Mother Nature was kind to them, but that was changing, and darkness was coming soon. Safe shelter was now a necessity with the relative proximity of the bear. Climbing over rock and ice and trudging through deep snow took their toll. But at least they had reached the shoreline in an area where they had a much better chance to find food.

They had not gone very far when John spotted two big slabs of ice, vaulted up against each other by the crushing pressure of the sea. The opening between them was hard-packed snow. He probed with the lance and dug between the slabs for a few moments. Luke was cold and was apprehensive about the bear. One close brush with the polar predator was enough for one year. To both of them, it was enough for a lifetime. Luke hoped that this place would suffice, but John rose again disappointed. "It might work, but it's just too narrow, and the snow is more like crust between the ice slabs." Eluk understood and was thankful because the space between the leaning giant ice shards appeared too confining. The last thing Luke wanted was to feel trapped again. The haunting memory of the encounter at Discovery Valley and Long's Glacier flashed through his brain.

Luke soon spotted a second potential shelter when John was looking the other way. They needed to use one of their flashlights in the deep shadows of the contorted ice. The light beam landed on a crystal clear triangle resembling a small thick window between two more huge slabs.

These large former pieces of sea ice were well over a meter thick and close to three meters high. The symmetry was excellent. The two slabs had been forced skyward by the stresses of waves, wind, and currents. They formed a rooflike structure. The near end was sealed by more ice and snow, but clarity of the ice at the apex of the upper angle gave Luke the hint he needed. He chipped away at the translucent area and broke through. Shining his light inside, he turned to John with a smile and said, "This will work, and it is more than big enough."

John looked inside and nodded his satisfaction. Snow sloped downward to a relatively flat frozen floor. The opposing slabs of solid sea glistened in his light. The area between the sides of the natural shelter was quite large, and though festooned with numerous other broken chunks, the depth was at least five meters.

This natural A-frame-shaped respite from the harshness besetting them was a welcome sight. Beautiful clear icicles hung like stalactites from the point where the opposing slabs joined. Formed during brief sun-warmed melting, the fragile beauty attested to the strength of the thick sea ice.

Luke turned and cut a block of hard-packed snow from the backside of the drift blocking the opening. He chipped away just enough ice to form an entrance to slither through. Both Inuits slid inside on their bellies. Once the block of snow was in place to close the entrance, they were safely sealed inside. Their newfound shelter resembled an ice cathedral from the inside. John enjoyed the familiar beauty when his flashlight beam pierced the darkness of the narrow recess at the rear of the room.

Eluk and John played in similar miniature ice structures as children. Warned by their parents of the dangers, they still ventured onto the sea ice and explored pressure ridges. But in their youth, the ice was thinner and far less pervasive.

John followed the beam of the flashlight to the end of their sparkling surroundings. A jagged block of white cut across the end of the triangular room. The pockmarked floor sloped gently to it. Moving gingerly to avoid slipping, Luke followed close behind.

The corner of the ice room had a familiar-looking appearance. The ice had a different texture. It was thinner and had the unmistakable characteristics of a seal breathing hole. Seals would go to great lengths to maintain openings in the ice at which they could surface for air. They could not tell if this seal or group of seals had left the area, succumbed to the extra harsh environment, or become a meal for a hungry Arctic predator.

Protected in the natural shelter, this seal breathing station was safe from hungry bears. Though frozen over and not recently used, the ice was thin and would serve the purpose of the hungry Inuits. If their luck was good, the hunters might be fortunate enough to attract a seal to the opening, harpoon it, and thereby feed them all for a while.

They had to act but felt the fatigue of their trek. Extra batteries would provide an attracting light, but they did not know how long their lights would last. Only one at a time would be used. They also had canned survival candles to provide a tiny bit of heat and illumination.

First, they settled back to rest. A few hours would have to suffice, but they needed to at least get some rest from the fatigue of their hike. After the respite, they planned to light a candle and go to work.

The phone rang every few minutes in Colonel Jenkins's office. He turned off the ringer and paced nervously. His secretary was screening all calls. The weather improved for a few hours, and he called for another rescue effort but was politely turned down. Every rescue unit was needed elsewhere. Another rescue to AWRB 1 was well down the priority list, especially since they lost a valuable asset and possibly a crew during the first attempt. The only thing he could do now was wait for help from the Navy, and Jenkins was not very good at waiting. His patience was often nonexistent. To Jenkins, it was always time for action.

"By god, Mason, we've got to do something." Mason had just stepped into his office.

"Yes, sir, I wish we could, but all we can do is wait for the Navy."

"Negative, Mason. Get home, get some warm clothes, get the best crewmen you can muster, and meet me at the landing area in two hours." Mason couldn't believe his superior's words. He hesitated by the door. "Wait, Mason. I've got a jet chopper on its way. The crew will have to do, and I've had food and medical supplies put on board. We'll land by your house and get what you need. We're going to get our people. Come one, we've got a flight plan to file, and we'll need Canadian clearance. Also, we'll need a fuel requisition."

"Yes, sir. I'm on it. Let's go."

Cliffside, the mood was somber. Carl and Becky began singing to keep their spirits up and to keep them warm. Malingering, Joe Stewart would not join in and became even more detached. Wayne did not trust him and kept a watchful eye on him. Becky feared him. They took turns sleeping or resting in front of the meager heaters. Dr. Hoffman kept an eye on Charise. He could tell he was slowly losing her. Brad produced a deck of cards from his jacket pocket. He and his pilot friend Wales played a game, and Jamo joined in. Bob was trying to read a book that Dr. Hoffman had stuffed in his parka pocket, but reading was difficult while shaking from the cold. Bob was not doing well.

In the ice A-frame shelter, John and Luke slept well, but not for long. When they awoke, Luke yawned a steamy long slow breath, uttered an audible yawn, and rubbed his eyes to focus. He lit the candle. They warmed their hands and then stomped around to warm up. The candle cast a soft but eerie light around them, producing long shadows. Because of the reflection from the glistening ice walls, the lighting was fairly good.

Luke wasted no time. He grasped the hardened steel chopper, shaped like a harpoon, and began chipping away at the thinner ice over the former seal hole. They took turns, switching when one got tired. Eventually, they broke through and began enlarging the hole. The water level was well below the bottom of the ice and dropping. The tide was going out. Their luck was holding.

As they enlarged the hole, Luke could tell that the level of the sea was continuing to fall. When he had the hole large enough, he leaned out and tested the depth. It was very shallow, almost ideal. When the tide fully receded, he would be able to drop through the hole safely and stand or crouch on the rocks below. It was their first stroke of good luck. They had the good fortune of finding a nearly ideal spot to venture under the ice.

They waited patiently as the tide continued to recede. Luke removed the hard snow block and peered into the blackness. No snow was falling. He briefly spied two or three stars, high overhead, but in a moment, racing clouds obliterated the tiny white dots. John decided that it was time to contact the base and spread a bit of good news.

The tide rapidly exited the fjord. Shaped similar to a funnel, the net change was less obvious at their present location near the wide end than the large tidal bore farther up the narrowing fjord. Before John could contact the base, Luke motioned him over to the hole in the ice floor. "Wait, John. Let's see if we can find what we came here for." Luke was ready to drop through to the seafloor below.

John wanted to contact the cliffside before venturing beneath the thick ice layer. He needed to know how they were faring, though he feared he already knew. Their brief trip back through the cliffside left him shaken. Words were not necessary because the faces told the story.

He plucked the walkie-talkie from his pocket with his ungloved hand and poked at the on switch and send buttons. He prayed that the weak signal would reach through the snow and ice, over the rocky crags separating them, and trigger a response from the mate unit cliffside.

He was greeted by only static and silence. On his fourth try, the static noise was broken by Carl's warm and familiar voice. John relayed the good news that they had reached the coast, rested, found a suitable goal for their quest, and were about to begin their search. He understood that the group needed good news, so he tried to be as cheerful as possible. Carl's voice brightened, and he signed off with a promise to relay their situation. John finished the brief message, switched off the unit, and joined his friend at the opening.

Descending through the narrow hole in the ice was an experience their ancestors described on numerous occasions. Both Inuits had wisely chosen to learn the ways of "the old ones," the revered elders of their ilk, the ones who truly knew and understood the ways and means of survival in a realm where modern man would perish when stripped of his modern conveniences.

For the Arctic "explorers" from the south to call it food, it needed to come out of a box, can, or package. Both John and Luke were raised with most of these conveniences, and both enjoyed them. But they also made a commitment to their heritage to study the survival techniques their ancestors used for centuries. That choice could provide the sustenance needed to help the others live. Without the Inuits' help, the cliffside group was doomed to not survive for long.

Luke dropped through the opening first. John chipped out two grooves on opposing sides of the opening and fitted the ice chopper harpoon across the orifice, just a little off-center. This would allow one to boost the other up to use the bar to pull himself back out of the hole from below. Once one was out, he could pull or assist the other back through. A rapid escape was a potential necessity due to the unpredictability of these seas. Even under the sea, sudden surges were a deadly possibility, and the incoming tide left no room for misjudgment or error.

Luke surveyed the underside with his light and located safe footing on the slippery rocks. He then guided John's feet to solid footholds. Luke had done this before, but this was a first for John. Both knew what they were looking for, and it wasn't long before Luke's eyes located their prey.

Familiar ocean odors permeated their olfactory senses. The normal sounds of crashing surf were humbled by the solid sea overhead. They removed their parka hoods in order to listen for the anticipated onrush of returning tidal sea. Their ambient surroundings were much warmer than the harsh conditions above the ice. Compared to the gales of wintry storm overhead, beneath the ice was a world of relative comfort without wind. To John, it was incredible, surreal, and remarkable in its relative tranquility.

Seaward, the rocks and storm-rounded cobbles sloped gently away from the abrupt rocky shoreline behind them. A deepening trench led directly to sea from their tiny window to the world above. It was an ideal protected path to a safe breathing haven for whatever creatures had used it. From the shallow depth and narrow entrance, a seal hole was confirmed. It was shallow and too close to shore to be a beluga whale breathing station.

The belugas had either migrated or perished because the multiyear wintry grip closed their necessary breathing holes. The more resourceful seals were now suffering the same fate. As the food chain became more disrupted, the predators too would leave or perish.

Disruption of the fragile Arctic ecosystem was now a reality, destruction a very real possibility.

Only a few feet from their crude entrance and exit, Luke stopped and stooped to pry with his blade. His quarry was an aggregation of pelecypods encrusting the leeward side of a protruding edge of now unsubmerged bedrock. Small mussel shells were soon loosened from their tenacious perch. Luke skillfully pried one open and scraped the raw contents into his open mouth. The chilled contents of the cold bivalve sea creature tasted wonderful. He opened a second for John, who eagerly gobbled it up. John was already shaking open a ziplock plastic bag to hold the remaining treasures.

Both Inuits began prying the tasty morsels from the slimy rocks and placed them in the bag. They stopped harvesting the morsels from the backside of the first rock and shined their lights about to search for more. Being careful with each step, they moved about snatching up every potential food source they found. In an hour, they filled a liter bag and began filling a second.

John captured a few scurrying crabs to add to his booty. He seemed to be enjoying this exercise in survival to the fullest. Both were hesitant to venture too far from the tiny opening. When two bags were completely filled, they tossed them up through the opening and resumed their search for more. Time passed fast, and the rewards of their trek and the location choice proved to be excellent.

Each took a turn to stop and open enough shellfish to satisfy their own appetite. John moved a fair distance from the opening in a direction parallel to the shore to find unharvested mussels for his own consumption. Luke remained close to the escape hole, having already eaten plenty. He was just about to shout a warning to John to not go too far when they both heard the distant gurgles and stared wide-eyed at the leading edge of the returning tidal bore. In their eagerness to continue searching, they both lost track of time.

To be trapped beneath the ice meant certain death. To be soaked meant a slow, chilling torture on the surface before death came. John looked up, turned, and began running as delicately as he could over the wet glistening litter of broken, storm-tossed rock and gravel beneath his feet.

"Hurry," Eluk shouted. "But don't fall."

"I'm coming. Get out," John yelled back.

"We have time. You can make it." Luke shot back, but he feared John was moving too fast. His fears were correct. John was two-thirds of the way to him when he lost his balance and slipped sideways from a large rock when he crouched to clear a protrusion from the underside of the ice. He fell hard and rolled through a shallow water-filled depression.

Luke panicked. He wanted to flee through the opening to save himself, but his nature would never allow him to abandon his friend. He was about to rush to John as the water gushed and rose toward him, when John rolled and rose, clutching his shoulder, and began scrambling toward him again.

John reached Luke as the first rivulets of seawater encroached upon their feet. The returning tide swirled up the mini-canyon leading to the hole and splashed against their boots. In one motion, Luke knelt and boosted his panicked comrade up to the ice chopper bar straddling the opening and nearly propelled him through the orifice. With his uninjured arm, John forced himself up and through and turned around to reach back for Luke. His fellow Inuit had already leaped with amazing strength and grasped the bar with his ungloved wet hands. His hands were now stuck to the now superchilled metal, further complicating their predicament.

The water was rising. Tidal surges in this funnel-shaped fjord and estuaries were very strong. Luke had been in too much of a hurry. John was finally able to free one of Luke's hands without injury and, after considerable effort, dragged him up and out to safety before anything other than his waterproof boots became wet. They both rolled on the floor of their icy home and laughed, relieved that they both were above the ice. They were safe, they had food, and had won this round from the spirits of the sea. They gave thanks for their good fortune and escape.

John's shoulder ached, but he did not care. For a few moments, he thought he was a dead man for sure. Now they both felt better about calling the cliffside survivors and passing along the good news before that group became any more despondent. John reached in his deep parka pocket for the two-way radio, but it was gone. The fall must have jarred it loose, and in his haste, John had dropped and lost it. Their brief reverie turned sour.

"It's gone, Luke."

"What's gone?"

"The walkie-talkie is not in my pocket."

"You lost it?" Luke now had a long face.

"Yes, it must have fallen out when I fell. What a dumbass. I'm sorry."

"Hey…don't…at least I have you back, and we got what we came here for. Case closed. Let's dry out a little and head back."

They lighted the candles and canned-heat source they saved for such an eventuality and removed their wet items in order to dry them as much as possible before returning outside again into the stormy deep freeze. It was a necessity to dry their outer garments as much as physically possible. A quick glimpse outside showed Luke that conditions were again a foreboding blizzard. It made the decision to stay put easy as well as mandatory.

CHAPTER 17

VISITORS

Aboard the USS *Longley*, the communications officer made an amazing and totally baffling discovery. His orders were to maintain a continuous multiband surveillance for any type of nearby communication signal in hopes of picking up a distress call from the AWRB 1 base.

They received an emergency long-band message from SUBCOM that the attempted aerial rescue had ended in a probable crash, only adding the urgency of their planned rescue mission. Captain Brevard closed the distance to the former base to only seven nautical miles.

"Communications officer to captain on the bridge."

"Captain Brevard here, what have you got?"

"Sir, I've picked up a totally strange short-range transmission in my search."

"What do you mean by 'totally strange'?"

"Well, sir, it came from south, thirty-five degrees east, sir, and it came from under the ice."

"That's the general direction of the base, but how could it come from under the ice?"

"I don't know, sir, but that's where it came from. The signal was weak and at maximum range, a handheld walkie-talkie, I think, and it could not have reached us from above it. I checked the analysis. It definitely came from below the ice somehow. It sounds completely impossible, but that's what happened."

"We're as close as we can get due to the shoals and subsea moraines in that direction. Is the SEAL team ready in mini-sub one?"

"Yes, sir" came the instant answer from the team leader, already preparing the smaller submersible.

"Launch as soon as possible and investigate the source, Mr. Meyers. We have a pinpoint triangulation on the signal."

"Aye, aye, sir. I am closing and securing the hatch and ready for launch."

In less than ten minutes, the first minisub with its Navy SEALS was speeding away in the direction of the weak radio signal. It maneuvered as close to shore as safely possible, at which point the two SEALS disembarked into the syrupy cold water clad only in their thick Arctic wet suits. They began following their compasses and swam at a steady pace toward the point from which the weak signal had emanated. It was eerie and dark, their lives dependent solely on their advanced rebreathing equipment. The water was crystal clear and cold. A few sea creatures scurried from their path when the beams of their lights shown upon them. The water began to shallow, and a soft glow appeared through what appeared to be a small opening in the ice.

Jenkins's commandeered jet chopper landed in the cul-de-sac at Mason's address. His assistant ran from the front door with his winter gear, brushing a quick kiss on his concerned wife's face. She meekly waved a worried farewell. In moments, the vehicle lifted into the air and sped north, away from the quiet suburban community.

Cliffside, Carl and Becky made several attempts to raise John and Luke. They waited for half-hour intervals and repeated their attempts to no avail. Their earlier feelings of encouragement once again returned to complete depression.

Luke and John spent nearly two hours holding the wet parts of their garments above the heat flames, watching the moisture evaporate and disappear. It was a slow and tedious process, but it also warmed them and allowed them a chance to let John recover from his fall. His shoulder was bruised and very sore, but he was fine. His ego was the most bruised.

The candles, canned-heat sources, and flashlights cast a pleasant glow about their ice room. Their precious food bundles were well away from the opening in the icy floor. Luke left his light sitting by the opening, hoping by some remote chance a seal might happen to be attracted and come to breathe. He kept the harpoon ice chopper at his side just in case.

After more than two hours of working John's shoulder and drying their wet garments, they checked outside and decided to rest briefly again before leaving. The food was stowed in equal amounts in backpack slings. The weather outside was still frightful, and they had at least two more hours until they would have a modicum of daylight.

John settled back in the sloping snowbank below their entrance, and Luke went to retrieve the light from near the hole in the ice leading to the sea below. He noticed the black movement in the murky ink-colored water and quickly snatched up the freed harpoon. He raised it as quickly as possible and plunged it at the shape below. The immediate loud *clank* caused John to bolt upright. It also startled Luke. He studied the hole in the floor between his legs and noticed the growing red stain in the water. Luke's eyes and ears were greeted by a blinding bright beam and a shout of expletives from the trashing masked face, which appeared in the opening.

As incredible as it seemed to John, a diver had just appeared in their ice-chipped sea portal. Luke staggered backward in abject disbelief. The wounded diver switched on his headlight. Luke sheltered his eyes from the blinding search beam. The diver was wounded and bleeding, gasping and grasping at the sides of the narrow opening. A second head appeared beside the first. There was just enough room for one additional arm to appear, and it held a rustproof forty-five automatic pointed at Luke.

The Inuit dropped the harpoon, sending ice shards flying, and instinctively raised his hands. The second masked diver struggled to support his injured comrade. John spun around and slid forward to help support the bleeding SEAL, a Navy SEAL, not an Arctic subsea Native. The gun disappeared, the second head with it. The wounded Navy SEAL, special operations frogman, emerged from the opening and slid forward in his glistening black wet suit into John's helping arms. His sleek breathing apparatus had deflected the sharp point, but the harpoon had cut through his wet suit on his side and opened a wound. Blood dripped from it.

Luke recovered from his shock and quickly offered assistance to the second diver. He too wiggled up onto the ice floor and removed his regulation mouthpiece and face-covering mask. His look was not pleasant, and his interest was focused on his wounded crewmate. No words had been exchanged.

With caution, the second diver examined the injury to the first. It was only a flesh wound. Fortunately, the glancing blow was deflected, and the thick thermal wet suit had allowed little more than superficial skin-surface damage. The wound was not deep but would probably need a few stitches. Peeling back the wet suit, the second SEAL opened his small first aid kit, applied three small butterfly bandages, and covered the wound with waterproof antiseptic bandage. This all transpired before a single word was uttered.

"Who are you? Where did you come from?" John asked when the second diver finished with the first.

Before the SEAL could answer, Luke added, "I'm really sorry. I had no idea. I could have killed you."

"It's okay," the second SEAL responded. "I'm Roger Singletary, USN, and this dumbass with me is Bob Johnson. We're US Navy SEALS from the US nuclear submarine *Longley*."

The wounded SEAL did not like his "dumbass" moniker one bit, and the pain in his side further aggravated the insult, but he knew in his heart that he deserved it.

"Look, I should have never let you or anyone else spear me. It hurts, but the crap I'm going to get for doing something as dumb as I did is going to hurt worse."

"Don't worry, Bob. They will not find out from me," Roger added. It was only slight consolation. "We saw the glow of your lights through the hole in the ice as we closed in on your bearing and turned off our lights to zero in on the opening. It made it easy to find it, but it almost got Bob killed. Twenty-twenty hindsight says that turning off our lights was a very bad idea, but here we are. Who are you?"

Luke extended his hand; so did john. They exchanged their introductions. John explained to the SEALs that they were from AWRB 1 and had come to this location to gather food from under the ice. That explained the mystery sub-ice signal intercepted by the *Longley* communications officer. John explained how he had tested his handheld radio beneath the ice before they searched for food. He also explained how he had then carelessly lost the communicator.

They gave the SEALs a complete report on the avalanche, the subsequent destruction of the base, the survivors, the crash of the rescue craft, and as much pertinent information as possible. The SEALs relayed the information to the *Longley*, where a complete rescue plan would be formulated.

Luke asked the uninjured Johnson if his communicator could be used to contact the cliffside. His response was a quick affirmative. With a few minor adjustments, he was able to contact the *Longley*, obtain the needed frequency and channel settings, and prepare his instruments for Luke. In the meantime, John and the other SEAL compared their injuries and traded stories.

Becky was ready to ask Dr. Hoffman to tranquilize or knock Joe out. His antics had everyone disgusted and flustered. He was now belligerent, nasty, and threatening. His overt comparison of their situation to the infamous Donner Party made everyone just about sick. When he began suggesting that Charise was the obvious choice, Becky reached her saturation point. She had enough of Mr. Joe Stewart. He was told, ordered, to keep his troublesome mouth shut. Her actual verbiage was much more succinct. The more she had to deal with him, the more upset she became. Wayne finally took over the situation with complete support from the others.

Just as the tense situation reached its worst, Carl's radio beeped and began to crackle. He only had one set of batteries remaining. The rechargeable ones were on the charger. It was Luke's voice on the other end.

"Luke to base," he began. "We found plenty of food and are on our way back. Prepare for a feast, over." Carl relayed the brief message, and Luke could hear the cheers in the background.

"That's great news, Luke! We are starving," as if he didn't already know.

Luke continued, "I've got even better news than that, over."

Carl couldn't wait to hear more. "What's that, Luke? Is the weather breaking?"

"Better than that, Carl. We have guests." A stunned silence followed.

"What do you mean by guests?" The familiar voice was that of Becky, the base commander.

"Here, I'll let him introduce himself." Luke handed the walkie-talkie to Roger.

"Good…what time of day is it?" he asked Luke, glancing at his wet suit sleeve to check his diver's chronograph. "Good morning, Becky. I'm Roger Singletary, USN SEAL, Special Forces, rescue and reconnaissance specialist, at your command."

Becky could not believe her ears. Emotion overcame the stress and tension. She handed the radio to Wayne, who had a perplexed look on his face, and lowered her head to sob tears of joy. He saw her smile and sensed relief, not despair, emanating from her slumping body.

CHAPTER 18

THE *LONGLEY*

Preparations were already underway aboard the *Longley* to launch the second minisub, a third SEAL, and another experienced medic. Captain Brevard monitored all radio traffic between his first team and the survivors at AWRB 1. He was elated when they made the first contact but saddened by the report of the deaths of several base personnel and concerned about the seriousness of the injuries to Charise.

Sea conditions at the entrance to the fjord were treacherous and dangerous for his ultrasophisticated piece of Navy hardware. Water depth varied due to numerous ancestral glacial moraines or submerged ridges. Rocky shoals were also present and pervasive, making navigation in the shallow waters both a challenge and a headache. Thick ice overhead further restricted maneuvering, and by any standard, the *Longley* was a huge vessel. She was the best in her class, most modern, and could outmaneuver and even outrun any submarine. Brevard knew that he needed the flawless functioning of all systems and the complete attention to every detail by his entire crew to complete the intended rescue. He hoped for a little luck to go along with that.

The area around AWRB 1 was ideal for the advanced weather monitoring base and a perfect location for the "hidden array" until the landslide. For a submarine, it was more of a nightmare. Landward from the base, the fjord was narrow with glacially smoothed sides and inadequate water depth. At the mouth were fringing tidal flats, submerged ridges pocked with large boulders or glacial erratics, jumbled ice and pressure ridges, and fearsome tides and surges, all creating an impenetrable barrier. The position of the base or remnants of it were landward of the most formidable barriers and therefore unreachable by the *Longley*.

Brevard positioned the *Longley* as close as he could safely bring the sub before he sent the initial pair of SEALs, but the present position was still more than seven miles from the base, and the ice was very thick. Even the reinforced sail of the *Longley* was not capable of breaking through the ice above without sustaining damage. Brevard had a perplexing problem. He could eventually blast an opening in the ice, but seven miles was a long way to transport seriously injured over the surface, a surface strewn with innumerable obstructions and continued miserable weather conditions. He could use the minisubs for part of the extraction, but the injured, especially the critically injured like Charise, would not survive. They ran rescue simulation drills many times, but for hardened Navy SEALS, not untrained civilians in already poor condition.

Captain Brevard knew that he had to make some tough decisions if he was going to rescue any of them. Otherwise, he would get them basic needed supplies, food, and medical attention, and they would just have to wait for another method of extraction. He also wanted to get his own people back to the safety of the *Longley* after they completed their secondary mission. His orders included getting his team into position to provide security for the secret sensor array and make it impossible for anyone or anything to tamper with, alter, or remove any part of it.

The second team was launched, and constant real-time communications with all members of both teams indicated that the second pair would arrive at the surprise rendezvous hole in the ice in less than thirty minutes. Brevard was still wondering about the initial comments of the first pair when they stumbled upon the two Eskimos. Only he and the SEAL team leader were listening to the chatter of the divers, the clatter of metal, shouts, expletives, and drama of the chance meeting. It was bewildering, but he let them do their job without interference. They would give him a full report later.

The second SEAL team arrived at the meeting point without incident. Brevard was concerned that he had two teams at risk and ordered the first team to return to the *Longley* because one had sustained an accidental injury, needing medical attention. The second team unloaded the essential emergency supplies and food, introduced themselves to the Inuits, and helped the first team back through the opening in the ice for their return. They had to leave before the tides changed again and were cutting it close. John and Luke hated to see the first team leave but were assured that they would be back as soon as they were given clearance to return. The Inuits were anxious to begin the trip back to the base. Along with their bounty from the sea, they now had additional food, a medic and medical supplies, and a heater brought by the new SEALs.

Rumors aboard ship were rampant. Not much was hidden from the crew, who had a heightened sense of interest in this very real rescue mission. The ship's surgeon was standing by for the returning first pair. Everyone wondered why, knowing that they would not have been recalled unless one was hurt.

The change of divers and initial part of the rescue mission was proceeding as planned when another unexpected problem came up. Tidal rises and falls were precisely known. The *Longley*'s position was strategically maintained at the optimum location to minimize tidal effects and to assure the safest and most direct route for the minisub. Whether because of weather changes above the ice or a shift in the ice itself, the outgoing tidal bore was more turbulent than expected.

The first two SEALs reached their firmly tethered minisub through the thick superchilled Arctic seawater. An arduous swim resulted in two tired frogmen working to their limits. They swam as fast as they could, but it was especially strenuous for the one with the now reopened and bleeding cut, which was non-life-threatening but very bothersome and painful.

They untethered their small watercraft and aimed for the *Longley*, planning to ride with the outgoing current to their rendezvous point with the mother ship. Instead of an easy assisted ride, they were tumbled and banged along the bottom by the unexpected ferocity of the strong current. They were momentarily stunned, but their training kicked in, and they regained control. Any damage to their minisub meant additional problems for the recovery effort. Narrow confines between the ice and the seafloor left little room for error.

Roger Singletary saw the rocky ledge on the small radar screen on the control panel of his craft. His injured companion strained to control steering and did not see it coming. Fabricated of high-strength composites, the subs were built to sustain some contact. A loud clang and crunching scrapes confirmed hard impact before Roger could warn his companion, Bob, or do anything to help him avoid the accident. Turning and twisting, Johnson ducked down while the sub ground forward and fought to gain clearance from the rocky promontory. It was over in an instant. Both SEALs felt the heat of perspiration beneath the thick thermal wet suits. Neither sustained any injury, but damage to the minisub was serious. They limped forward at the speed the wounded machine could sustain.

Brevard monitored every step of the effort, watching and listening in the control room. He had not rested for a moment since their arrival and was showing signs of fatigue. The dangers of a mishap were always present. "STAND BY RECOVERY," he shouted. "HELMSMAN, GET US OFF THE BOTTOM. WE NEED ROOM TO MANEUVER."

Crew reactions were immediate. Power was shifted to propulsion, ballast tanks filled with enough air to provide necessary buoyancy, and the submarine began to rise from its present resting place on the bottom. He planned to shorten the distance between himself and the returning men, having backed off from their departure point to a place with favorable room to maneuver. His divers regained control and were shortening the distance to his ship from their direction. They were now out of the dangerous narrow approach channel near shore and heading into deeper, less confining waters.

Aboard the *Longley*, Brevard needed a situation report. "SEAL leader, what is your situation?" he inquired.

"I am Singletary, Captain. We are inbound range nine hundred meters. Bob is hurt, and we had a bump on the rocks with minor collision damage to the sub. That current was really tough. Our propulsion is okay, but we are taking it slow because the diving and steering planes are bent." He finished his comments and looked over at Bob, expecting a thumbs-up. Johnson was not inside the sub but was clinging to the handles on the outside, inspecting the underside guidance controls. He was trying to straighten the planes. Roger knew that his teammate was showing signs of fatigue, but something else was wrong. He had not had time to check over Bob since the collision. Then he saw the fluid emanating from Bob's seat area.

"Bob, you okay?" No reaction. "Bob, answer me!" Singletary stopped the sub.

"Johnson, this is Captain Brevard. What is your situation?"

"I am having a bad day, sir." His response was clear and strong. "It's the minisub, sir. I'm afraid this side is pretty torn up. We have hydraulic fluid leaking, and we didn't see the tear in the stern. That hit on the rocks was a lot worse than we thought. I'm fine, but our transportation is not. We may have to swim the rest of the way." At that moment, the lights and electrical systems failed, and the minisub began sinking to the bottom.

The recovery chamber on the *Longley* was ready with divers standing by. They were immediately dispatched to assist the inbound SEALs. Recovering the minisub for repairs was their next assignment, but that would not be an easy task due to its size and weight and present location.

"Captain, this is Munson here."

Brevard was happy to hear his other team checking in. "Go ahead, Munson."

"We've got good light and a slight break in the outside weather. Winds have decreased a bit with only light blowing snow. We'd like to make a go for the base. Between the four of us, we can carry the food and medical supplies. The Inuits think that we can be there in five or six hours if the conditions hold." Brevard wondered if he should give them the green light to go or wait for additional support, but the damage and loss of the minisub meant that they would not be getting more help in the foreseeable future.

"Captain, John and Luke say that the conditions at the base are getting desperate, and the wounded woman is pretty bad off. They also have one wild-eyed bozo ready to go off the deep end."

"Go, Mun. Godspeed and please be careful. Keep us apprised of progress and your sit. We'll do all we can from this end and try to get relief to you ASAP."

Luke knew that they had to leave because Becky said that Charise's condition was steadily going downhill. John had already made up his mind to leave. Luke peered outside, seeing the noticeable improvement in the weather, and said, "Let's go." They stuffed their heavy packs with everything they had and set them outside the ice A-frame shelter. In ten minutes, they were ready to move. The SEALs brought folding snowshoes with them, or they would not have been able to make the return trip to the base with the Inuits. Once they put them on, Luke gave a thumbs-up, and the other three responded in kind.

"Team two, are you moving?" Brevard checked in.

"Yes, sir. We have marked our exit with a transponder and should have no problem finding it again. If the light is adequate and the weather holds, we will recon the area to see if a return closer to the *Longley* is possible. Damn, it's colder out here than it was in the drink, sir. I'm going to have to really haul butt to keep up with the Eskimos. They're used to this shit and already leaving us in their dust. Out for now." The silence after the message left Brevard pensive again. The recovery of his first team replaced thoughts of the second.

It took much longer than expected to recover the first team. Singletary's buddy swam Bob to the submarine where he was greeted by the new divers dispatched to help them and to recover the damaged minisub.

CHAPTER 19

CAPTAIN BREVARD

Decisions of command by officers and their subsequent repercussions invariably took a toll. Captain Allen Brevard was not an exception. As commander of the world's most lethal vessel, potentially the most deadly machine ever built, he carried a heavy burden of responsibility. Around his neck hung one set of keys needed to launch Armageddon. In his possession were codes needed to launch or recall his arsenal of destruction. In his mind, the captain often revisited and replayed his most difficult decisions, re-evaluating them over and over in his head, seeking to analyze every facet. He wrote his reports in his head long before he entered them into the permanent ship's log.

Captain Brevard rose through the ranks from a modest beginning. He grew up in western New York, in a small town called Watkins Glen, most famous for its beautiful park and annual auto race. He was bright and a good athlete in high school, captain of the swimming team, and a starting pitcher on the baseball team. His dad was a tough former Marine, and his older brother continued the family tradition by joining the corp. Mom was a stay-at-home mom who raised the boys to have excellent manners and respect for all people. The younger Brevard boy applied to and was accepted by the Naval Academy at Annapolis where he eventually graduated with honors near the top of his class.

His career at sea began with graduation as an ensign from Annapolis and being assigned to a destroyer. His superiors noticed his ability to solve complicated problems during war games early in his career. He was promoted to lieutenant in two years and lieutenant commander in eight. He received his commander rank while serving on a nuclear aircraft carrier after twelve years of naval service. His meteoric rise to that of captain took only eighteen years in the Navy, a position normally attained after at least twenty-one years. He was there when the *Longley* was launched and completely overwhelmed when he was assigned to take her out to sea on her maiden voyage. The ship was part of him now, and he an integral part of her. After three years at her helm, he knew every inch and idiosyncrasy of the behemoth. His crew had the utmost respect for him. They all realized the incredible responsibility he carried on his shoulders every day. In stealth, speed, deadliness, and technology, Brevard's submarine had no equal.

Brevard completed numerous world cruises since he was given the command of the *Longley*. On several instances, the submarine was brought to full alert, battle stations manned, all weapons armed, and launch codes entered. He had unlocked the second set of keys and placed them in their ready positions. Personal feeling and emotions became secondary. He acknowledged his orders with swift decisiveness and stood by to destroy his targets and perhaps kill millions. He never doubted that he would follow orders to launch if the order was given.

The captain's personal life was uncomplicated. He was married to the Navy and stayed single for his entire career. Life ashore consisted of a warm apartment decorated with neutral furniture and pieces of art he collected from all over the world. Art was his third passion. His second was his girlfriend of over ten years. They met at a restaurant he was attending with several of the ship's officers. They dated every time he returned from duty, and he asked her to marry him after one long weekend together at a cabin they rented in the Smoky Mountains. She politely turned him down, explaining that their relationship was fine as it was since he was gone so much of the time on long voyages. He understood and accepted her reasoning without question, and their relationship remained strong to this day. She was a career intelligence specialist who also loved her job and had risen to a position in charge of coordinating various intelligence-gathering services. They loved each other, and absence made the heart grow fonder with each passing day that they spent apart.

Brevard's parents accepted the relationship too, but like most aging parents, they hoped for a marriage and grandchildren. His older Marine brother retired from the corps, married and had two children, a boy and a girl, who loved their Uncle Allen. Captain Brevard always brought them presents on the occasions when the family was able to get together. He and his girlfriend, whom his parents just loved, had no plans to have children of their own.

Early in his career aboard the *Longley*, his fiber and mettle were tested. Following orders, he had the *Longley* remain in silence at periscope depth, watched helplessly, and videoed while innocent civilians were robbed of their boats, machine-gunned and dumped into the sea. The sins of the drug lords and their thugs were witnessed and documented, but Brevard had to wait until much later to make them pay for it. He had the unpleasant task of retrieving bodies and returning them to the proper authorities through mysterious channels. His orders were always the same: observe, document, remain hidden, do not interfere.

On one occasion, the crew felt a bump after the periscope was lowered. They heard a crunch and the sounds of a vessel breaking up. When the captain left the bridge, the first officer of the bridge raised the periscope to see a pirate boat breaking up and sinking. Brevard's official log entry said, "Anomalous sounds heard while leaving the area."

The captain relived the agony of being forced to be passive and stand by while atrocities were committed. That ended when the drug war moved into the most active phase. After that, he was NEMO, captain of the famed *Nautilus*. He unleashed hell upon the drug traffickers caught in his crosshairs. The volume of data collected to that point proved to be worth the long wait. Target vessels and routes were already identified and cataloged. The intelligence was gathered. They knew the boats, when and where they traveled, and which ones were the best targets to stop or sink. Lethal darts loosed to sink a cartel-owned and cartel-operated freighter, the first of several kills.

Brevard's most classified mission involved a scheme to bring out and destroy the maximum amount of drug cartel assets. The submarine was a mystery vessel to the drug lords and their henchmen. Its origin was unknown; it was never seen and only rumored to exist. Captain Brevard planned a facade. The operation took the *Longley* into shallow coastal water where he allowed the sub to be spotted by the cartel's light aircraft tailing a drug-laden high-speed yacht. The powerful drug cartel's huge profits allowed them to obtain sophisticated weaponry, aircraft, and high-speed watercraft with crews capable of firing shoulder-launched missiles. The captain even simulated running the *Longley* aground in his overzealous effort to stop the target drug shipment.

The kingpins of cocaine pulled out all the stops when they learned about the submarine and sent everything they had to damage or eliminate their greatest detractor. High-speed drug-runner boats sped from every port within miles. They listened on all frequencies for news of a grounded submarine seeking assistance but knew that it was likely being kept quiet. They wanted to strike the sub before anything came to its aid.

While the *Longley* pretended to struggle and churn up sand and material from the sea bottom, the encroaching attackers were identified, illuminated by multiple radars, prioritized, and swiftly eliminated. One particular drug lord, in his own drug-crazed state, was brash enough to go along for the kill with his most trusted crew. He was fond of killing, and this attack looked like that could be in large numbers. His life, many of his mongrels, and most of his empire's air assets were knocked from the sky, blown from the water, and decimated with precision in less than two hours. The trap was sprung with complete surprise and uncompromising thoroughness. Officially, the *Longley* was in no danger, but in reality, she came very close to receiving serious damage from a missile that sailed over within mere feet of the sub's superstructure.

Brevard went on to deliver several crippling blows to the cartels. He also rescued Captain Wales after torpedoing the freighter responsible for shooting down Wales's helicopter. His task now was to rescue him again along with the rest of the people his two-man team was attempting to reach at the crippled base.

CHAPTER 20

THE TREK

Scudding clouds streaked overhead, moisture laden and low-lying but not ominous. Light snow was falling, and the air was clearer than it had been for a while. The wind speed was way down. An aircraft with an experienced pilot could safely land, even with the low ceiling. Luke thought about the Grey Lady crash. Had they attempted an approach and landing in conditions like those at present, they would all be gone from their present predicament. He also realized that no others were coming, so he had to make the best of this rescue attempt.

Trudging forward through the crunching deep snow soon removed the chill from Munson's body. The second team brought two pairs of snowshoes from storage aboard the *Longley*. Without them, progress would have been almost impossible. Even with them, the going was very tough. Munson realized that his high-energy supplement bars were not going to last very long. They were expending a tremendous amount of energy with every sliding step. He was already feeling hunger and began to calculate how long he could sustain this pace and have enough energy to also maintain his body temperature.

Munson communicated with his fellow rescuer, Medic Ybarra, but had no way to talk to the Inuits. They remained stoically silent, plodding ahead up a rise of several meters. Munson could hear Ybarra breathing heavily, though he too was in excellent physical shape. He was thankful for the strict physical training he went through with the

SEALs. When Luke stopped to check on the Navy men behind him, Munson wanted to see and hear fatigue. There was no sign of any. "Tough little SOBs," he muttered.

"What's that?" Ybarra sputtered, obvious panting following.

"Nothing," Munson added.

Luke's sharp ears picked up the conversation and brief exchange. He took their comments as a compliment and feigned indifference. His legs already ached, and his lungs burned too from breathing big gulps of the frigid air, but he would never let the new guys know that. They continued to move on at a steady pace, John leading, with Luke close behind. The two Navy men began to slow down. On the incline, the snow was less packed, but walking in their snowshoes with heavy backpacks became pure drudgery.

Single file, they surmounted the first big rise and felt the ground beneath their feet begin to level out. They were at the top of the first set of cliffs, with more to come. Munson beheld the expanse of the white wilderness landscape around them. With a level trek ahead at least for several hundred meters, their energy was bolstered. Munson pulled out his binoculars and scanned the icy fjord bottom below. Even if the *Longley* was able to get this far up the fjord and blow a hole in the ice, getting to her with injured or weak civilians would be pure hell. He hoped to spot another way to reach the *Longley*, but those chances looked bleak. He decided to wait to make his report until they were farther along, and perhaps he would find a better vantage point to scan the area below.

Munson was head down for most of the walk, well over an hour, obediently following the Eskimos, but now looked up to see gray above and white everywhere else, except for a few rocky crags sticking through the snow. It was a bleak, barren landscape. He had no sense of direction.

"Rest break," John interrupted his thoughts. Munson watched Luke flop back in a nearby snowdrift without even removing his pack. Luke pulled out several nearly frozen shellfish and began munching them raw, handing some to John. He offered some to Munson and Ybarra, but they already had power bars in their gloved hands.

Using the SEAL's radio, John attempted to contact the base. He knew that they still had a long way to go uphill in difficult conditions, with the worst climb still ahead. Toward the base, the valley narrowed, and the sides grew steeper where the last cliffs towered. Though only one hundred meters in height, they were steep and treacherous with lose unpacked snow in places. Once they cleared the final rise, the flat walk to the base would be much easier atop the cliffs.

After several tries, John was surprised that no one answered. He passed the news to Luke and the SEALs. All agreed that the rest stop was over. John wondered why there was no reply and began to fear that something else had gone wrong for the already desperate survivors at the base. Returning the communicator to the Navy man, John signaled to Luke to take the lead and break trail for the rest of them. Luke was pleased to lead for the present and began doing so with determination. Luke knew that they had to reach the cliffside. He felt a little better after the rest but knew that the weather, fatigue, and time were his enemies.

He checked behind himself and waited for the others to catch up. In his brief reverie, he had plodded ahead of the others and realized he was making a mistake by setting too hard a pace. He let them all catch their breath. Rest stops were important, and pacing themselves in these conditions most important of all. Breathing too much chilled air was not a problem for the Inuits, but the Navy men were not acclimated to the extreme chill effect in their lungs.

Luke turned and resumed their march, noticing a swirl of large snowflakes a short distance in front of them. He recognized the signs when a stronger puff of wind tossed loose snow into the air beside him. He and John stopped to discuss the situation while the Navy men caught their breath. Both were starting to cough from the frigid dry air. The landscape ahead began to disappear, larger flakes falling around them. Luke had no way to call the base and check on conditions there. Communications were just not working. They checked their GPS position and compass, both not entirely reliable at this latitude. A few seconds later, they were all buffeted by a stronger windblast, whipping snow into their faces. Goggles protected their eyes.

John moved to Luke's side. "What do you think, Eluk? I don't like it."

The answer was a quick 'I don't like it either." He began scanning the area in all directions.

Munson moved up next to them and asked, "What's up? Weather problem?"

"Always weather problems," Luke returned. "Can you contact the *Longley* and get a fix on the topside weather?" The frogman almost laughed at the Inuit's wording but checked his communicator and asked Captain Brevard, "Captain, could meteorology give me a stat of the local weather conditions? It seems to be getting stormy again out here."

"I'll put you through to him," Brevard answered. The *Longley*'s weather forecaster, a young meteorology specialist named Sanger, gave them the bad news. "The ceiling is dropping, the clouds are thicker, the wind is picking up in velocity, and the barometric pressure is falling. Things are deteriorating fast, and it looks like another storm is brewing."

Munson said thanks and signed off. He relayed the message to Luke and John. The other Navy man had listened in to the conversation through his headset. The Inuits had a choice to make. They could make an all-out dash for the cliffside or chance the present pace and seek shelter or dig in when conditions made further progress impossible. Being caught out in the open in a total blizzard meant that none would likely survive.

They pushed ahead, tightening their parkas around their faces. Munson's hands were cold. He wiggled his fingers and blew warm air into his gloves, but he was losing heat. The falling and swirling snow, a white disappearing landscape, and white above, below, and everywhere were disconcerting to the men from the *Longley*. For the first time, fear began to fill their minds. Munson did not relish freezing to death in the middle of nowhere.

Luke led on, plodding through the swirling snow gaining elevation with each forward step while pondering the question whether they should stop or continue on. He felt a tap on his shoulder. It was John pointing out the turn into a side ravine where they could ascend the cliff to the top of the plateau. Once between its steep walls, the wind mitigated enough to see ahead. They climbed through thick drifts. Luke listened for sounds of stress from his colleagues. The weight of his pack and deepening snow made walking difficult when the path steepened. He could not hear the others over the sound of his own heavy breathing. He wished that the SEALs had provided him his own communicator so that he could listen to them. Looking up and ahead, Luke could scarcely believe his eyes. He held up his hands to stop the others. A cloud of steam emanated from each parka, small warm puffs of vapor that froze and disappeared. His three companions stared at him, not knowing what to expect, but John quickly realized that their path was blocked. The snow overhang ahead was dangerous. If it failed under its own weight, they would all be buried. Enough had already broken off the block to stop further progress. It was an insurmountable, very threatening barrier.

John and Luke pondered the situation and discussed the possibility of a climb through and over the obstacles in their path. They decided that it was just too dangerous and that they had no choice but to turn around and retrace their steps out of the side canyon. They had to go back to a previous possible place to ascend the cliffs, a place passed on earlier, or go on to find a better, more suitable location closer to the base. John's familiarity with the terrain suggested going on. The canyon where he and Luke climbed down was just ahead, and though steeper, it was wider. The SEALs just accepted the decision, turned, and began retracing their path, their earlier footprints already rapidly filling with fresh snow.

Exiting the side canyon, the winds increased again. The ambient conditions only worsened. Luke began to worry that he was leading the entire weary group to their deaths. The frustration of retreating made him angry. He thought of Anook the Great One and of his dad. The memories gave him renewed strength. It was his call, and he had no intention of stopping for no more than a brief rest. He was not about to falter.

Forty minutes passed without a word exchanged. John slipped and fell headfirst into a deep snowbank. He was embarrassed but not hurt. The others dusted him off, and they continued onward.

Munson toppled over under the weight of his unsteady heavy pack. Luke was ready to stop at that point. John pushed on, and his terrain knowledge and instincts proved dependable. Only a few yards farther on, they found the side canyon they sought. It looked good all the way to the top of the cliffs. After stopping long enough for water and to catch their breath, they decided to make an all-out maximum effort to reach the top. In twenty minutes, they were halfway to the edge of the windswept cliff top. Munson stumbled again. His heavy pack shifted, and fatigue made him unable to keep his balance. He fell backward, breaking one snowshoe, and began an uncontrolled tumble toward exposed rocks. He waved his arms, trying futilely to get a handhold but to no avail. His pack broke the slide and fall, that and a dive from John, who just barely got a grip on his other snowshoe. He hit the rocks hard and winced in pain, but the skilled commando took the fall in stride and, though in pain, pulled himself to his feet.

At this point, they all realized that they had to stop, eat something, and rest more than a few minutes. Munson's snowshoe was broken and would need rudimentary repairs. To Luke's surprise, everyone was in favor of pushing on to the top, even Munson. Luke muttered a prayer to himself and moved ahead, hoping that there were no more obstacles or accidents before they reached the top. Twenty minutes farther on, his prayer was answered. He stopped to catch his breath and observed a vertical wall of snow ahead, the edge of the plateau top. Fresh snow was whipping over the edge, adding to a growing drift at the end of their path. The drift was no more than twenty feet wide and not too deep. They had to cut their way through it to escape the valley, but it was very hard packed. The shelter to the leeward side was the perfect place to stop and rest, even dig in if they had too.

The three others reached his side and surveyed the path ahead. Their spirits improved appreciably with their first and most difficult goal in sight. John approached the snowbank and looked for any signs of the danger of the bank sloughing off or giving way, carrying one or all of them back down the canyon. They had already climbed over several small avalanches on their way up to their present position. As tired as he was, John hacked out a path and rough steps for their snowshoed feet, working his way through the final drift. They all helped John and watched him break through. Beyond the drift, the terrain was flat and relatively clear of deep snow.

John checked his watch and could not believe that almost eight exhausting hours had passed since they left the ice pack shelter, and they were about halfway to the cliffside base. Everyone was relieved to see the relatively flat path ahead. Tapping John, Luke said, "John, we have to rest, eat something. I think that the weather is going to get worse, and it is getting even darker. I'm looking at the wind change and thicker clouds."

"Me too." John was direct. He also recognized the signs. "We better fix up some shelter fast. We can make a suitable place on the cliff top by hacking out a few snow blocks and using the SEAL's survival tent for a top." They all began cutting out blocks of the hard-packed snowdrift and stacking them. Within minutes, they made a wall and had the side toward the wind of a rudimentary snow shelter. Stretched and anchored over this, the survival tent formed a suitable ceiling. Supply packs blocked the simple crawl space left for a door. In a half hour, they were all inside, had ignited the canned heat, had a long drink of water, and were enjoying the satisfaction of high-energy snack food. This time, the Inuits took the offer of the chocolate-covered bars over the shellfish. Leaving the confines of the shelter to relieve themselves was their most difficult task. It was so cold that their urine froze before it hit the snow-covered ground. The decision to build a shelter on top of the cliff instead, digging into the face of the drift, would prove to save their lives.

They rested while the wind howled. A storm like the newest one could last for hours or days. Huddled together, they held down the tent roof and knocked snow off as it accumulated around them. After only three hours, the winds died down. Luke thought it was a sign that their luck was changing. They stuck the radio outside and tried to raise someone at the base. After only two tries, they heard a few crackling sounds and then a human voice. It was Wayne who heard their message on their working walkie-talkie. He was elated that they would be there within a few hours if the weather held.

The four would-be rescuers were ready to repack the tent, struggle into their backpacks, and with renewed determination, begin the final leg of their mission.

CHAPTER 21

NEW PROBLEMS

The earthquake hit two hours after the good news came in from the frogman rescue team and their Inuit guides that they were more than halfway there. The first shock wave was preceded by a slow rumble sound. The survivors in the cliffside refuge were elated at the news of the nearby submarine and their real potential to leave their trap in the near future. Food and warmth were their greatest hope. The tremor broke the upper door glass, and rocks tumbled from the cliff. The first landslide that destroyed and buried their base was likely caused by a minor quake. This one was much more serious and lasted over two minutes. The ground shock beneath their feet, and the entire cliffside retreat seemed to sway from side to side and then up and down.

The terrified survivors clung to one another. Dr. Hoffman held Charise down to keep her from falling off her makeshift bed. As soon as the shaking stopped, Wayne and Becky ran up the stairs to assess the broken door situation at the top. Joe Stewart reacted like the madman he had become. He began raving that they were all going to die. Wayne told Wales and Brad to get him under control. For now, he was their problem. Jamo was still hurting, but he knew that he had to somehow control Joe. He sat with him and tried to strike up a conversation to no avail. Dr. Hoffman could spare no tranquilizers for him. When the news from the Inuits and Navy men came through, Stewart calmed down and resumed his brooding by himself.

Perched shivering by the midstairway portal, he remained quiet and stayed away from everyone.

The shaking from the ground wave was intense and unnerving to all. The air filled with dust, and the broken door to the outside at the stairway top let in very cold air. At the ice chamber where the Inuits first encountered the first pair of SEALs, one of the slabs shifted, and the natural shelter collapsed. It would have crushed them all had they been inside. Seawater splashed and soaked what was left of the interior of the former shelter from the hole in the ice floor. The submarine was jostled and hit by intense turbulence below the ice cover. Captain Brevard was forced to withdraw to deeper water well beyond the entrance to the fjord. He nearly lost control of his vessel, which almost ran aground twice in the narrow, shallower part of the fjord.

The earthquake emanated from the Gakkel Ridge. A sudden surge of magma triggered the shock at the nearest point of the ridge to their location. Intense volcanism followed, with a huge eruption of lava splitting the seafloor open. The sea boiled in an otherwise frozen part of the planet, and a huge plume of smoke, gases, and ash was exploded into the air by the subsea eruption. With their situation far from stable and an undersea rescue now aborted, the survivors in the cliffside faced the prospect of a huge growing ash and debris cloud descending toward their position. Just when things were looking up, the situation turned in an instant to pure despair.

Wayne hugged Becky while the shaking took place. Afterward, they tried desperately to stanch the cold air entering their haven with anything they could find. The outer heavy door was jostled off its hinges and crashed through the inner door. The thermo-pane glass doors were a wreck. If they had not run up the stairway when they did, one or both of them would have probably been killed. A large section of rock ceiling broke loose and tumbled onto the stairway where they had been sitting. It missed Carl but crushed Bob's foot when it came to rest at the bottom. He was unable to avoid it after the ground shook. He was screaming in intense pain, holding his right leg. Blood was oozing from his boot, now split open by the impact of the rock. Another few inches and it would have come to rest on him, and instead of his foot, his head would have taken the brunt of the impact.

Dr. Hoffman and Jamo rushed to Bob's side, and with all of his strength, Jamo pushed the rock debris off his foot. It looked bad, but Hoffman wasted no time in trying to keep Bob from going into shock. He looked up at the rock ceiling that was smooth and finished with sprayed-on concrete before the quake to see several large cracks and what appeared to be other loose pieces ready to fall if another trembler hit. Wayne was looking there too and knew very well that there were always aftershocks. He could not believe their luck.

Jamo stood up after helping Dr. Hoffman and Bob. He seemed to be still swaying, though the ground was no longer moving. His head began spinning, and his vision went blank. He tried to speak, but no words came out. The doctor noticed and tried to steady him, but he was too late. Jamo went down in a twisting fall, blood gushing from one ear and from his nostrils. The cerebral hemorrhage was extreme, and he became unconscious and unresponsive. There was nothing they could do for him. Dr. Hoffman checked his vital signs, looked into his frozen stare, and closed his eyes. Jamo was dead.

All four of the rescuers were shaken awake from their fatigue-induced sleep. Snow blocks shifted, and the protective wall collapsed around them. Even with their fur-lined park hoods pulled close around their resting faces, the ice and snow that hit their faces woke them. Shuddering earth brought them to their feet. Pushing the tent roof aside, they grabbed gear and food packs and moved away from their shattered shelter, away from the cliff edge. After the first ground wave lifted them several inches and dropped them to their knees, moving while standing became difficult. Snow and ice began to slide away into the icy chasm they had climbed to reach the top of the cliff. An avalanche formed, pushing ice boulders down the slope that they had climbed only a few hours before. There was no doubt that they would have been swept away and buried, much like the recently discovered Eskimo man.

The shaking was over as fast as it started. The four men looked at one another. All four were covered with fine snow and ice particles and began shaking it off like freshly bathed dogs. Luke and John feared the worst for those trapped in the cliffside. Luke worried that they could not withstand the forces of another avalanche. "WE WAIT UNTIL THE SNOW DUST CLEARS AND MAKE A DASH FOR THE BASE!" he shouted. The others immediately nodded assent. They checked their bearing from several satellites because even a simple compass was sometimes unreliable at this latitude.

After three minutes, they formed a line with John leading. Heads down against a serious headwind, they pushed forward, at times touching the man's shoulder ahead to keep close in the blowing snow, now falling harder as if on cue. A communications check with the base and the sub proved useless. They were able to communicate with each other using their headsets, but beyond that, nothing was getting through. The clouds were so low that they seemed to be walking in only a slot of light between earth and sky. Several times, they had to backtrack a bit to go around obstacles or find a way to cross open crevices. The sharp edges of one crevice were evidence that it was newly formed during the earthquake.

John came close to taking a very bad vertical fall into a new crevice. Luke was able to steady John and prevent him from falling over the edge. John was shaken enough for Luke to take over to lead the rescue party. After another exhausting hour, Luke and John stopped to discuss a large boulder field with rocks as big as houses scattered among a huge pile of car-sized blocks. They had reached another physical landmark, indicating that they were going in the correct direction. Luke would have killed for a dogsled or more modern snow machine. His body ached from the constant strain.

Luke stopped and jumped straight up in the air, swinging around 180 degrees to come down facing a startled and puzzled John. "That's it, John! We will get the injured out by dogsled and rendezvous with the sub down the coast. There are two behind the hangar covered by tarps."

"Great idea, Luke, only one problem: no dogs. But inside the collapsed hangar are snow machines and snowmobiles. If we have a target and can get them out and working, maybe we can use them. We have discussed this. Let's get there first." Darkness was approaching, and they still had a fair distance to cover. The SEAL's headlamps cast a pall of light on the monotonous white surface. The only real way to navigate was by pure Inuit instinct. There were no stars to use, and most of their other equipment was frozen or inaccurate.

Five more extremely arduous hours brought them close enough to try to communicate with the base. Their only stop was to hydrate, urinate, and ingest a few calories. Legs ached with fatigue. Subzero air burned their now sore lungs. Frostbite was becoming a serious problem at their toes and fingertips.

"AWRB 1 here." It was Becky, and she sounded very upset. "Are you anywhere close, over?"

"We should be there in a couple of hours if it doesn't get any worse." John made himself sound strong, but his bones ached, and he was beginning to feel the signs of frostbite. They had all been exposed to the elements for too long without real rest. "Hang in there," he added.

"It's bad here. Jamo is dead. Bob has a crushed foot from a broken-ceiling rockfall but is coping.

"We had to sedate Stewart with the last painkillers. He freaked out and made a mess. He jumped out of the hatch naked. We almost let him freeze to death but finally dragged him back in when he was too cold to struggle anymore.

"He was ranting and running up and down the stairs screaming that we were all going to die. The quake finished him off and sent him into a raging fit. We struggled with him as long as we could and tried to talk to him and calm him, but he would not listen. We thought that Wayne was going to kill him. He finally sat by the midstairs hatch and rocked like a madman, threatening anyone who came near him with a hammer. More of the ceiling tumbled down, but no one else was hit or hurt. Now the upper door is destroyed, and the stairs are cracked and crumbling. We can't hold out here much longer, especially if there are aftershocks. Hurry!"

"We are a couple of hours out but freezing. Is the generator still working?"

"Yes, we are conserving use, but it is keeping us from freezing in here. We can't get the door open to check on it now. The quake jammed the door completely, but it is still running, and we have lights. We are glad you are bringing food because we are all really hungry." Becky did not know what else to say.

"Will you check to see if there are any charges in the supply cabinet by the upper door?" Becky was surprised at that question. She had seen the box marked Danger, High Explosives but wondered why he would ask such a question.

"Yes, the emergency charges are still there."

He told her that he would explain when they got there, that they had to keep moving. He was planning to use them to open the hangar to get to the snow machines.

The SEALs had a separate agenda: orders to eradicate certain parts of the array and power source before leaving. The technology was too important to leave behind intact and unguarded. They had told the Inuits that they had specific orders to complete that task. The specialists were not too keen on following that order, only in surviving at this point, and both knew that those odds were getting worse with each step taking them farther from the safe confines of the submarine.

Luke never said anything about how difficult it would be to even reach the array from the base in the deepening snowpack, and to John, the idea was ludicrous. The numbness in his hands and feet was getting worse with each step. He could only imagine how horrible the military men were feeling, but these particular men were trained to ignore and endure hardship and pain. The SEALs had not said anything about the fact that if they could not reach it and destroy the key components, a missile would accomplish the task.

Unknown to them all, a team of Russian commandos was already on their way to what they thought was the abandoned and destroyed base. Transferred from a Russian icebreaker, now dispatched from their own nuclear sub on a parallel fjord, they were slowly making their way to the base on an even more difficult path. But they had highly specialized snow machines that were capable of making headway in even the deepest loose snow and fourteen heavily armed, well-supplied men with excellent Arctic gear. Neither side anticipated the eventuality of meeting any opposition. The last thing either expected was to run into an adversary, but the Russian team was well prepared and had orders to eradicate any resistance and leave no traces that they had ever been there.

It was over four hours before the frozen four reached the base. They could not open the upper inner door, and those inside quickly realized that they were even more trapped than they thought. The glass was broken and shattered but still held together by a heavy mesh where it was not broken completely by the falling outer door. The ice-chopping bars were extended from inside through the large crack after hauling away the outer door. Expending the last of their energy pulling it, they had the door finally give way with a large creak and swung inward, leaving a gaping hole. Stepping inside, they secured the entrance from the howling wind with a thick tarp while those inside assisted.

Becky greeted the frozen figures with mugs of warm water, heated on the failing hot plate, the only thing she could give them. The four arrivals clutched the cups in their shaking hands and sipped the warm liquid with a relish. They all huddled around the still working space heater at the base of the stairs. The SEALs opened their packs and passed out food bars to the personnel from the base. They gobbled them down with an eagerness they could not believe. The food that the Inuits brought was frozen solid and would take time to thaw out.

It took quite a while for the rescuers to warm up in the chilled ambient surroundings of the cliffside shelter. Once the shaking stopped and the feelings came back in their extremities, they began to assess the condition of the stairway occupants and to begin planning for their escape. The first aftershock frightened them all, but it was not severe and caused no more problems. The cracked and broken ceiling held together. Inspecting the damage to their cliffside shelter, the military men and Natives realized just how precarious their situation had become. Loose ceiling chunks protruded everywhere. The SEAL medic and Dr. Hoffman together checked over the unconscious Charise, and both realized that her condition was very poor and that her chances for survival on an arduous journey were minimal.

CHAPTER 22

ADVERSARIES

The Russians wanted to know the secrets of AWRB 1, the part that the US military maintained did not exist. They understood from aerial and satellite surveillance before the perennial overcast skies that it had more than one purpose. The array, almost invisible from above and assembled in the dark, was still detected. When a story was somehow leaked to the Western press, they began blaming the base for somehow adding to the weather disaster affecting the entire northern hemisphere. The rumors spread that it was a radical device to somehow influence the weather. When communications with the base ceased, the Russians knew that something had gone awry.

An icebreaker was dispatched to get in close, drop off a commando team, and get a close look on the ground. Since no call was received indicating that their assistance was needed, the team was sent in to gather information and, if possible, remove apparatus for inspection back home. It was a simple plan with basic orders: get in, do not get discovered, steal what you can, get out.

The icebreaker would have been a better way to attempt a rescue of the surviving base personnel. Because of the nature of the base and its more secretive use, the Russians were never considered for a rescue. The US authorities did not consider that the Russians would be as interested in the more clandestine nature of the base and attempt to launch a mission to inspect it on the ground.

Now only a few miles away, the Russian team ran into their first major obstacle. Their lead Arctic machine broke through a snow layer that disguised a deep crevice that was undisturbed by the earthquake. It and two of their team plunged into the abyss and were killed and buried. Two others barely escaped the plunge, clinging to the side of the crevice until pulled to safety. There was no chance to rescue or recover the bodies of their two lost comrades.

The first aftershock caused the remainder of the snow covering the large and extensive crack to fall in, forming a serious barrier to their progress and forcing them to search for a way across or around the obstacle. Their state-of-the-art vehicle and snowshoes made moving onward reasonable even in the ever-deepening drifts. The SEALs had their own equally impressive footwear, but one pair was damaged and made the wearer work even harder. The Inuits preferred their more traditional means of traversing the powdery white.

Within less than three hours of their arrival, the new members of the cliffside began preparations in earnest to head for a chosen point on their maps where the submarine could potentially rescue them all. Becky and Wayne listened to the plan with trepidation. Luke and John slept after consuming needed replacement calories. They also needed time to rest after their arduous two-way journey. The resilience of the Navy men impressed all the surviving base team, but they too were in desperate need of rest. The toll from the fatigue of the trip, near frostbitten condition upon arrival, and stress of their assignment was obvious on their chapped reddened faces.

While they were pondering the fate of Charise, Dr. Hoffman brought the dreaded news that she passed away. They did everything possible to stabilize her and make her as comfortable as possible, but her wounds and the near-freezing conditions finally proved too much for her to overcome. They covered her face and removed the things that they used in a desperate attempt to keep her warm. These would now be used by the survivors to add to their insulating layers. The chill of the cliffside stairwell had slowed down her metabolism and lengthened her survival, but she remained unconscious until her death. There was little time for sorrow, only a brief prayer and a few tears.

GLOBAL WARNING

When Luke and John awoke, their bodies ached, but they insisted on going back outside with Wayne to see if they could gain access to the collapsed hangar and assess the condition of the snow machines inside. Bob and Wales had already ventured out and made an attempt to dig and smash their way in. They considered using the explosives in the storage locker for that purpose, but none were well versed in the use or placement of the charges or detonators. Both Navy men were trained in their expert use. They slept for several hours, ate, and then turned their attention to evaluating the small charges they brought with them and those still in the locker. They were pleased with what they found. Their own explosives were enough to knock out the key components of the array and purposed for that only. The plastic explosive and C4 would finish that job and easily tear open the remnants of the hangar.

When the snows and wind slowed, they took the opportunity to exit the confines of the stairwell, examine the crushed building close by, and set three small charges to tear open the bent metal walls. The explosives had to be placed with precision and small enough to do the job within, causing enough concussion to bring down more of the cracked and loose rock in the cliffside. The muffled detonation was barely audible to those huddled inside, away from potentially deadly falling fragments of the damaged ceiling. The Navy men completed the task without any additional problems, and the jagged shredded hole they created in the ruined hangar was large enough for one to crawl inside.

After ten minutes of exploration, he emerged to report that one snow machine was mangled and useless, crushed beyond hope. A second was pinned but serviceable, and the third-largest one appeared to be fine and started as soon as he turned the key. A feeling of jubilation filled the survivors. Hope replaced gloom.

Now only two miles away, the Russians stopped to rest and eat in the silent glistening white wilderness. Their sensitive equipment picked up the sound of the explosion that was insulated and dampened by the soft white surroundings. They shrugged it off to earthquake-settling aftershocks. But in case something had exploded in the area, the specialized commandos went on high alert. Expecting no one to be at the destroyed base, they did a weapons check. One hour later, they broke camp and zeroed in on the location of what they came to reconnoiter and steal.

At the remnants of the base, the survivors enlarged the opening in the old hangar and wrestled the snow machine through the jagged new entrance. Those inside packed all their provisions and prepared as best they could to begin their journey to the planned rendezvous point. Not wanting to use any fuel for the snowcat to go to the array, Luke and Munson donned their snowshoes and began a slow walk to the secret array. Suspecting nothing, Luke and the SEAL disappeared into the white armed only with the SEAL's sidearm and Luke's knife. The Russian group approaching from the opposite direction had enough firepower to hold off a small army.

Had they used a snow machine, the Russian commandos would have heard their approach, and Luke and the frogman would likely have been gunned down. Instead, the sharp ears of the Inuit picked up the sound of their counterparts just as the two crested the small ridge on the east side of the array where the controlling software was stored. The low drone of the approaching machines was now discernible. The first machine stopped, and two men got off to survey the area, one with binoculars. A scoped weapon slid off one's shoulder. The owner scanned right and left. Another snow machine pulled up close by. Its occupants looked to be using some type of GPS.

Luke and Munson froze and dropped into the snow behind the ridge. It did not take long for his companion to realize that the men they faced were not friendly and that they were not there to help them but to garner and take what they could from the secret array. The two had said very little while trudging through the deep powdery snow. At first, Luke thought that the cavalry had just arrived to rescue them all and rose to wave his arms and shout. Munson pulled him back to the ground and silenced him by covering his mouth. He whispered in a hushed voice barely audible over the ambient sounds of the wind, "Luke, those are not friendlies! From what I can tell, those are Russian special forces, and they are heavily armed. They are not here to help us." He heard Luke's audible gasp.

When more adversaries showed up, their only choice was to beat a hasty retreat before they were discovered. The new arrivals were highly trained killers on a mission and would show no mercy. Munson knew that much. Outnumbered and outgunned, the two men backed away, turned, and shuffled back toward the base as fast as conditions allowed. Munson clicked on his communicator and called Ybarra. "Bar, there are Russian special forces at the array. We are heading back. We have to boogie, now!"

"Roger that, Munson. We'll be ready by the time you get here." He wanted to say more but could tell from the edge in Munson's voice that the situation was serious. He clicked to the frequency that they used to talk to the *Longley* and tried to link up. "*Longley*, this is Ybarra. Do you read me?" No response. "*Longley*, come in over."

After a third try, his earpiece came to life, and Captain Brevard himself answered, "Go ahead Ybarra. What is your situation?"

"Captain, we have a problem. We are leaving as soon as Munson returns. Condition two scenario is an affirmative. I repeat, condition two is active. Boots on the ground at the array." Brevard had specific orders if the condition 2 scenario took place. Leave nothing if the top secret listening array was compromised in any way. His orders included the launch of a cruise missile to eradicate the array if his men could not destroy the nonessential parts and retrieve the critical pieces. Condition 1 was out of the question and condition 2 now in effect. He had to find the thinnest ice, break through, and launch one of his harshest nonnuclear weapons, and that would take him farther away from where he hoped to meet with his returning men and those stranded at AWRB 1.

His orders caused a bustle of activity throughout the ship while most of his crew were lounging.

"Maneuvering, find me the thinnest ice and prepare for breakthrough. Weapons Control, prepare tube three for immediate launch. Set target for the following coordinates. When we clear the surface and are on top, be ready to launch!" Brevard was sure that the *Longley*'s reinforced sail could break through the ice covering the sea above at its present position, but suffering any damage so far from assistance made it very dangerous.

Since the warming Southern currents switched their course from westerly, swirling toward the pole, to more easterly, the Arctic ice pack had returned. The heavy cloud cover and cooling associated with it after the Indo-Pakistani conflicts further exacerbated the problem. Now there was a plume of ash to deal with, and if the wind shifted again, the folks on the ground would have to deal with that too.

At the base, they were loaded and ready to depart by the time that Luke and Munson returned, sweating in their parkas in the bitter cold. They wasted no time warming the loaded machine and checking their bearings for the planned rendezvous point with the submarine. John chose to lead the way. He would walk ahead of the lumbering snow machine, looking for hidden dangers, probing with a long pole. He estimated that it would take at least a day and a half to reach their destination if all went well. He also clearly understood that fuel for their machines would run out before they got there. He and Ybarra found full extra cans of fuel in the collapsed hangar, but those would only lengthen the time before that too ran out. The machine would have to work extra hard to make any progress in the deep, loose snow.

Once the snow machine was clear of the sagging hangar, they strapped on the gas cans and attached their meager supplies to the outside. Except for loading those who would ride first and Carl to drive, they were ready to roll. Luke stopped in his tracks and looked around. He could not believe his eyes. Those outside working on the machine all became aware after seeing Luke hold up his arms. The snow coming down had turned from white to gray. The ash cloud from the active volcano was now drifting toward them.

The Russian soldiers scrambled over the snow-covered array, probing wherever their metal and electronics detectors signaled that something significant was located. They dug up the strange-looking buried equipment and cataloged everything. Photography was almost useless in the constant snow, but they photographed all they could in high resolution. Progress was slow, but they continued their work for hours, guards keeping a vigil for any unwanted activity.

The *Longley* moved to a new position. Brevard gave the order to surface, and the ballast tanks filled, adding the positive buoyancy needed to cause his multibillion-dollar megamachine to rise. Orders to close all watertight doors and brace for impact blared throughout his vessel. The breakthrough went as planned. "Open outer doors tube three and arm warhead." The tube-covering hatch swung open. "Launch on my command." Brevard opened his key holder and inserted the card it carried in the slot-marked launch. He typed in a brief code and sent it to the northern fleet command. The lights on the launch control panel turned green. He signaled the okay to his launch officer, who pushed the button for tube 3, and the missile engines roared to life. The ship rocked slightly, and the deadly bird cleared the ship in a blaze of fire and smoke. It streaked skyward, turned, and dropped to a terrain-skimming altitude, rocketing on its way to deliver its lethal blow.

On the ground, the surviving base staff and their rescuers heard the missile pass overhead before they were a mile from the former base. The Russian commando force never knew what hit them. The explosion directly in their midst destroyed them and their equipment in a blinding ball of fire, snow, and rock debris. There were no survivors. Their mission ended in an instant, and no record of it would ever be made.

After the launch, the *Longley* slipped silently beneath the ice and waves and set a new course to return to the most favorable position to enter a relatively narrow ice-free fjord where it was possible to pick up his men and those accompanying them. He planned to push the limits of his vessel and enter very dangerous water where he had little room to maneuver, but the *Longley* would not need to break through thick ice.

His frogmen could set charges to crack the ice from below if they had to get close enough. The main necessity was to shorten the distance that those ashore had to travel.

CHAPTER 23

THE RUSSIAN SUB

Captain Brevard had no idea that a Russian antisubmarine sub was close by, and the Russians did not know about the *Longley* until it launched the cruise missile. The Russians detected the launch and went to full-battle stations thinking that the missile was meant for them. By the time they determined its true direction, it disappeared, causing a panic among its crew. The missile delivered its deadly blow before the Russian captain could warm his doomed men at the array.

But now, the sub killer had the position of the American vessel, and his stealth technology gave him an incredible advantage over the American vessel. He could avenge the loss of his men and eliminate the enemy sub without being detected. He had the chance to deliver a blow to a menace to the motherland and make it look like the American ship had suffered a terrible accident.

The United States Navy, largest and most powerful of any maritime country, took great pride in tracking as many of the naval vessels of Russia as possible. The submarines were difficult to find and track, and Russian technology for muffling propulsion systems got better with each new sub that was launched or refitted. Satellite tracking was good, assisted by subsea tracking by sub killers, surface tracking, and ship-launched helicopters with magnetometers all helping keep track of most. Once under the thick ice, tracking was all but impossible. At present, all Russian subs at sea were accounted for except for one, commanded by Captain Alexis Petrovic.

Captain Brevard had earned his command of this powerful nuclear submarine because of his ability to calmly make the tough decisions he faced and because of his intelligence. He did not like the precarious position his vessel faced by being in shallow water with little room to maneuver. As a precaution, he had antisubmarine and countertorpedo measures loaded into the Landry's fore and aft tubes and kept his entire crew at battle stations. He felt trapped but secure that they were as safe as could be under the present circumstances. Brevard wanted to be safe in deep water, where speed, stealth, and all his weaponry would protect his sub from almost any threat.

Captain Petrovic was a proud, egotistical tyrant who hated the Americans with a passion. He came from a maritime family with a long list of sailors and officers dedicated to life at sea. He rose through the ranks like a rocket, helped by others in his family who preceded him. He was bold and decisive and followed orders without fail. After surviving a wreck and sinking of a surface ship, he decided to try underwater submarine life and found out it was the perfect fit for him. He demanded absolute loyalty from his crew and earned it.

His submarine was sleek and fast, but the Americans badgered him and played games with him at times, sneaking up undetected and then making him look foolish when they sped away. It was a cat and mouse game beneath the waves, one that he seldom won. It was all good for training his crew, but he was enraged by the fact that he seldom felt victorious. But today, he had a critical tactical advantage, one he could not help but use. He made no contact with his superiors, not wanting to do anything to give away his advantage. The American sub was a sitting duck waiting to die, no escape possible. He fought his own impulse to simply return to his planned course, but the possibility of hurting his enemy was just too much for him to ignore. Petrovic knew that it was an act of war, but he could not help thinking, *Who would ever know?*

Petrovic had four Mark 5 torpedoes loaded and armed, the deadliest ship-killing weapons ever developed by any country. These torpedoes could avoid obstacles in their path and home in on the titanium outer shell of the *Longley* with deadly effect. He smiled and cursed the enemy ship. He dreamed that he would be secretly honored and decorated for his decision by his superiors. He had no plan to pick up any survivors since he was sure that there would be none. The torpedo outer doors were opened. His second-in-command warned Petrovic that what he was doing could and would produce an international incident, maybe even start a war. Petrovic's look silenced him immediately. "Fire one and two!" were the captain's only words. The *whoosh* of air that signaled the release of the two fish was the only sound the crew heard. They were at nearly the maximum range of the torpedoes, but the high-speed killers picked up the target and closed the gap between the two war machines.

"High-speed propellers inbound!" The sonar officer on the *Longley* could not believe what he was hearing. "Torpedoes closing fast!"

Brevard wheeled around at his position on the bridge and asked for range. "Twenty-five hundred meters and closing fast. They have a lock on us!" There was excitement in his officer's voice but no panic.

Brevard felt a knot in his stomach but reacted with calm professionalism. "Fire all countermeasures and jam all frequencies. Fire torpedo tubes five and six back along the path those fish came from. If that bastard out there hits us, he is going to die too." All six forward tubes emptied, gently rocking the neutrally buoyant machine.

The first inbound torpedo was jammed by the countermeasures, lost its lock, and exploded harmlessly on contact with the rocky side of the inlet. The second suffered the same fate, in close proximity to the *Longley*, rocking the sub wildly but causing no damage.

Russian Captain Petrovic suspected that this might happen, so he fired the second pair of torpedoes soon after the first, knowing that the American sub would not have time to rearm. He then made a quick turn and dove deeper into the syrupy cold Arctic Sea. At flank speed, he wanted to escape fast in case the enemy ship fired back.

The Russian torpedoes were set for explosion on contact; the American ones for proximity detonation. Two passed so close to each other coming in opposite directions that the American warhead exploded, damaging and sending the Russian one to the bottom. That left one killer fish from each sub still on course to destroy each other.

Only one tube of countermeasures was loaded and ready when the last Russian torpedo was detected. "Captain, there is one more high-speed fish inbound, and it is very close." Brevard did not panic. With the push of two small joysticks on his console, the boat spun on its long axis.

Brevard ordered, "Ahead flank!" The entire crew felt the submarine lurch, roll several degrees, and pitch forward. The high-pitched sounds of the screws of the inbound torpedo were evident.

"Fire control, whatever is ready, fire now." The countermeasures had hardly cleared the tube when there was a horrendous explosion rocking the boat from end to end. The torpedo outer door was twisted and jammed, and the fore torpedo room began to flood. Two men in the torpedo room were thrown off their feet and seriously injured by the blast. Several other members of the crew were also injured but none hurt badly enough to require more than a quick trip to sick bay. There was very little serious damage to the *Longley*. "EVERYBODY, OUT OF THERE AND SEAL THE FORE TORPEDO ROOM!" Captain Brevard shouted. He knew that if there were more inbound fish, they were doomed, but no more came.

The Russian sub fired its countermeasures and also received minor damage when the last American torpedo tracked the sub but exploded too far away to sink it amid a swarm of metal chaff meant to lead it astray. The incident was over in only a few minutes. Captain Petrovic whistled a merry tune, and his men sang a military song to celebrate the destruction of the American sub. Captain Brevard, being a patient man, swore to himself that this was not over.

The flooded torpedo room was pumped out and cleaned. Divers were dispatched into the inky darkness of the polar sea to make necessary repairs to the torpedo hatch. Neither side made any immediate report of the incident. Brevard's sonar experts identified the telltale signature of Russian torpedo sounds, but the captain was already sure of who fired them at his vessel. He sent a report of the incident to fleet command, expecting them to order him to abandon the pickup of the survivors from the weather base and get to a safer location. There was no reason to point blame because the Russians would deny that it was them or that they knew anything about it.

Instead, fleet asked him to now use his own discretion about picking up the people from AWRB 1. They also informed him that the attack could only be the work of one submarine commanded by a dangerous rogue captain named Alexi Petrovic.

Fleet command began an analysis of what had taken place between the two submarines. The entire Navy was moved to a state of alert. Finding and tracking the suspect Russian boat became the highest priority. Destroying the array should have never been a reason to attack the *Longley*, even if the Russians somehow understood its more sinister purpose.

The collateral loss of Russian personnel at the site of the array was the Russians' fault, not theirs. What prompted a Russian captain to attack an American submarine on a mercy rescue mission became a matter of utmost concern. It was clearly an act of war. Unknown to the general public, tensions on both sides rose to a peak.

CHAPTER 24

THE FJORD

It was deep, very deep. The smooth sides were shaped and carved by the valley glacier at its head. The tidal bore current and twenty plus foot tidal change from low to high tide kept it open and free of ice except for bergs in midwinter. A magnificent arcuate wall of crystal-blue ice at its end marked the present location of the ice-water interface. Towering 400 feet or 120 meters above the sea, a large calve of ice could literally create a small tsunami in the narrow fjord. Combined with the strong currents and lack of maneuverable space in the narrow confines of the rocky walls, this could damage or even destroy his machine.

The captain knew it was the only open water nearby. If his men and the survivors of the snowslide could make it to this fjord, he had volunteers to go meet them and bring them back to shore. Brevard's only option was to maneuver the sub through the narrow winding fjord to where his maps and charts indicated that a rendezvous was possible. An ice-free side valley led down to the fjord. It provided a path the survivors could take to meet his landing party.

Once in the fjord, there would be few places to easily steer his vessel. The tides and strong bore, first in one direction, and then the reverse would be treacherous. It would take all his skill, that of his navigators and propulsion team, and every trained member of his crew to pull it off. If a rescue using his vessel was the only option for the foreseeable future, *We can do it*, Brevard thought.

He did have an amazing new feature on his submarine. The hull was equipped with stabilizing planes similar to those used on a cruise ship. They could be deployed to stabilize pitch and yaw and were expendable. The planes could also minimize an enemy hit by absorbing energy. In addition, the submarine had steering thrusters fore and aft with which the captain could make extreme and fast turns, literally turn the vessel on a dime. That feature he knew likely saved the *Longley* from the one Russian torpedo that had come so close.

Brevard made the final decision. Following renewed discussion after the Russian sub encounter, SUBCOM had said no way. They determined that it was too risky for the ship, captain, and crew. The *Longley* would be incommunicado with fleet command within the sheer fifteen-hundred-foot-high walls of the glacially carved canyon. Sonar and radar would paint the walls of the canyon with their rays and provide a near-perfect picture of his subsea path. Depth data would also be excellent as the sub's transponders gave instantaneous depth readings at three points on the keel of his sub and automatically calculated safest clearance of obstacles in their path. Charts accurately predicted the high and low tide times inside the fjord for the captain. He understood that the path ahead would be difficult for both the rescuers and those rescued.

When a glacier moves forward or backward over eons within its chosen path to the sea, it grinds and pulverizes the rock in its channel into fine silt. The resulting smooth U-shaped valley enlarges by direct carving by the crystalline ice and by erosion and collapse of its sides by weathering. Side valleys are common and drain upland areas through narrow, steep chasms cut into the fjord sides at right angles. When not frozen, these types of fjords create magnificent scenery with beautiful waterfalls of every imaginable shape and size cascading from many hanging valleys. But these side valleys also bring in landslides and boulders and any loose rock detritus broken off from their sides.

Above water, the fjord was relatively smooth sided. The mostly granite walls are hard stone and grooved deeply by rocks and boulders dragged and towed along inside the ice. Below water could be a different story altogether. The sides were still relatively smooth and would cause a bump or scrape but no real damage to his sub if they slid against one. It was the jagged bottom Brevard feared or was at least was very apprehensive about. In places, there were debris piles and huge boulders rafted by icebergs and dropped. There were old moraine piles and ridges, places marking other advances of the glacier. The mouths of those many side cannons would likely have debris fans, small deltaic cones of rock talus. All were potentially dangerous obstacles.

This glacier was sourced from an ice field over one hundred miles long. Barren lifeless mountain peaks in that area were the only rocky crags protruding from the glaciers and ice field. Its recent advance was fueled by more and more snow falling in those ice fields. The snow compresses and crystalizes over time. As depth increases with burial in the ice, it clarifies and begins to move. Absorbing all but blue wavelengths of daylight, the ice appears beautiful blue and clear where exposed. Pressure at its source created by additional ice and snow falling makes the solid ice move downhill, aided by gravity, on a long and timeless journey back to the sea.

Ice caves are often present. Inside one of these is where the iceman was found. Some of the people he was trying to bring out discovered that iceman. Brevard did not know failure, and it was never in his thought process. His ship and men depended on his tenacious attitude to always get the job done. They were a well-oiled killing machine, but purposes like this were what made his job so satisfying and why he captained the world's most advanced underwater vessel.

The glacier at its head had no name on the charts. The course was set for the entrance to the fjord. It was in the hands of his chief navigator and friend, Amos Redford, and his chief mate with him at the helm was another seasoned veteran of subsea missions. The die was cast, and Brevard could only sigh and secretly cross his fingers. The chaplain had led a prayer for their safe passage and for bringing back the missing crew and their survivors. To the captain, it rested in his own hands and that of the Almighty.

On land, things were no different for the two Navy frogmen, the Inuit guides, and survivors from a crash and the catastrophic snow—and ice slide. Their dash for survival would be miserable and arduous, trudging through deep drifts and crossing hazardous snowfields with dangerous pitfalls. The more barren rocky places would be a welcome respite even with the swirling snow. There were enough snowshoes to equip everyone and ski poles for balance and assistance.

Luke, Wayne, and John were surprised by the SEAL's insistence that they leave immediately after the two Navy men contacted the submarine. Wales and Bob had the snow machine ready and all the extra fuel bungeed to the side. It seated as many as four and the driver with minimum comfort. Between digging and strapping things onto the snow machine, they were tired. Brad was busy keeping the near-madman Joe Stewart occupied inside the cliffside and out of the way. Relieved by Bob, Brad had fresh muscles to help complete the preparations to leave. They planned to take turns riding in the snow machine where they could also warm themselves.

The group making the final trek for survival were Becky and Wayne, Luke and John, the two Inuit guides, Brad and Wales and Dr. Hoffman from the crashed helicopter, Munson and Ybarra, the Navy SEALs, Bob and Carl, and a crazed Joe Stewart. Left behind in death were Jamo and Charise, who survived the hellish snowslide onslaught, only to succumb later. Pilots Mitch and Francois and scientists Blake Edwards and Richard Hall died during the base destruction. No trace of them was ever found.

Captain Wales, Brad, and Doc Hoffman were eager to do something besides shiver and keep Joe Stewart from causing any damage to their frail situation or to himself. They came up with the idea of lashing the dogsleds together and to tow them behind the snowcat as far as possible. There were twelve humans fighting to survive, and only six could ride in the snowcat packed in tight. The driver needed room to steer and avoid obstacles. Their meager supplies and any extra materials they needed for heat had to be strapped to the sides or carried in the sleds. Becky was the only female, but she planned to carry her weight and told everyone else that she wanted no privileges.

Two of the group took positions to ride the tandem dogsleds towed behind: Luke because of his experience and Becky because she had done it before. She and Luke were riding like they were mushing a team of husky sled dogs. They could use the brakes on the sleds to stop forward momentum if the snow machine lurched to a quick stop.

John and Munson took point and planned to walk ahead of the snow machine using probes where the surface conditions were in question. Carl was their driver. He loved driving the snow machine, but this time, his and their lives depended on his skill. He was secretly very glad that they would be moving slowly. Inside the cab with him initially were Bob, Doc Hoffman, Ybarra keeping a close eye on Joe Stewart, and Brad charged with keeping the window clear. Captain Wales and Wayne decided they were starting afoot.

Munson tried several times to raise the submarine, to no avail. All that he heard were static and a few words at one point, but it was garbled. The ambient weather was not too bad. The normally menacing winds were still swirling snow but were at least below-gale force. John studied what he could of the weather—signs, wind direction, present conditions—while Munson tried to get through to the *Longley*. On the last try, he realized his simple message that they were moving somehow got through. He heard the brief "On our way to rendezvous" in the captain's voice followed by "God bless and Godspeed."

CHAPTER 25

ESCAPE DAY 1

Munson looked at his chronograph to see the time and pressure information that it recorded. He and John talked, comparing their weather info, both realizing that they were on the back side of a serious low-pressure system that was slowly sliding eastward. Conditions were already improving by degree, but still not great for starting their trek over the lowest pass in the ridge separating their disastrous fjord from the rendezvous point to the west.

The path was level for the first section, but the snow was deep. Beyond that, the grade rose steadily with conditions in the low pass, unknown. Beyond that, in turn, it was downhill all the way to the fjord with a difficult descent from the side valley, finishing a tough route. John just shook his head and uttered an old Inuit prayer for guidance to the powers above. He and Munson gave each other a final 'thumbs up,' pulled their parkas tight to their goggles, and plunged ahead on the bearing they planned.

The artic snow machine groaned to life, and the wide treads dug into the powdery white and creaked ahead. If it dug in too much, two more passengers were going to walk. Carl moved forward, checking the snow depth, watching each cleat as it made its turn back under the cat. No one looked back. The bodies of Jamo and Charise were wrapped in several layers of plastic and left in the collapsed hangar. Doc Hoffman had said a few words about her valiant struggle and led the group in the Lord's Prayer. They had no time for anything else. Everyone knew that they might be the next to freeze to death or succumb some other way to the merciless Arctic environment.

When the dogsled tandem jerked forward, Luke and Becky hung on and let out a whoop. It eased the tension of leaving the partial shelter that they still had cliffside. The rocky outline of the base disappeared into the gray falling snow behind them. The generator was shut down, the light turned off, and the upper door wedged back in the closed position. Without clearing, everything would soon be blanketed, and only soft mounds of snow would mark the base.

The first issues appeared only forty-five minutes into their foray. When Brad and Ybarra threatened to hog-tie Joe Stewart, he calmed down and just sat whimpering. "Are you going to behave? Just take it easy. We're all going home." Doc talked to him and kept it simple.

The fact that Joe responded by nodding yes gave him hope. They jammed him against one side in the rear row of seats, preventing him from the incessant rocking that filled his time cliffside. Dr. Hoffman was almost certain that he was now getting close to being completely mad. He feared that any new or additional trauma on their journey might push him over the edge. Joe was fine in every way except his mind, which was temporarily a mess. He was strong and fit and would be difficult to handle if he went into fits.

Hoffman was snapped out his reverie by Joe, who began coughing and gasping. He screamed, "YOU ARE ALL SUFFOCATING ME. I CAN'T BREATHE!" It was already stuffy in the cab, they all acknowledged that fact, but the warmth was wonderful. The meager heater kept them comfortable, while the outside temperature dropped, and the wind picked up.

Brad cracked a side window and held Joe's face close to it. The cold air calmed Joe, and he settled back into the seat satisfied. Doc leaned close to him and spoke into Joe's ear. "You just talked and are doing fine, Joe. We all have to pull together. You can do it. Just hang in there. We may need you. You're doing okay." He squeezed Joe's gloved hand, and Joe responded with a meek smile and eye-to-eye contact. The doctor let out a big sigh; that was a major step in the right direction. Ybarra did not miss any of the entire episode. He winked at the doctor and turned his eyes back to the windshield and the terrain ahead.

The group moved on at a steady rate for over two hours, covering a good distance. The first stop was a pee break for Becky and Carl. Relieved, Carl returned to the snowcat with Becky in tow. "She's freezing!" he yelled through the window. Brad climbed out to take her place, while she clambered into the welcome warmth. Brad checked with Luke when he took his position on the sled.

Luke gave him a few pointers. "Watch what I do. It's pretty easy while we are being towed at low speed. Hang on tight on the bumps and be ready to bail if the cat has trouble." That was the total of Brad's lesson.

"You still warm enough? Brad asked.

"Yes, I can handle it just fine. Button up because it looks like we are about to get going again. Don't want you to fall off and look stupid. Nobody is looking back. You fall off, I gotta run up there and stop them. Don't want to have to do that." Luke pulled his parka tighter.

"Roger that one, Luke. If I fall off, leave my sorry ass behind."

"No can do," Luke responded. "We don't make that pickup and get stuck out here. We may have to eat you."

Brad laughed. He pulled his parka tight and muttered a muffled, "Definitely leave my ass behind." Luke never heard it.

Day 1 passed without major problems. They set up a rotation to take turns inside the snowcat for warming and to ingest calories. Each received a small ration of food brought by the SEALs supplemented with the raw shellfish procured by the Inuits. They sang songs within the machine to keep their spirits up. Joe even mumbled a few words to one before falling back into a trancelike sleep.

When John gave up his position at point and climbed stiffly into the cab, Carl asked him if the snow was getting heavier or if his eyes were playing tricks on him. "No tricks." John's voice was unsteady while he shuddered and shivered to get warm. "The weather is getting worse again. The wind has shifted, and the clouds are even thicker. We go on one more hour, and then we stop to rest." No one uttered a sound. No one wanted to stop. "The machine needs a rest, and Carl is a better driver than Wayne." No one questioned John's authority.

Luke was dozing on his sled. He needed a few minutes in the snowcat to warm. Ybarra was riding shotgun with him on the other sled. It happened so fast that Luke had almost no chance to react. The giant white monster charged the two men clinging to their sleds. An eight-hundred-pound bear appeared from the blowing snow and nearly got to Luke before Ybarra screamed. Luke dove from the sled as a huge paw swiped at him. Ybarra stood there shouting like a madman, waving his arms. He was now bear bait.

Luke rolled, scrambled for the cover of the sled, and pulled his rifle from the case tied atop the tarp in one fluid motion. Having lost his goggles, he was partially blinded by the snow in his face. He chambered around and fired blindly in the direction of the beast.

The loud report scared the creature, and it ran away, stopping only yards away to grunt in frustration before disappearing into the frigid white. The bears that could not get to seal or whale breathing holes were starving, and humans were now prey. The snowcat lurched to a halt, and John sprang from the vehicle. Before him, he counted two, no, three, no, four hulking figures skulking nearby. They were sniffing the snow-filled air and pacing, standing on two legs, nostrils flaring.

He heard a second shot and watched the bears disperse. As brave as SEALs were known to be, Ybarra almost wet himself. He and Luke joined John and now Munson beside the machine. Munson had his pistol drawn, but it was no match for a full-grown polar bear. Brad was taking his turn walking outside with Becky at the time the bears showed up. She gulped at the thought of another bear encounter. The one in the ice cave had resulted in a close escape and two serious injuries. Luke and John conversed in Inuit for a minute. One bear was serious; four adults together seemingly hunting as a pack was unprecedented.

"The weather is not cooperating, and we need to hunker down pretty soon. The bears are a serious threat, so, everyone, stay alert and look around at all times. They can attack with great speed, and we have only three weapons, two of which will do little good but to make noise. We are almost to the foot of the pass through to the other fjord and have made good time. I think we should go on for two more hours with caution and stick as close together as possible.

The snow is getting deeper and less stable. We can't afford to overwork the overloaded machine."

John repeated the message to those inside through a partially opened side window. Joe Stewart's eyes were red with fear. He had lost his nerve again and was looking about with nervous trepidation. Doc was inside again and tried to steady him. Joe pulled away, curling into a ball in the corner.

When they came to a deep crevasse directly in their path, Munson and John returned to the machine and told the others that this would be their rest stop. Those cramped in the cab needed to stretch again. Luke and Ybarra walked a short perimeter to look for bears but saw nothing but white. Luke planned to kill one of the bears with his next shot to leave its carcass to be cannibalized by the other hungry bears. It could also provide meat to further add to their foodstuffs.

Luke looked around and realized John's idea. The crevasse would block the approach to their encampment from one direction. They could park the snowcat and use it for protection from the wind and allow them to build a quick shelter against the leeward side. Two would sleep inside: driver Carl because of his age and Becky in the back seat. Bob stayed inside too because his injured foot made it impossible to walk in the deep snow. Spreading and anchoring a tarp and attaching it to the cat provided an inclined roof. Snow block walls were built at each end, and additional blocks were placed against the windward side to provide a minimal shelter. Wayne prayed that it would work, knowing it had to suffice.

Luke volunteered for first duty as a lookout atop the snowcat. The bears scared him, but he was determined to face down the next one rather than run. He took a seated position, cleaned his goggles, and hunkered down for some serious discomfort. Luke checked the weapon, removing any ice buildup. He thought of the great hunter Anook, who faced the great bears alone, without a rifle. He thought about his parents and friends from his village. He gritted his teeth and made himself as comfortable as possible.

Most of the rest of the party had considerable trouble trying to get comfortable and to get some rest. They huddled together as close as possible to conserve heat. No one could sleep. A couple of hours went by when Munson relieved Luke. Munson was sure that he spotted a bear as soon as he settled onto the top of the cat. Senses on high alert, he scanned in all directions, but darkness made it impossible to make anything out for sure.

Shortly before John planned to get everyone moving again, Joe Stewart exited the tented, letting all the slightly warmer air escape. He needed to relieve himself. Munson warned him to stay close, but he ignored the warning and ventured a few more feet into the darkness.

The roar of a nearby bear brought them all to their feet. Joe Stewart came running, but he had not pulled his pants and leggings all the way up. He stumbled and thrashed through the deep snow with terror in his eyes, slipping and sliding. Munson raised his rifle and fired shots at a charging bear. He wasn't sure if he scored a hit, but the bear was on Stewart in seconds. He screamed a bloodcurdling scream of agony as the bear's jaws closed on his torso. The animal flung him in the air, picked up his bleeding body, and dashed away with him into the increasing morning light.

He was gone in an instant. Luke gave chase with Munson's nine-millimeter automatic pistol, but John tackled him only steps away. He shouted in frustration and cursed the bears. There were two blood trails leading away into the snow. Munson had hit the polar bear, but the starving beast prevailed. There was no sense in going after Joe. By now he was dead and would soon be torn to pieces and consumed. The bear danger was over for now, and another life ended by the unforgiving Arctic wilderness.

No one knew what to say. Doc Hoffman wept, consoled by Becky, who wiped freezing tears from both of their cheeks. Day 1 had ended with more tragedy. They were in deep shock, hearts rendered, and could only wonder who was next.

CHAPTER 26

THE SECOND DAY A SOMBER START

The surviving eleven broke camp and began their second day contemplating their fates. No one could eat even though they all needed the sustenance. They started the second day exactly how they started the first, minus one sick young man. His death hit them all hard. Luke spent considerable time sharpening his hunting knife. Munson and Ybarra did too. Wales cleaned the rifle and carried it over his shoulder facing down to keep snow out of the muzzle while walking beside the struggling machine. They had to go almost a mile out of their way to eventually cross the large rocky crevasse.

Once on the other side, the ground began a perceptible rise. The Arctic cat bogged down several times. They refueled it and realized that almost half of their fuel supply was already expended. Loaded down and pushing through the slippery snow consumed fuel at a higher rate than they expected. They needed enough to reach the summit of the low pass. It was still a four-hundred-meter relatively steep climb in very difficult conditions. They found the entrance to the valley and began the ascent.

Everyone walked except Carl, who skillfully piloted the cat around boulders and drop-offs. It nearly slipped sideways over the edge of a steep ravine hidden by drifts, but he forced the machine to cooperate, and it edged along until safely on stable rocky ground swept clear of snow by the now howling winds. The valley was a wind tunnel focusing the currents and doubling its ferocity.

After climbing at a steady rate for two hours, everyone was chilled to the bone. They stopped and used the snowcat as a warming hut, taking turns to remove some of the chill. Luke and Munson scouted ahead and were the last to warm themselves. They returned with bad news. The summit was not far ahead, but the path was blocked by deep drifts and heavy rock detritus. Great boulders, glacial erratics from a warmer time, littered the canyon floor. John broke the news gently while they all gathered for the final assault.

He began, "There is no way that the snowcat will fit through where we have been. It can make it three-quarters of the way, but from there on, we will have to leave it behind. We will transfer what we can to the sleds and make up teams to haul them to the top and over. That means we again take turns warming and riding until we can do it no more."

Munson agreed with John's assessment and added a few comments about the fact that the steepness was not too bad. That was fine for everyone but Bob, whose foot was swollen again. They took his foot out of his boot and, just short of frostbite, chilled it in the snow so it would fit back in. He insisted that he would make it, but they all knew that there was no way he could.

"Bob, you will ride in one of the sleds. The decision is made when it comes to it, so don't argue." Wayne was adamant, and everyone concurred. Doc removed Bob's sock and examined the injured foot before easing it back into his unlaced boot. He agreed that Bob could not walk and had to ride. He did not want anyone to know that if Bob survived, his foot likely would not.

Brad was limping noticeably when he returned for his warming time in the cab. Dr. Hoffman insisted on checking his feet and discovered what he expected: frostbite. Brad would have extra warming time or lose some toes. It was that simple. Warm up or not be able to walk at all very soon.

Luke and Becky rode the sleds now tied farther behind the slipping machine at a safer distance. Bob was tucked in with supplies in one. Heads down and single file behind the sleds, the other seven shuffled their snowshoes in stride with a hand on the shoulder of the person ahead. Munson led with the scoped rifle with John at the rear. It was up to Carl now to lead the way in the struggling machine. The fumes behind the machine were strong, but the exhaust was at least warm.

On one steep part of the climb with ice and barren rock showing, the snowcat began to slip backward. Carl applied the brakes to both treads, but they were losing any grip. Luke and Becky rushed to unclip the ropes from the sleds and pull them to the sides. Munson rushed to help Becky first, and Ybarra assisted Luke.

"Get out of the way. Move, fast!" Wayne shouted. The vehicle was sliding backward and picking up momentum. Carl was fighting for control but stopped the tracks in case someone got too close. Any of the survivors crushed beneath the heavy rubber treads was not something he wanted to see. All eyes turned to Carl's face in the frosted window. He looked scared for the first time. He managed the machine in some tight and difficult places, but this time, he had no control.

They had transitioned into an area where ice was pervasive. It was only a short distance ahead where Munson and John had turned back. John recognized the change underfoot as soon as they arrived there. He was about to caution Carl when the snowcat began to lose traction. Munson rushed over and hopped onto the moving machine, opening the door, and shouted at Carl, "Get out. Jump for it!" Carl ignored him. He was looking out at the side mirror through an open window. Snow was blowing in. Carl was breathing fast, and with each breath, a cloud of steam blurred his vision.

Munson was about to reach in and yank him out when Carl applied full throttle to the left tread and full back on the right. The machine skidded in a tight turn and spun to a stop on a slight uphill-facing bank. Carl's maneuver was timed perfectly. The snow machine coughed and belched smoke, and the left tread snapped in two. He had saved the machine from destruction, but it was not going any farther. Carl became despondent that he had broken the tread with no way to repair it under the present conditions.

Gathering around the snowcat, everyone rushed to see if Carl was okay. "I'm fine," he said, sweat dripping from his chilling face. Several pats on the back later, he donned his woolen hat and joined the others for a brief powwow beside the wounded machine.

John spoke first. "This is about where Munson and I turned back. From here to where we found the spot where the snowcat would not fit through is probably only a hundred yards. We would have had to abandon it there anyway. I say we stay here to eat and rest and use the cat for one more round of warming. The engine runs. We still have a little fuel. Let's make the best of it before we push on." Heads nodded in agreement.

They all knew the drill. Bob was transferred from the sled to the cab, and Dr. Hoffman joined him there along with Brad and Becky. Carl insisted on staying outside and helping pitch their shelter. He claimed that he needed some fresh air. It was fresh but very cold, and snow was lashing hard against any exposed skin on their faces.

They were in a narrow part of the canyon. When they first arrived there, the wind battered their parkas with blasts of hard-driven snow and ice crystals. Luke noticed it first. In this area of the Arctic, it was common to have multiple layers of wispy clouds between storms, blanketing the coast in moisture-laden fog. Between the layers, there often appeared more quiescent layers of misty but mostly clear air. They found themselves in one of those.

The wind died to a gentle breeze. The snow stopped. The air twinkled with tiny ice crystals. A veritable calm settled over the camp. Faces poked out of parkas, eyes agape. Smiles appeared in near disbelief. They spoke and were actually heard without shouting.

"Let's get this done," Munson interrupted their reverie. It could change back in minutes. Luke and John understood this better than the others. Munson was right. They returned to the task at hand, but spirits were raised. The four in the snowcat opened the side window to see for themselves. Warmer air escaped for a few moments, but no one cared.

Their luck held. The wind and bad weather abated for several hours. They feasted on a healthy portion of their remaining food supply. Over the top was rescue, or at least the chance. They needed the calories for the final climb. Ybarra knew well that the downward descent could be very tough even with snowshoes and cleats. Tomorrow was not going to be easy, but if all went well, the goal was to reach the fjord where the *Longley* would hopefully be waiting.

CHAPTER 27

DAY 3

By the time, they ate, and all took turns warming and getting some badly needed rest; full darkness had descended. The upper cloud layer parted, and a starry sky appeared. The aurora borealis shimmered with beautiful greens in waves of vivid hue from cloud to cloud. Hyperexcited oxygen atoms painted an unforgettable picture across the sky, moving like a living creature.

Awake, outside the tent, and stretching was Luke. His upbringing told him that this was a good omen. He searched the small area of exposed stars for ones he recognized, but the aurora was too bright. He woke John and told him what was happening, but John was exhausted and buried in his warm gear. He acknowledged with a grunt and closed his eyes. Wayne stuck his head out and just stared, never uttering a sound. Becky was looking out from the steamed cat window. She smiled and blew him a kiss. It was over in minutes. The opening in the clouds disappeared, and blackness returned.

It took little time to break camp. Before they finished, the inclement weather moved back in. There were no cloud layers, just the bleak white of blowing snow and the intense cold that returned with it. The abandoned cat was switched off and closed up. Bob was eased into one of the sleds; the other had what was left of supplies, and a second rider with hurting feet, Brad, was added.

Brad's feet warmed when it was his turn in the snowcat. He pulled off his boots and peeled off two layers of thermal socks. He put one foot at a time on the heater outlet. Circulation returned to his almost frozen feet after both warmed enough to rub gently. Needles of pain and tingling replaced the deadened nothing. They gave him extra time. When he emerged from the cab, he stepped gingerly but with confidence. "No way I'm riding. While I can walk, I walk."

They formed two teams of four to pull the sleds. Luke took point this time. It was glare ice ahead but not steep. No more soft snow to plod through. They did not have enough ice cleats to clamp onto everyone's boots. Brad walked by himself with the help of two poles for support and balance. The going got tough. It was relatively flat with a slow rise for several hundred yards. They moved at a steady pace. But then the ground rose into a rocky crag, perhaps the jagged remnant of the cirque at the head of an extinct glacier that once occupied this valley.

Dragging both sleds up the steep embankment looked futile to Munson. Luke stopped at the bottom of the steep spot. He was looking up for the best climbing spot when the rest caught up. Bob said, "Whew, that looks tough." Brad, not too far behind, showed up looking very nervous when he lowered his goggles.

John and Wayne breathed heavily, emitting wisps of steam from the strenuous task of getting Bob and his sled this far. Luke was about to start climbing when Munson grabbed him by the shoulder. "My job, I'm going. I'm an expert rock climber, and I have cleats. Get me the rope from the one sled I suggest that we leave behind. All of it and a carabiner." He waited while Wayne undid all the tie points, freed a long length of rope, and brought it to him.

With the rope coiled over his shoulder, Munson scrambled up the rock face like a mountain goat. Luke was impressed. He disappeared over the edge kicking a large piece of icy snow off that edge. It cascaded down on to those waiting below. He returned shouting, "WE ARE THERE! THIS IS THE TOP! IT'S NOT TWENTY PACES TO WHERE IT STARTS TO GO DOWN."

He dropped the rope to Luke after securing it with two loops around a large exposed rock. Luke tugged twice and began to climb with its assistance. Once he was at the top, they tied a climber's loop in the end and lowered it down so each could in turn climb to the top, pulled steadily by Munson and Luke. Lashed into the sled with John last in line to steady its ascent, they pulled the sled with Bob up the face of the short cliff. It was blustery and extra cold at this summit point. Bob needed to be moved to a more sheltered location.

With everyone safely on top and one sled, they wasted no time moving toward the downward-sloping area ahead. Going down this side was even more difficult than ascending. They slipped and slid everywhere on the glassy surface of ice coating everything. Becky landed on her butt twice with Wayne struggling just to stay upright. He could not help her, but she refused assistance anyway.

After two hours, all hell broke loose. A furious wind whipped up the canyon. Their progress came to an immediate halt. John spotted a small opening not completely filled between several large rounded boulders. "There." He pointed. Crowding around the sled, they huddled together while the howling wind whistled. "We hunker down and ride it out for a while," John added. "We can't go on in this. If it doesn't get better pretty soon, I'll go on alone to scout ahead."

"Not alone," Munson added, and then silence fell over the group. Shivering was palpable. After no more than thirty minutes, the storms weakened, and they started moving again. Leaving the rudimentary shelter scared everyone. It looked bleak ahead. They picked up their pace when the loose snow appeared again instead of ice underfoot.

No more than a mile beyond that first sheltered spot, they needed another. The wind picked up again, and the snow came at them at a right angle to the ground. Digging into the side of a snowbank was their only option. Again, ten people hunkered down. One did not. John continued on ahead by himself. An unwise decision, he knew, but he had to see what they faced ahead. In silence together, as close as possible to conserve any heat, no one missed him.

John struggled against the wind going on for another two hundred yards to where he almost fell over a precipice. It was a place where in warmer times a waterfall fell from the cliff to a box canyon below. He could not see the bottom in the swirling snow. He searched for a rock to drop over, but there were no loose ones around. "S<small>HIT</small>!" he yelled into the screaming wind. He turned to head back to the others, muttering a curse in Inuit at first, but then he prayed for a little luck. Their time was running out. He knew that.

By the time John returned to the group, they had discovered that he was not there. Luke was angry, Munson too. The weather eased up again, and whipping snow was replaced by more gentle flurries. They all trekked on to the new cliff edge and peered over. John found a small rock on the way and tied it securely to the end of the one-hundred-foot length of rope. He tossed it over the edge, and it did not hit a solid bottom. He hauled it back up and tried several other places along the drop-off. On the last attempt, it landed on something solid. He only had a few feet to spare, so the closest bottom was over ninety feet down.

Bob got out of the sled and started untying their last sections of rope from it. Brad and Becky helped him. With the sled disassembled, they now had another one-hundred-foot length. Munson volunteered to go over and climb down while the strongest held the loose end like a tug-of-war team, and was about to, when they all saw another dark cloud and felt the wind increase once more.

The new gust of wind hit the sled, and it started sliding toward the precipice, knocking Bob off his one good foot. Munson was closest to the edge. He lunged and half dove into its path, stopping it just short of going over. From his unzipped pocket, his communicator fell and disappeared into the white below before he could grasp it. There was nothing he could do. He hoped that Ybarra's was still working, which it was, but the low battery indicator on Ybarra's was flashing.

CHAPTER 28

ABOARD THE *LONGLEY*

Inside the fjord, the nuclear sub moved at a snail's pace. Around every bend, the subsurface terrain changed again. Captain Brevard altered course and direction often, barking commands in rapid succession. The navigation system was close to overload with so many conflicting returns bombarding their sensors. The signals ricocheted in every direction when below water.

He blew the ballast tanks and ran on the surface when the ice broke up in the channel. It was too bitter cold outside to man the conning tower on the sail, so he ran with two periscopes, looking fore and aft. The tide was moving them along still inward bound. He wanted to get far in before he had to fight the bore on the descending tide.

Progress was slow but sure. Icebergs were everywhere in the fjord. The ship performed flawlessly. The crew remained glued to their posts and duties. All information passed through the con loudspeakers throughout the ship. Brevard preferred it that way. He never held any secrets from his crew.

"Captain, problem ahead." The chief navigator studied his screens, and Brevard crouched at his side. "Wow, that's going to be tight. What do you think, Captain?"

"There is a big berg stuck on the right side too. That doesn't leave us any room to spare. I will use the thrusters if we have to make any moves to avoid that berg." Captain Brevard stood and picked up the small console with two red joysticks used to operate the thrusters. "All ahead dead slow!" The giant submersible crept forward.

Brevard looked at the data streams and clearance calculations. An obvious landslide fan protruded from one side of the narrow gorge and was piled up above the water surface on the other side too. "We can make it on the surface if the current holds." He looked at the tidal chart for lowest tide. If they returned at low tide, he could see that, based on water depth below the keel, they would not safely clear it.

Passing over the debris fan, the channel narrowed with one side much deeper. The captain avoided the iceberg by swinging the stern of the sub and increasing speed. The port side was too close to the smoothed rock, nearly vertical, side of the fjord. The loud scraping sound reverberated throughout the sub. It groaned and creaked, but no damage other than superficial was done to the submarine.

They were over halfway to the planned pickup point. The water deepened again. Ice was building up on the hull on the surface, so while they had adequate depth, they proceeded submerged. Ice on the periscope was eliminated by a defrosting element, so they had a clear vision of their surroundings, but everything was white. The surface storm was intensifying. The barometer readings taken when on the surface were dropping.

Brevard asked his highest-ranking SEAL on board to meet him on the bridge. His name was Jacob Barnes, a young iron-jawed muscular Texan who grew up hundreds of miles from the sea but fell in love with the ocean the first time he saw it as a child. His dark complexion shined with sweat, having been summoned from a workout. He wiped his brow and stood at attention. They called him Barney since it fit with his name, and he grew up in one. "Barney, we are almost there. Is your team ready? It's colder than a well digger's ass out there. How many are you taking?"

Barney answered with confidence. "Four of us are going, sir, all volunteers, all know the risk. You call it, and we are into the rafts and heading for those people. Hell, excuse me, sir, Munson is my best friend, and his butt is freezing out there in the middle of absolute wilderness in the worst weather you can imagine. I can't wait to jump into it with him. Don't worry, sir. We'll be fine, and we will bring those folks back. At least nobody will be shooting at us this time.

"I'm taking Gonzales. I think she's a little sweet on Ybarra, and she's one hell of a climber. She grew up in the mountains and likes it cold. At cold survival school, she stayed in her T-shirt when we finally got heavy coats. She's tough and sees in snow conditions better than anyone."

Brevard answered with a smile and a crisp salute. "Go get them Barney. We will be here to pick you up, waiting and ready with hot biscuits and coffee."

"I'll take a T-bone and a dozen eggs, sir." With that, Barney saluted and spun in a crisp half circle, exiting the bridge. Brevard went back to checking their progress on the digital maps and multiscreen presentations on his main command console.

For over three more hours, they made slow but steady progress toward the pickup point. Slowing to keep a safe distance from multiple icebergs, the smaller ones clunking and bouncing off the titanium hull, they submerged and ran just below the surface.

He saw it on the periscope screen at the same time his chief navigator turned to face him. Coming around a sharp bend, in the sub's path, stood what resembled a dam spanning the valley just below the waterline. The tide started to fall, and the tops of obvious large rocks on the crest of the ridge protruded from beneath the blowing waves.

"We're screwed, sir. We're not getting by or over that." The helmsman was right. This was the proverbial end of the line. Not on the incomplete charts, the hidden barrier of moraine debris was just the kind that wrecked many an early sailing vessel. Brevard ordered all stop. The sub glided closer and settled neutrally buoyant just below the surface less than two hundred feet from the earthen dam. The behemoth could go no farther. Brevard shook his head. The helmsman shrugged his shoulders. The new SEAL rescue team had to fast-boat the rest of the way to the rendezvous point. There was no other way.

Conditions topside were deplorable. Brevard could only imagine the plight of the surface survivors and did not want to put more men at risk. But that was his job.

"Captain here, surface and deploy the two fast boats. Rescue party, prepare to disembark in fifteen. Take your long johns. We calculate that running on one motor at half speed, you have one hour and forty-five minutes to the valley entrance rendezvous point. Check in often. Good hunting."

The team going ashore consisted of two crewmen to each fast boat. That provided space to bring back multiple passengers. The lightweight but structurally strong Zodiac-type boats were propelled by twin redundant high-speed rechargeable electric motors. To conserve charge, and in the event that a motor was damaged by hitting floating ice, only one motor would be used at a time. The front person in the raft aimed a searchlight, while the other steered.

With his team on the way, Brevard tried the communications channel again. He tried Munson's unit, but nothing happened. He tried Ybarra's and two backup channels: nothing. Ybarra had turned off his radio to conserve the dwindling battery. The captain had no way to know; instead, he expected that he would be able to reach his men ashore. Both sides were in the dark.

CHAPTER 29

CONTACT

The fast boats were coated with a special treated fabric so that snow and ice would not stick to them. At top speed, the craft skimmed the surface of the water. At slower speeds, they glided without wallowing in any way. Going ashore by stealth, the SEALs often clung to handles on the side to have the minimum profile. Under the present frigid conditions, the two-person teams were lying low in the boats, peering over the front and sides. Snow and ice crystals stung open skin, but with their thick wet suits and goggles, they had good protection from the elements.

The lead boat bounced off one low-profile miniberg hidden by the blowing waves even with the water surface. Barney tried to avoid it and swerved hard as he made contact. Gonzales went airborne. Her firm grip was the only thing that kept her from flying out. The prop of motor 1 hit the car-size chunk of submerged ice, making a loud clank sound. Its protective slotted cover was ripped off, but the blades continued to spin at normal speed.

Boat 2 avoided the potential hazard and took the lead. "Crap, I never saw it!" Barney was mad that he made the mistake.

Gonzales interrupted him. "My fault, Barney. I had the light aimed at the rock wall to see how far we were from it."

"I was going too fast, didn't have time to react." A wave of brackish freezing water broke over the side of the boat, leaving a salty taste in his mouth. Conversation over, they put it behind them in mind and situation and sped on toward the goal ahead.

The next hour and a half seemed like a week. Their thermal undergarments and cold-water suits provided a modicum of help staying warm, but that heat was pulled away by the bitter cold air, wind, and water. Trained for extreme environments, everyone reached their limit against cold at some point. They had extra layers and parkas in the dry bags, hand and foot chemical heaters, and heat packs for onshore use, but they were no help on the way.

Barney checked his watch GPS often. When he slowed the boat, the other one eased to a stop, and he let them glide alongside. They were at the right coordinates. Gonzales swung her light to the right. The beam from the other boat joined hers. Tracking back and forth, Barney spotted the low-sloping convex shape of the break in the smoothed walls of the fjord. They surveyed the shore and entire area, hoping to see waving arms. There were none. No lights, no sounds, only dark silhouettes of rocks and drifts of blowing snow.

"This must be it. We land there." Barney pointed to a shallow place where the boats could easily be pulled from the water. He noted the high-tide mark twenty feet up the rock face, marked by a change in color like a bathtub ring. "We'll have to pull the boats above that high-tide mark." One at a time, they landed and pulled the two craft to a safe distance above the changing water-rock interface.

"First we change into land gear and warm up." That meant getting out of the cold-water suits and into dry gear over their thermals. The men all used chemical heaters to warm themselves. When offered one or two, Gonzales said, "Save them for the folks we are here to take home."

She donned her snowshoes and was the first ready to move out. Gonzales told the others that she was going to look around, reconnoiter a bit. She switched her high-intensity light from lantern mode to flashlight mode and strode off into the falling snow.

"She's got to pee," one of the two SEALs from the other boat suggested.

"Nope, she's not that shy," Barney added.

"She is making us look bad. Let's move," the last SEAL implored. Geared up, the three men switched on all lights and followed in her tracks.

Gonzales was not far ahead. They could see her light though the near-blinding snowfall. She stopped and waited for them to catch up. "If they came through here, I haven't seen any kind of tracks, nothing disturbed, but this wind would cover anything in no time anyway."

Barney decided to contact the submarine before they ventured very deep into this side chasm. The sheer rock walls could eradicate any signal from their handheld communication equipment and headsets. The captain acknowledged in seconds. "We are ashore at the rendezvous point and starting up the valley. No sign of anyone or anything so far. We may lose signal in here but will check back in sixty."

"Roger that, Barney," the captain came back. "Good luck!" he added.

Their path steepened within a quarter mile of the water exit. There were signs of small recent avalanches all along their route. In several places, they were forced to smash their way through drifts and clamber up over icy boulders. Progress was slow and steady. At check-in time, there was no signal. Barney tried to reach the ship to no avail.

Brevard waited for their check-in. He had finally made contact with Ybarra, who explained that he had very little battery life left and so just turned it off. He reported that they were still all okay but that a couple of folks in his charge were in bad shape. Munson checked in with the same story but was delighted to hear that help was on its way. They switched to an emergency signal from the still energized communicator to maximize its useful life and hunkered down again. Munson had no way to know when help would get there, but he spread the word that his fellow SEALs were on their way.

In beacon mode, voice contact was now impossible between the rescuers and Ybarra. Munson's unit was switched on, but it was now stuck in the snow far below. Barney had a signal from it but received no response after multiple attempts to contact Munson. He worried about his friend as he plodded onward up the valley.

Munson's signal strength was getting weaker, and the sophisticated phone was also in and out of beacon mode. A signal was sent when the phone detected massive trauma as would happen in an explosion or hard fall. At initial detection of the signal, the four were 1.5 miles from the location of Munson's device. They could home in on it if the signal lasted.

They pushed ahead again, but each step forward now came with a half step backward. Panting heavily, all four hunched over in fatigue, one hand on a knee after another hour passed. Barney again checked the signal and activated his heads-up terrain display. They had covered half of the distance to Munson's device.

Barney pulled off his outer heavy thermal glove to use the greater dexterity allowed by his inner glove liners. He unzipped his parka and reached inside. First from one inside pocket and then the opposite, he produced four foil pouches. Peeling one open, he handed it to Gonzales first. She could not believe her eyes. The other Navy men stepped forward, each receiving theirs.

"Eat them before they freeze." Barney bit into his.

"I love you, Barney!" a voice yelled. They eagerly devoured them, savoring every bite. Barney brought with him the chef's specialty chocolate chip cookies. They were one of the many perks that came with serving aboard the *Longley*. Barney was particularly fond of them.

Each member of the team hydrated from the straw tube connected to the water pack against their back. "Let's go. I'm ready." It was Gonzales's turn at point. They buttoned up, groaned, felt the fatigue in the arms and legs, and moved forward up the canyon. Their arms ached from pulling one another up and over hard spots.

With each step, Barney told himself that he was warm and thought about a tropical island. The four rounded one wide bend and, through brief interludes between periods of blustery flurries, shined their lights at a solid rock wall and towering cliff blocking the canyon. A tremendous fan-shaped pile of snow at the base filled the entire gorge.

"We are here," Barney reported. "Munson must be here somewhere within one hundred feet." He shined his light to the top of what was a two-hundred-foot waterfall during thaw times. Above that, another cliff rose almost another hundred feet. "Let's search the immediate area. Spread out." Their beams on wide-angle, they fanned out to begin a cursory search. One went left to the rock wall only feet away. Two went to the right where the canyon was much wider.

Barney began searching the area ahead, probing the snow pile. He turned off his light to adjust it to lantern mode. In the darkness that ensued, he spotted a faint glow in loose snow on the right side near the top of the enormous mound. Working his way to it in the extra deep snow below the cliff face, he dug into the snow and retrieved a communicator. It was Munson's. He knew it at once. "I GOT IT!" he yelled, but the others didn't hear him until it crackled through their earpieces.

They gathered around their leader, acknowledging his find with the same certain recognition. Barney felt a knot in his stomach. He looked up again at the cliff, knowing no one could have survived a fall from there. Their eyes followed, returning to his face to see the deep concern etched in his snow-covered brow.

"Do we climb it, Barn?" Gonzales, their climbing expert, already had her pack off and was pulling out her rope and climbing gear. In good weather, the overhanging waterfall would have been a near-impossible climb. Frozen solid with lose ice ready to fall, the climb looked like suicide. They again all shined their lights up and down both sections of waterfall covering every point with converging white beams.

Luke was wide awake and shivering, watching on quasi guard duty. He blinked and cleared his eyes. He backed out of their huddle, stood, and ran to the edge of the first precipice. He crept to the brink and looked over. Four rays of light focused on his face when he knocked a small snowfall over the edge. He cried out, "We're here. Thank God, you found us."

Alerted, the others who could move shuffled to near the edge and leaned to look below. Barney looked up and shouted, "US NAVY SEALs AT YOUR SERVICE." Becky collapsed into Wayne's arms. Doc Hoffman never left the side of Bob and Brad, who were nearly frozen.

Munson leaned over the edge and yelled down, "BARNEY, MAN, AM I GLAD TO SEE YOU!"

John inched forward on his belly to peek down. He did not like heights. Through the snow, he could just make out Gonzales, who was laying out her gear and preparing to start climbing. She had spikes on her boots and ice pick hammers in both hands. He rolled away from the sheer drop and looked at Munson. "He will never make it."

"It's a she, and she is the best climber any of us have ever seen." Munson knew that John was correct. The water fall overhang was vertical and sheer, one slip meaning more injury or even death.

"We will come down. Don't try to come up. We need to get down there to you." Looking up, Barney realized that Munson was right.

CHAPTER 30

DOWN AND OUT

The group at the top of the frozen waterfall stomped and did anything they could to generate body heat. They consumed all their remaining high-energy bars brought by the first two frogmen. Rationing was over, rescue within sight. Spirits among them went from sullen to soaring. But the weather turned worse once more. The wind howled, and snow blew up the cliff face. Large pieces of snow and ice broke off and fell crashing downward. The four below retreated to a safe distance.

Munson rigged up a boatswain's chair to lower the first person to at least the middle ledge of the waterfall cliff. They needed someone there strong enough to receive Bob, who would be the second person to be lowered. They did not have enough rope to get to the bottom of the second lower waterfall. They stripped every bit, even short lengths from the last sled, leaving it in pieces. Tied together, the rope was only enough, when doubled, to reach the first ledge below, where ice covered any vestige of rock.

Munson reported the rope situation to Barney. "We have enough to get folks to the first ledge but not enough to reach from there. It looks like adequate room for all of us on that mid flat area but too dangerous for more than one or two below that. It's blowing like a wildcat up here again."

"I'm going up. The wind will be at my back and snow not blowing in my face so hard." Gonzales moved to the snow fan and began making her way to the most advantageous climbing approach. She had two hundred feet of climbing rope wrapped around her body and over her shoulder. Barney did not stop her this time. It was the only way.

Munson, Wayne, and John still had plenty of strength to lower the others one at a time. In spite of the awful weather conditions, Luke was chosen and readily volunteered to make the initial descent to the middle ice-covered ledge. Once there, he was on his own. He backed very slowly over the edge and swung out so that the chair would clear. He closed his eyes and prayed as they lowered him. Becky, Carl, Brad, and Bob, who could hardly move, anchored the rope while the three men inched him lower.

Luke reached the narrow ledge and untied himself from the makeshift chair. Back against the wall, he tugged three times, the signal that he was free and settled. The chair began to rise. Alone in the near darkness, he wondered how John was going to make it. His fear of heights was very strong. Luke had no light. Leaning forward, he saw the glow of an ascending beam. The SEALs spotted him and shined their lights close to him, providing some nonblinding illumination. Someone was on their way up to him. Looking at their path ahead, Luke could not believe what he was seeing.

Gonzales made it past the first major obstacle. She was halfway up to Luke when she lost her cleated footing. Hanging free by an ice ax, she sank her second one deep into the ice, pulled herself back against the cliff, and began climbing again.

Munson shouted down to Luke, "WE ARE STARTING TO LOWER BOB." Luke already realized that because of the cascade of ice and snow that rained down on him. Bob arrived slumped over and nonresponsive. Luke struggled mightily to free him from the harness and move his body to a safe position on the narrow ledge. Luke removed his parka and wrapped it around Bob's core. Stranded on the ledge shivering, he again thought of his ancestor, Anook. It gave him hope and strength but rekindled fear.

Gonzales was getting close, but the last stretch to reach Luke was a formidable task. She was within shouting distance. The swirling snow filled their mouths when they tried to communicate. "I'M going to throw the end of the rope to you. If you can anchor me, I'll climb to you." She threw the loose end, but Luke was not able to catch it. The second time he caught it but almost tumbled forward over the brink. A handful of fleece undercoat grasped by Bob was the only thing that kept him from falling to his death.

Luke's heart was in his throat. He gasped and wrapped her cord around himself. Bob tugged hard with his dwindling strength. Gonzales swung free of her perch and landed against the cliff below Luke. He strained with all his strength to hold her while she climbed to join him. She hugged Luke. He sobbed. He was never so happy to see anyone. Bob passed out.

Over the next two hours, one at a time, they lowered the survivors to the middle ledge and, in turn, lowered them into the waiting arms of the men below. Bob's and Brad's frozen feet were placed in chocolate chip cookie pouches along with a chemical warmer. Given fresh dry socks and sock warmers, Bob regained consciousness, and Brad attempted to walk. John made the trip by keeping his eyes closed the entire way. Once they had enough rope, the last three went from top to bottom.

Munson had no strength left after the others were down. He was the last on top. Gonzales was still on the middle overhang. With the rope firmly anchored, hand over hand, he began his climb down. His gloves were worn through from the exertion of lowering the others. His hands ached; his muscles were spent. Once on the overhang with Gonzales, he rested. She gave him water and two energy bars. Rejuvenated in strength and spirit, he followed her over the edge and slid most of the way down from there, landing on his butt in the cushioning snow. His close friend Barney and Wayne helped him to his feet. Reunited, they celebrated their good luck and, with little time lost, prepared for the last leg: the return to the submarine.

All those brought down from the top received cursory treatment for frostbite. They all suffered from it to some degree. The respite was brief. Gathered around Gonzales, they patted her on the back and hugged her, sharing words of thanks. Her super effort made the rescue operation possible. No one wanted to wait or take more time to warm. Led by Barney and Munson, they headed back down the valley. The weather was cooperating. The snow was light, and the wind bearable.

Still chilled and bone weary, the journey back to the shore went well. Bob was carried by the Navy men as much as possible. Brad leaned on Gonzales the entire way, developing a fondness that would soon grow.

Carl and Dr. Hoffman made it unassisted but literally crawled the last couple of hundred yards. Becky's face was partly frozen, and Wayne could no longer feel his fingers when the Navy men pulled the boat from behind an ice berm. Miles was quiet as usual. He flopped on his back, exhausted. Ybarra felt a twinge of jealousy about Brad and Gonzales, but his total fatigue made him ignore it. Barney contacted the *Longley* and reported their success and the fact that the first six rescued were in the fast boats and on their way.

When the first group departed for the sub, Barney turned to Munson. "Man, I am looking forward to that T-bone steak with a stack a foot high of fresh cookies on the side."

All Munson could say was "Me too, and anything hot."

CHAPTER 31

HOME

Once all those rescued and the crewmen were on board the *Longley*, Captain Brevard gave the orders to leave the fjord behind and head home. The new arrivals were escorted to sick bay and given warm tea or coffee. Bowls of steaming soup wafted a wonderful aroma that permeated the vessel.

Of greatest concern to the *Longley*'s medical team were frostbite and exposure. Bob had first priority because his condition was now very serious. The medical personnel rushed him into surgery to see what they could do to save his smashed and frozen foot. He was unconscious, and his breathing was very shallow and labored. With IVs inserted and a respirator helping him to breathe, the surgeon did what he could, but the condition of his foot was hopeless. They had no choice but to amputate the foot and remove three severely frostbitten toes from the other foot. His condition was downgraded to grave, but if he made it through the night, the prognosis for survival was considered good.

For his age, Carl was doing fine. He showed signs of exhaustion and stress of the trek from the weather base that gave him a heart arrhythmia, but medication and bed rest were his best option. He showered in the luxury of warm water, gorged on two plates of steak and eggs with pancakes and maple syrup, and passed out on a bunk in a crewmen's cabin.

Munson and Ybarra were greeted by the captain who embraced each man and thanked them for their bravery and exceptional devotion to their duty and to those they helped to rescue. They were surrounded by their comrades and showered with praise. Munson got his steak and a huge pile of fresh baked cookies. His toes and fingertips were blackened by frostbite, but the damage was minimal and would heal with time. The blisters caused by lowering person after person down the cliff face were cleaned and bandaged. The glass of Jack Daniels and ice was a surprise that he relished and downed with cheers from his fellow crewmen. He too looked forward to a long shower and plenty of sleep.

Captain Brevard wanted to greet and talk to each of the survivors but let the medical staff do their jobs first. Ybarra was famished, and frost damage to the skin on his face was treated as soon as he sat down. He ate everything they served him and let out a burp that brought cheers from everyone in the mess hall.

Barney told the story of Gonzales's dangerous and fearless climb to the middle ledge. She shrugged indifference but admitted that she was terrified when she made the final swing to bring the rope to the Inuit on the ledge. The crew listened to the story and patted her on the shoulders and back. When the captain arrived in the mess hall to congratulate her, it was he who saluted her.

Wales and Doc Hoffman were suffering from the cold and extreme fatigue, but good food, warmth, a long rest, and minor medical attention were all that they needed. Brad had come through the ordeal well and, though exhausted, was in good shape. They all enjoyed a large mug of steaming coffee and piles of chocolate chip cookies. The doctor insisted on spiking their coffee mugs with a healthy shot of bourbon. It worked to revitalize them and lower their stress levels.

Luke and John ate and drank hot tea by the mug full. Each suffered mild frostbite and burns to their exposed face parts, but they were in very good condition for the time they had spent in hellish conditions. They became the center of attention. The SEAL who was injured at the hole in the ice was the first to greet them and hug them both. Assigned two bunks in crew's quarters, they were asleep in minutes.

Becky and Wayne were tired beyond weary. Becky collapsed and had to be carried to a bed in the medical center. When they removed her boots, her little toe on her left foot was beyond saving. How she had walked at all amazed both doctors. Wayne was ready to drop but accompanied her to sick bay. Sipping on warm coffee helped reinvigorate him enough to stay awake while they checked Becky's vital signs. He could wait. He was so afraid that she was spent and that the last few days had brought her to the brink.

They started an IV and forced her to drink a little warm liquid to help swallow pain pills. They added those to Wayne's menu too. Dr. Hoffman showed up at the door to see how she and Wayne were faring. He had a patch of bandages over one frozen ear. He had changed into fresh clothes and was finishing his second cup of coffee laced with brandy. The doctor in charge ordered him to get some rest.

"Doc, is she going to be all right? She's been through so much and I fear was pushed too hard." Wayne's face told the story of his complete anxiety.

"Her vitals are okay. She is completely dehydrated, and her body temperature is still pretty low. She may have pneumonia too because she is having respiratory problems. I think that we can give her vitamins through the IV, get her fluids in better balance, and start some antibiotics right away. She will lose that toe, but the others should eventually be okay. I don't think that she would have lasted another day out there."

Wayne felt slight relief, but his stomach ached, and he felt like vomiting. His insides hurt so badly, and his head was spinning. His vision blurred, and he felt a pain deep within.

The doctor continued, "She needs lots of rest and more to eat when she is able. We'll continue the liquids and see how her body responds. She's a tough lady and, from what I've heard about your ordeal, pretty darn strong. Give her time and don't worry too much. We need to take a close look at you too. How are your feet?"

Wayne stripped down and shivered. He felt weak and dizzy. The doctor gave him a warm blanket and began his check. Wayne had insisted that he be last. He felt faint and could hardly keep his eyes open. The doctor steadied him and seated him to listen to his heart and lungs. After two deep breaths, his world went blank. He toppled forward toward the doctor, who stopped him from sprawling on the floor. His assistant helped push him back and lay him prone on the examining table. The extreme hypothermia and complete exhaustion caused his heart to stop.

"CODE BLUE!" the doctor shouted. "GET ME A DEFIB! HE'S GONE INTO COMPLETE SHOCK. HIS INTERNAL BODY TEMP IS STILL TOO LOW." He continued instructions to inject a stimulus and try to restart Wayne's heart. Hooked up to the monitor, he still had no pulse. He tried CPR, and they gave him pure oxygen, but he was not breathing. "For God's sake, we're losing him. Stand clear!" He turned on the defibrillator to high and stretched out the paddles. Wayne's body lurched and heaved in an arc, almost arching off the table. The monitor showed no pulse, just a telltale flat line.

His assistant was continuing CPR. "Clear!" the doctor repeated. "Another 20cc please." Two intense pulses and no heart activity. Precious minutes were passing, and Wayne was not responding. They inserted a breathing tube and shook his body, rubbing his hands, and speaking into his ears. "Come on, Wayne. Becky needs you. Come on, man. You can do it."

The flat line flickered, and a weak but uneven pulse showed on the monitor. "We got him! Come on, Wayne." The ventilator began pushing precious oxygen into his lungs. The chemicals injected to shock his heart back into rhythm began to take effect. He was alive but just hanging on by a thread. His bravery to go last in sick bay almost cost him his life and he was far from out of danger. It turned out that he was in the worst shape of any of the survivors.

*****

The *Longley* proceeded on a southerly course around and out of the Arctic Sea. They had to detour around the volcanic activity on the Gakkel Ridge. They planned to rendezvous with a US Navy surface ship where the arrivals could receive further treatment or be transported by helicopter to hospital facilities ashore. Once all the new passengers were situated and made as comfortable as possible, they were allowed to send out messages to any family or loved ones.

Bob and Wayne remained in the onboard hospital rooms under constant scrutiny and supervision. Wayne remained unconscious, and Becky, though still in pain, never left his side. Bob was kept heavily sedated, having no idea that he had lost a foot.

The SEALs were debriefed and filed their reports. Each of the rescue party who could was asked to write or dictate a brief report about the experience at the base and subsequent time until rescue.

Captain Brevard took time to sit down and interview each member of his teams and all of those they brought aboard. Much of it was incorporated into his logbook and a supplement to it. He filed a daily report with his superiors at the Pentagon now that his submarine was not in its stealth mode.

Two days under the sea and one running on the surface brought the *Longley* to the meeting point with the destroyer escort sent to meet them. The at-sea transfer went without a hitch, and all those rescued were moved to the destroyer. It had a large helipad where the helicopter sent to take them to land was waiting. Captain Brevard was there to send them off. Munson and Ybarra were at his side. Each took a moment to thank the crew and captain and the medical staff who had cared for them all so well. Becky hugged Munson and Ybarra with tears of thanks streaming down her cheeks. Wayne was awake and talking by the time they underwent the transfer. Wayne saluted them military style from his stretcher. "How can we ever thank you?" were his parting words.

Bob had recovered enough too, but his pain was serious. They all boarded or were carried to the helicopter, and once comfortable and secured, the chopper lifted off and moved away from the two Navy ships, circling once for those aboard to wave their last thank you. The copilot moved to the second row so Captain Wales could sit in his seat. Silence filled the cabin. The whirr of the massive turbine engine and vibrations left each survivor quiet, pensive, and thankful for the rescue and excellent care each received.

They landed in Halifax, Nova Scotia, where ambulances and cars were waiting to take them to the hospital for another round of checkups and needed additional treatment. Canadian customs officials welcomed them and whisked them all through a quick check-in. The hospitality they displayed made everyone comfortable. After their medical checks, the Canadians—Captain Wales, Brad, and Dr. Hoffman—all being ambulatory, said their goodbyes with hugs and headed for their connections home with escorts. They had many questions to answer, but rehabilitation and recovery were the present directive from the authorities. They had already filed preliminary reports.

Luke and John were also Canadian citizens and were welcomed back as heroes even though very little of the story of their adventure had leaked out. They refused to leave until they were sure that Wayne and Becky were fine and that Carl and Bob would make a complete recovery. Arrangements were made to send the two scientists and Wayne and Becky back to the US. Carl and Bob both needed more time under hospital supervision and were to be transferred to Bethesda Naval Hospital for their convalescence. Becky and Wayne had long reports to write but were given permission to choose their place for some needed rest and recovery time. Becky wanted nothing but warmth and sunshine.

After recovering his strength and stamina enough to walk and take care of himself with a little help from his sweetheart, Wayne was happy with her choice. After saying temporary goodbyes to Bob and Carl in DC, they boarded a plane for warmer climes. They insisted that Luke and John go with them with complete blessings from their superiors. Luke and John had never been to a warmwater beach. Becky assured them that they could leave their parkas behind. Their first stop would be in Destin Beach, Florida, at the Hilton. A second stop in the Florida Keys was planned with a final stay in Cozumel on the Mexican Riviera.

After two weeks of sunbathing, snorkeling, boogie boarding, fishing, and eating, the four had formed an even stronger bond that would last the rest of their lives. Luke and John, tanned and relaxed, eventually left for southern Canada but had no intention to return to their tiny village anytime soon. They stayed long enough to celebrate one more special event with Wayne and Becky. They were married on the beach at the resort in Cozumel. Their family members were flown in care of the US government. Luke and John were co-best men, and Becky's dad gave her hand in marriage to Wayne. Two of Becky's closest college friends stood with her as bridesmaids. It was a beautiful breezy day with small puffs of white clouds drifting aimlessly across a spectacular blue sky. Becky's proud mom videoed the ceremony. A group of nearby tourists clapped and cheered when Wayne placed the ring on her hand and kissed his new bride.

After everyone departed the next morning, they had a quiet breakfast together at a small beach café. A gentle breeze moved Becky's hair, making her more beautiful than she had ever looked before to Wayne. They had conceived their son the night before, and the blush on her cheek melted Wayne's heart. He grasped her hand and kissed the back. "I love you, Becky, and will until the day I die." He had tears in his eyes.

She smiled at him and, squeezing his grip, responded, "I love you too, more than ever, and will never leave your side again."